MW01124790

NO TRIVIAL PURSUIT

JOHN ELLSWORTH

Copyright © 2019-2020 by John Ellsworth

All rights reserved.

No part of this book may be reproduced in any form or by any electronic or mechanical means, including information storage and retrieval systems, without written permission from the author, except for the use of brief quotations in a book review.

This is a work of fiction. Names, characters, places, and incidents either are the by-product of the author's imagination or are used fictitiously. Any resemblance to actual persons, living or dead, events, or locales is entirely coincidental.

1

─────

Los Angeles, 1955

The LA County Morgue called just after nine that night. Harley Ellis answered on the first ring. Since Wendy had gone missing, Harley always answered on the first ring.

The morgue said they had a Jane Doe who could be Wendy—the tattoo matched. They put Jane Doe at about fourteen. Wendy would've been fourteen. Harley was Wendy's mother and knew her age to the day.

Tattooed on Wendy's belly, in red and blue ink, was the warship *USS SAINT PAUL*. It was her father's ship, Korean War, 1952. She had no other tattoos, marks, or identifying scars. Her dental records were on file with Central Records downtown, too. So far, there hadn't been another body with teeth. This new one was different: Jane Doe had all her teeth. Harley knew it might come down to the teeth. It all depended on decomposition. Harley was a Los Angeles Police Department Detective Sergeant. She knew all about decomposition.

Harley told them, "Look again." The morgue came back and said Jane Doe's tattoo was a match. Harley struggled to calm her rising panic when she hung up from the call. The chance some other girl bore the same tattoo and was found dead less than twenty miles from where Wendy had gone missing, was beyond coincidence. Except for one thing: many of the *USS Saint Paul's* crew had acquired the same tattoo and then many of their children were allowed to get the same one, becoming known as "Paul's Saints."

Harley jumped into her Ford and drove twenty over. She held her detective shield in her hand all the way, ready to badge any traffic cop asking for her license and registration. The shield said LOS ANGELES POLICE DEPARTMENT along its bottom half. No matter what speed they clocked her at, she walked.

The morgue, located on Mission Street, operated 24/7. Hollywood Division dealt with it day and night. Asking a relative or witness to ID John or Jane Doe could happen during waking hours or during sleeping hours, it didn't matter.

Harley pulled into nighttime parking.

She double-stepped the fifteen steps up to the main entrance then jogged to the end of the hallway, its dim overheads flickering, threatening to quit. She took the elevator to the basement and was immediately assaulted by the smell of the autopsy floor. A mixture of chemicals and decay violated the nose. Dry cleaning wouldn't eradicate the odor.

She turned right and jogged again. This time to the double doors marked *Authorized Personnel Only*. It was the place where the bodies were kept. There was a guard on duty just outside. Harley flashed her shield and dashed inside before he could nod at her or say her name because, of course, he knew her from Vice. Those were the bodies long dead before they died.

"Come in, Harley. God, I'm sorry to make that call," said Garcia, the attending.

She ran to him and he held her by the shoulders. She was crying. Garcia had worked night shift since before Harley started with LAPD. He was medium height, a burly native from South Central. Educated at UCLA and battle-tested in World War II where he worked Graves and Registration, Savi Garcia had seen and done everything when it came to the dead. He also knew Harley from Vice, knew her and her kid's story, and liked her.

Garcia stared into her teary eyes. "I have Wendy's tattoo memorized and I owe it to you to call like I always promised I would. She's down here in level four. Please tell me if you need a minute first or when you want me to open her." His face twitched. This was going to get rough.

"I'm ready, Goddamit," Harley spit out. She was ready, too. She'd dreaded this moment since Wendy's disappearance when, as Harley was busy catching calls, Wendy had opened the outside house door and let a taxi driver in who came back out with her heavy duffel. Wendy followed him outside and down to the cab at the end of the driveway. They climbed in and that's all the nosy-Nellie neighbor knew when canvassed.

Two weeks later, one of Wendy's friends had called, a girl, who said she'd spotted Wendy over the weekend in Las Vegas, poolside at the Sands. "Wendy looked fourteen going on twenty-one," said the friend. "She was hardly covered up in that two-piece, Mrs. Ellis. I'm sorry, I shouldn't have probably said that. But it was all those guys she was hanging out with. They were way older."

"Has she been back to school?" If Wendy were in Vegas, it was not a smart question since she lived and went to school in LA. But

Harley was beyond asking only smart questions. She was desperate for any news, any fact, any scent of a trail.

"No. Huh-uh. No one's seen or heard from her, nothing."

"But you're certain it was her at the Sands?"

"Yes."

"Was she working there?"

"No, just relaxing around the pool. She and some guy in a black cowboy hat were playing grabass. He'd push her in and then she'd run up and toss a glass of water in his face when he was on a lounger. It went on for an hour. I was there with my dad. My parents are getting their divorce and I had to be there to pick a parent. I'm fourteen and they said I had to choose. It was horrible."

Harley came back to the moment. Garcia was about to open the stainless-steel drawer. Inside would be a length of white plastic wrapped around a torso. Which is exactly what she saw when the drawer actually was pulled open. Not only the torso was wrapped, but long legs, too. Jane Doe legs that looked like Wendy's. Harley's nostrils flared when the wrapper was opened. Death smell. She wasn't watching, could not stand to look, not yet. Looked at her Bulova watch and noted the time. 9:57 p.m.

Garcia paused, waiting, while Harley steeled herself. Then she spoke, "Just her tattoo. Let me see that first, please."

"Sure."

He peeled apart the plastic at mid-line and spread it for viewing. Harley slid up to the drawer and opened her eyes to view only the tattoo. She looked at the ship, then stumbled back. "Oh," she said. "Oh, God."

"Should I show the face?"

"Yes. It's her, I know it's her."

Garcia went through the same procedure with the face, peeling back and then spreading, this time a much larger area. Jane Doe's entire bluish face was observed.

Harley looked.

"Oh, Sweet Jesus, thank you!"

Garcia shook his head. "Gracias, Dios, gracias."

He resealed the viewing port and began sliding the body drawer back inside its receptacle.

Harley turned away. She suddenly crossed her legs and settled onto the floor. She was wearing Levi's and a gray sweatshirt. Her penny loafers contained pennies in the slot—Wendy's contribution to mom's style. She put out a hand to steady herself as she sat on the floor, rocking.

Garcia pulled over a chair and sat beside her. He removed his left glove and tenderly lay his hand on her shoulder. "Thank God for someone else being dead besides Wendy. What a terrible prayer. I'm sorry other girl's mom and dad. I'm sorry for your loss."

Harley skidded a wooden kitchen match across the tile floor and lit a Camel. Garcia made no effort to enforce the No Smoking rule, despite the morgue's many flammable chemicals, as well as saturated towels, and clothes and papers. Wastebaskets full of incendiary materials were everywhere. But still—he let her smoke. It had been too much, even for a body hustler like him.

"Where can she be?" Harley asked. "I must ask that ten thousand times every day. When I first open my eyes until I come back eighteen hours later and close them to sleep. In between it's every other thought. *Where is Wendy? Where is my baby?* And, *how did I fuck up so royally that she ran away? What part did I leave out? What didn't I know about that I should have said to her or done for her?* I kick myself all day long. Guys in the unit ask me why I'm not married. I say to myself, I am married. I'm married to my shame for having driven my daughter off. How could someone like that ever be ready for a man? How could I turn all my attention to a man? And if you don't pay attention, they don't stay around long. Men are funny that way. They never need only a woman's love, they need her full attention, too. They're always *on* for her. Did you know that's the difference between men and women, Garcia? The woman is thinking about laundry and meals and taking out the trash. But the man? He's just always *on* for her. I can't do it."

"It's better if you try to let go, Harley. Some of us agreed on that. Some of us down here at County."

She reached and touched his hand, still on her shoulder. "That's sweet, Garcia. If you ever find one of these stiffs who wants to trade brains, call me first, okay?"

"I will, Harley. I'll call you first."

She stubbed her cigarette on the tile floor and snapped the butt in half. She held it in her left hand and stood and finger-kissed Garcia's lips with her right forefinger. They were never this touchy-feely, she would later remember just before sleep came. But it had been a special time.

A very special time.

It had almost been Wendy.

But that thing that kept young girls safe and alive, that thing she persuaded all day every day, that her daughter should live, that thing she prayed to and raged at for answers...that thing had delivered for her tonight. It hadn't been her turn tonight, it had been someone else's. She thanked the thing as she closed her eyes in bed that night.

She thanked the thing.

2

Harley Ellis locked her Fairlane in the parking lot shared by the police and fire departments on Wilcox Avenue in Hollywood. She passed through the Hollywood Station's rear entrance under a sign that read POLICE ONLY. Security looked her over: tall, thin, burned out eyes, straight chopped black hair, a cop struggling not to hit someone because she knew she wasn't going to get Robbery-Homicide.

"Smitty," she said in a low voice as she walked past the security officer.

Today she'd receive her posting for the next twenty-four months. Coming off two years on Vice, painted up for lonely businessmen, Harley had put in for the Robbery-Homicide Division. However, she was realistic because it was 1955 and the LAPD wasn't sending females to RHD. In fact, LAPD had a rule under Chief Parker that a female's highest attainable rank was sergeant.

She walked into the virtually empty squad room. Just as she'd done for months, she checked her mail slot for the green assignment sheet sending her to West Valley. No such sheet was waiting. Actually, West Valley wasn't the worst that could happen. That basement-level job was reserved for Financial Crimes—bad checks—the most mindless, boring detail. FC was usually assigned only to the most difficult, cantankerous, hard-to-get-along-with detectives on the entire force. Anyone drawing that assignment should likely begin considering other career choices right then and there.

She sat down at her desk and opened her bag. She snapped open her compact and checked her lipstick. Her eyes were dark and recessed from so many sleepless nights on Vice. But she was still tan from days off at the beach playing volleyball, where she played on the front line because she was tall: five-nine. However tall, her ankles and legs weren't the thin, delicate legs of a ballet dancer. Her legs were stout and muscled and were capable of kicking-in hotel room doors—which they'd done more than once while making Vice busts.

She hadn't seen her desk in days and began checking pink message slips. Nothing much of interest there. A request for an interview from Channel 4 news. A departmental memo on new leave policies. Status of the LAPD picnic—yesterday's July 4 bash, which she'd purposely avoided.

Charles Van Meter—CV—her partner, hadn't arrived. CV was not only her long-time partner, he was also her off-hours best friend. Harley lived two blocks from the beach; he lived clear across the Valley in his ex-wife's duplex where he'd been invited to live and help her share expenses. With CV living so far east, getting together was difficult but always worth it as they crawled bars, watched the Dodgers (who, it was rumored, might be moving to LA) on TV, stopped in at Bob's Big Boy and all the stuff you do when you're young and have a headful of streetwise and a belly full of Monday night beer—the night least likely to catch Vice call-outs.

She headed to the coffee station. She ran hot water into her Navy mug and returned to her desk. She had just dunked her first Lipton tea bag, when CV came up behind and playfully clapped his cupped hands against her ears.

"Motherf—" she caught herself. "My ears are ringing, turd head!" She brought her fists down on the wooden table she and CV shared as a desk. Everything jumped.

"I just wanted to see if you were awake. Heard anything about West Valley?"

She leaned back in her chair. "I have not. Which tells me it's a done deal. I'm soon going to be the undercover equivalent of an over-sexed Minnie Mouse on the hunt for theme park johns— though why anyone would go to a theme park to make a pickup is beyond me to begin with."

"Because mice hate pussy?" CV said in low tones.

"You just won the *$64,000 Question*," Harley said referring to the brand-new TV game show. She couldn't help but smile at CV, anyway.

The squawk box on Harley's desk crackled. "Harley, come in here a sec, would you?"

"I'm on my way, Lieutenant."

She shook her head at her partner. "Here I go. West Valley. But I'm going to fight it, CV. Damn them!"

Harley stood, squared her shoulders, ran her tongue over her teeth, and headed down the four-door hallway to Lieutenant

Chall's office. She stopped at the far end and knocked on the frosted glass.

"Entrez!" he cried out.

Harley twisted the knob and stepped inside, a determined smile on her lips and shoulders fully square for any action he might have for her.

Jamison S. Chall had twice received the LAPD Mayor's Medal over his impressive career. He had the inside track and thus feared no man. Or woman. Chall was tall, black, bald from the ears up and carried himself like a drill sergeant. He was a no-nonsense guy all week—but when Friday night came, the coats came off and the beer steins were hoisted down the street at the Irishman's Pub. At those times he became just another one of the troops and his underlings loved him for it. Mainly because anything could be said to him at the Irishman's without fear of repercussions. "The Irishman's is a say-what's-bugging-you pub," Chall told his coppers. "It's a free-fire zone," he added for the benefit of the cadre's ex-military, which was plentiful. "Just tell me what's on your mind and don't hold back."

Harley met the lieutenant's gaze upon entering and didn't break eye contact as she made her way to the visitor's chair. She settled easily on the metal chair and folded her hands in her lap. Then she remembered where she was and the image she meant to convey and she leaned back, crossed one booted foot across the other leg, and sat up. "Yes, LT?" she said in her command voice.

He held up a finger. "Wait one."

He stood and switched on the window air conditioner unit behind him. Harley knew all about the lieutenant's fear of eavesdroppers in the air ducts and electric wires. She knew it came from his days in the Army's Signal Corps but didn't know much more than just that. No one did, in fact. His military days—his actual duties—were confidential. Harley and the other dicks, after many attempts at him both drunk and sober—had finally given up and stopped asking.

He took his seat and sighed heavily, a troubled look on his face.

"Look, Harley, I know you put in for RHD. Don't think I don't know."

Her heart fell. "Why do I think Robbery-Homicide isn't happening for me?"

"There's something better. There's a special slot for you. The gods see you in Unsolved Crimes.'"

She jiggled her booted foot and reached down to scratch her ankle. A million thoughts raced through her head, the most consistent one being *Hey, this isn't Robbery-Homicide, but before I go out and jump off a bridge, let's listen to what LT has to say. The alternative is banging a cash register at FedMart.*

"So, you're going to dump a stack of unsolved crimes on my desk and order me and CV to solve them?"

"Not CV. Just you."

"You're splitting us up?"

He spread his hands. "It can't be helped, Harley. CV is going to Robbery-Homicide."

Harley's head snapped back. "What?" she exclaimed. "My partner gets Robbery-Homicide, but I don't? What the hell, Lieutenant?"

"I know, I know. We just didn't see RHD as a good fit for you, Harley."

She was one of a handful of female detectives on the force at that time. A good fit? He meant she was an inferior model, the one without testicles. That had to be it. The idea caused her blood pressure to climb. Harley had once operated heavy equipment for her contractor father in the Valley. This was before he lost it all when he got sick, but she'd done her eights right along with any man. She could operate anything from a backhoe to a road grader to a forklift. RHD would be a perfect fit for this woman.

She asked the obvious. "Am I not a good fit for the job because I'm a woman?"

"I can't deny that. I won't lie to you, Harley, but you know management's policy says women will not be admitted into certain departments. Robbery-Homicide is one of those."

Harley wanted to tell him to take the Unsolved Crimes job and shove it—she was that angry. But she also needed to keep a roof over her head and buy groceries. Her one and only job paid the bills and did it well—compared to other, menial jobs a woman could hope to land in 1955, jobs such as secretarial, waitressing, and secretarial again. That was about it, unless you had inherited a business from your father. But that wasn't Harley's case. Her father worked in the city sanitation department. He'd become a garbageman after losing the construction company and hadn't been able even to send his daughter to college. Harley swallowed hard and forced herself to shut the hell up. Losing RHD was bad enough; losing her job would be horrible. She even managed a half-smile.

"Okay, no RHD for me. Now tell me about Unsolved Crimes, Lieutenant."

"That's my girl," he said with a smile. "So here goes. We have a backlog of ten-thousand unsolved crimes in the LAPD. Obviously, we can't assign all ten-thousand to you, but we can assign the more egregious felonies."

"Egregious? How is a felony anything *but* egregious?"

He nodded. "Agreed. But in your case the egregious crimes will be those that are getting us into trouble with the citizens of LA."

"I'm getting the cases that come with bad publicity attached?"

"Your words, Harley. Not mine. You're going to be working the cases that are the high-profile ones. Ironically enough, this also includes homicides. Many homicide cases."

Which stopped her cold. What? How on earth could they keep her from an official RH assignment but then turn around and assign homicide cases to her?

"I know what you're thinking. How can we give you homicides, but we can't give you the title? The answer is simple. The public wouldn't approve of a woman working Robbery-Homicide. Maybe it will never happen, either. But that isn't your concern. You start your new assignment tomorrow. As does CV in Robbery-Homicide. You'll be getting a new partner."

"Let me guess. My new partner is female?"

"Bingo, Harley. You're going to be working with Marcia Meriwether."

"Oh, shit," Harley groaned. "Not Marcia Marry-Me-Somebody! Nobody wants to work with Marcia."

"That's not your call, Harley. Working with Marcia and making it smooth—that's your job. Besides, Marcia has a year of law school under her belt. That might come in handy some time."

"Is this because her uncle is on the city council?"

The lieutenant winced. His eyes flashed. "Please don't go there, Harley. We don't need that in our station."

"So it is. Marcia's uncle gets her a new assignment with another woman. What's the point, Lieutenant? Oh, wait, I get it. We're the new face of LAPD in the Hollywood Division. Our job is really a public relations one. Am I right?" Suddenly, the interview request from Channel 4 made sense. Word was already on the street.

"There will be a certain amount of interaction with the press. There always is."

"Marcia and yours truly are being setup to be the cheerleaders for the LAPD where it can't solve high profile cases in Hollywood. Why not just come right out and say it, Lieutenant?"

"Enough, Harley, I have your first case I'd like to personally turn over to you. Reason is, I'm drawing heat like July asphalt. Here's the deal. Ira J. Spielman over at Capitol Pictures? He was known all over the county as a grandfatherly type to orphans and disadvantaged kids. But someone didn't like him, the murder is pretty gruesome. All over the papers last April, remember? Anyway, Danny Sullivan has pissed off the widow, going in and telling her he figured Spielman was chasing young pussy. He all but told the press the same thing. Well, let me rephrase. The widow called and reamed me up one side and down the other. She wants a new crew on the case. She never wants to see Sullivan and Black again. So, I need you and Marcia to take it over and make it a priority. Find something new to crow about and call a press conference. Make it into something. We've done this and that and found out this and that—you get my drift. I don't give a damn whether you solve it by next Monday, but, dammit, you girls solve it and I'll demand RHD for you in two years. Give it everything for me, okay?"

Harley thought long and hard. The answer she was looking for wasn't an easy one. But in the next moment, she decided: she wasn't going to tell her lieutenant that her own daughter had screen-tested with Spielman before she disappeared. There seemed to be no reason for Lieutenant Chall to know that. It wasn't germane. She was sure the two weren't connected. 99.99% sure. Besides, she wanted the case. No matter what else happened with it, it might move her closer to finding Wendy and bringing her home. Wendy had been with Spielman. In the investigation there might be a word that led Harley to her, maybe a passing reference, maybe some key piece of evidence—who could tell? Whatever, Harley suddenly wanted the case more than she wanted Robbery-Homicide.

"Is that all? Solve the biggest case of the year? I can do that." She knew she sounded too cocksure; she didn't mean it that way. She cautioned herself to slow down, just get the case and get out.

"Don't let me down. I'm pleased to see you're eager to take this on. That's all I have for you today."

Harley sprung up and began leaving before she'd say something she'd later regret. Something that could cause him to suddenly change his mind and renege on giving her the case. Harley said, as she was leaving, "Thank you for having faith in me Lieutenant. I won't let you down."

"I know you won't, Harley. Have a good day now."

"Goodbye."

She stepped out and shut the door. Her stomach churned and her face burned like glowing embers. She was angry—she was pissed beyond anything she'd felt in a long, long time, about the male/female differential treatment. Which meant it was time to head out for the gun range and shred some targets with her department-issue gun, the Smith & Wesson K-38 Combat Masterpiece with six-inch barrel. Harley's own Model 15 revolver was modified to be fired double-action only. This was accomplished by the department armorer grinding the full cock notch from the hammer. She trained to shoot combat style, without ever cocking the weapon. She'd never fired her gun on duty but she had no doubt she was ready.

Instead of retracing her steps back to the squad room, Harley went straight ahead, emerging outside, where she stood under the portico and lit a Camel. She sucked the smoke deep into her lungs and the nicotine bled away some of her anger. She exhaled a boiling cloud of white smoke into the morning air. *There*, she thought, *much better. Settle down, Harley, you haven't found her yet.*

But it's a start, isn't it?

3

Harley gave birth to Wendy on July 20, 1941 in Vallejo, California. It was wartime in Europe, and her husband, Robert Ellis, was a welder at the Mare Island Naval Yard. He'd been working at Mare Island since before the European war. When war broke out for the U.S. in December, his job was listed as exempt. He could neither be drafted nor could he enlist, as his job helped keep America's fighting fleet afloat. He was told he was indispensable to the war effort and that he wasn't going anywhere. Robert was stuck and he was crazy with rage, so much did he want to be fighting alongside his buddies from high school, the kids who went into the Marines and Navy from the Bay Area.

They lived in base housing, a perk of being a vital, though civilian, part of the fleet. Base housing at the time consisted of 102 rows of wood-frame structures of two bedrooms and one bathroom each, all connected in long rows of twenty dwelling units each. The units were World War I builds. One universal color, sea blue, covered them all.

One night, the gas range in one unit exploded, killing four children who'd been asleep in one bedroom while their parents slumbered in the adjoining room. Fire crews immediately brought the blaze under control and there was no other loss of life that night. But several more units had been destroyed, including that inhabited by Robert and Harley Ellis, and their baby, Wendy. While their unit was hastily repaired, they'd been housed off-base for ten days before being allowed to move back. During that time, Harley Ellis had just happened to see a job board at the Mare Island office where she had gone to get new keys to their new front door. On the job board was a picture of a woman. Not so unusual, but this woman was wearing a uniform. The uniform of the US Navy, and she was serving as a member of the Navy Shore Patrol, riding herd on the Waves—the women of the Navy—who sometimes tippled a little too much and got in trouble with the local constabulary. At least, this is what Harley found out twenty-six weeks later, after she had completed boot camp and was ordered to report to the SP at Mare Island, where she would spend the war working in Naval law enforcement. There were only seventeen of them, women SP's, assigned to keep the peace among two-thousand Waves during wartime. Harley soon found out she was going to be just as busy as she wanted.

During this time, when Robert was working days and Harley was alternating shifts between days, afternoons, and graveyard, toddler Wendy was left in the care of the mother next door, a woman who had three kids of her own and who all but begged for the job of tending Wendy, so badly was the money needed in her Navy household. Her name was Bernice. Her husband's name was Douglas. Unbeknownst to Robert and Harley, their neighbors fought like cats and dogs, never screaming or yelling but hissing terrible insults and accusations of broken marital vows and affairs.

Douglas, it seemed, was a man's man who liked men. While he worked a normal Navy dayshift at the shipyard, he often came home from work after midnight and even once, just as the sun was coming up. Bernice and Douglas knew if they fought out loud and the SP were called, they could very well lose their on-base housing and suddenly be facing rents and prices no one-income military couple could afford. It would mean the end of them.

One afternoon, just as she was ready to complete her shift, Harley got a *See the Man* call from an address that was—as she read it for a third time—next door to her own house. It was where Douglas and Bernice lived, the same place where Wendy was lodged and babysat while mom and dad worked their shifts. Harley's stomach fell and she was dizzy. Her heart raced.

Harley ran for the SP Jeep she'd just parked and tore out of the SP substation parking lot, gravel spewing against the side of the modular unit as she sped away. Her radio blasted a second call and added, "See the man. Do not knock, go directly inside the unit." Harley didn't need to be told that twice: her daughter was inside. What in God's name? she prayed and wondered as she screamed around the base on two wheels, the subject unit now dead ahead.

Harley slammed to a stop and ran for the front door, which she burst through without first knocking. Just as she entered, she heard a loud whirring overhead, which was when she saw that the front door was attached by a series of pulleys and parachute cord to an overhead pulley in the middle of the room. Opening the door caused a stool on which the man was standing, to suddenly topple. Dangling beneath that overhead pulley hung Douglas by the neck, dying from asphyxiation. Harley whipped her K-BAR knife from her utility belt and reached to cut the line holding

Douglas. She found the cord was actually reinforced with a heavy twisted wire, the type commonly used to tie aircraft down, rendering her knife useless.

There, his feet scissoring as he died, hung Douglas—but that wasn't all. He was wearing a woman's swimming suit and a hairnet. Around his midriff was a strong, black belt. His hands were hand-cuffed in front. A line ran from the handcuffs, down through his legs and up to the belt in back. A face mask covered his eyes and nose. She took it all in and realized it was a suicide. Elaborate but foolproof since the line he'd chosen couldn't be severed.

Harley broke off and looked frantically for Wendy. The entire entry and attempt to cut the cord had consumed less than five seconds. She rushed toward the second bedroom but stopped when she saw Wendy was actually seated at the kitchen table, in her high chair, eating a pat of butter with her fingers. The girl looked up and smiled when her mother entered and ran to her.

There, at the last minute, she raised a butter hand and pointed to the now unmoving Douglas. "What dat?" asked the child. Harley gathered her up and swept her face around to where she couldn't see the dead man and ran with her from the housing unit.

Out to the Jeep she ran, where she jumped in, Wendy on her lap, and called for a medical response team. Within a minute she heard the sirens heading her way. They weren't able to resuscitate Douglas. His widow moved out the next day.

Different babysitting arrangements were made two doors down in the other direction that night. Wendy would now be staying with the young wife of a Navy ensign fresh out of the Naval Academy. The woman had a degree in early childhood education and that pedigree satisfied Harley and Robert.

Wendy moved on without a trace of trauma. Harley was slower to recover. It was her first dead body. She kept telling Robert how helpless she felt and how angry she'd been Douglas decided to kill himself leaving Wendy alone in the house without an adult when Bernice left with the other kids. On the other hand, she was very grateful and prayed for Douglas and thanked God he hadn't hurt her baby.

SP gave her a day off for personal leave, given what she'd been through. Meaning they really wanted her to have some time to just cry it out. It turned out that wasn't customary Navy practice, but it had been done because her child was involved.

Robert was of the opinion they should try to rotate their shifts opposite each other so one of them would always be home with Wendy. He would be able to change shifts almost at will because he was not Navy, he was civilian. With Harley, however, it was a different story. Her job was pure Navy and her shifts changed erratically. "They never want us to get too comfortable in our jobs," she told Robert. "We're always being shifted around for training purposes. It's never going to end."

By Wendy's fifth birthday the war was over, and sailors were leaving the Navy in droves. Harley's job was becoming easier because of the decreasing numbers but at the same time harder because so many of the men were coming home with emotional problems that were virtually going undetected and untreated. Shore leave was thus often violent in the bars around Vallejo and Mare on weekends. She worked twelve-hour shifts Fridays, Saturdays, and an eight on Sunday.

All during these years, Wendy became a daddy's girl. She squealed when he got home from work and threw little tantrums when he left to start his day at Mare Island. When he was home, they were inseparable and did ice cream outings, the zoo, the waterfront, the library, the toy stores together, an outing of some sort each and every day. Robert was just in love with his child; he hated leaving her when he had to go to work and stomped into the house as a monster, a delightful monster, when he returned home. Harley was equally active in Wendy's life, but it was different, more measured, more tempered, less exuberant, she would have to say. Which was fine. She did everything she could to encourage father and daughter and politely stepped back and watched and allowed daddy the stage when it came his time to perform.

After Harley had served four years, she wanted out. So, the family packed up and moved to Long Beach, where Robert got a welding job in the shipyard. Then, Long Beach NSY was placed in an inactive status on 1 June 1950. The Korean War began less than one month later, and the shipyard was reactivated on 4 January 1951. But, this time, Robert lucked out. He had sought other work when NSY went inactive and, when the Korean war broke out, he'd been able to enlist. He went into the Navy on 20 July 1950, his daughter's ninth birthday. Following her celebration, Robert reported for duty. He shipped out to Korea in September.

Harley wasted no time getting back into law enforcement. She applied for a job with the LAPD, took the physical and mental testing, and went to work in the Traffic Enforcement Division in January 1951. Her usual beat was downtown LA, where she spent most of her days writing enforcement citations and investigating fender benders. The work was stultifying to Harley after the excitement she'd known serving in the Navy Shore Patrol. She kept taking tests and moving up in her ranking.

Wendy was missing her father terribly. By the age of ten she'd taken to spending long hours in her bedroom writing letters to her father and looking up his duty postings on the world globe Harley got her. He wrote her at least every week. He did the same with Harley.

Robert and Harley were in love and, by early spring of 1951, his letters took on a tone of one who has made a grave mistake by separating himself from his family. His ship was involved in heavy combat; his letter-writing suffered. Which caused terror in the hearts of his wife and daughter as they more and more lost touch with their husband and father. Harley attempted to lessen the distance between herself and Wendy. But, Harley discovered, Wendy had begun blaming her for Robert's service. "He wouldn't have gone if you loved him more," she accused her mother.

"Nobody has ever loved your dad more than I love him," Harley repeated countless times.

They argued everyday about who loved who more. Wendy could go days without speaking to her mother. Harley suffered terribly from what she saw as loss of her daughter to silence. Then the real fighting set in, Wendy calling her mother terrible names that Harley wasn't aware she even knew. So, Harley doubled-down, trying to take Wendy on adventures she thought she would enjoy, including the Santa Monica Pier, weekends with the grandparents, movies and ice follies, and dance lessons so Wendy learned the latest dances, for she had started looking at boys and having light dates with other twelve-year-olds—as a group. But, try as she may, Harley just couldn't break through Wendy's defenses. The girl missed her father, her mother was to blame, and nothing was going to change her mind.

Harley took Wendy to see a therapist. It was paid for by Harley's LAPD insurance. The psychiatrist reported back to the mother that Wendy was stubbornly refusing to hear reason about her father's service. The little girl maintained that her father loved her so much that nothing could have separated them other than an unhappy marriage.

"There's no evidence of unhappy under our roof, ever," Harley told the doctor. Which, again, didn't matter.

Wendy had her mind made up and she was going to blame Harley for her loss.

Then it happened. Robert was lost in Inchon Bay on 11 June 1952. The telegram from the War Department came late on a Friday night. Harley was just off work and had just been paid. She had the record player blaring the soundtrack from *South Pacific*. She was having the first of her two allotted vodkas which she consumed every other Friday, on payday. Then the courier knocked at her door and handed over the yellow message.

With the telegram in hand, Harley somehow got to the vinyl couch and plopped down. She read the telegram a second time, a third, and each time it was the same. Robert was missing in action. Wendy happened into the living room, having heard the bell ring and hoping against hope it was Robert home from the sea. She found Harley in tears, unable to speak. The mother handed the message to the daughter. She read it. Wendy cried out and ran from the room. Harley heard her door slam. Ordinarily she would approach a closed door and knock softly, asking permission to come in so they could talk. But not this time. This time, she downed her vodka and poured a third. Two days later came a second telegram. He was, indeed, dead by hostile enemy action.

She couldn't eat or sleep; she cried for weeks—but only outside the presence of Wendy. Wendy's response never wavered. She stayed in her room, refusing to come out even to eat and see her friends. She refused to attend her father's funeral. At that time, the idea of children of that age attending funerals was not favored anyway, maybe because of the war and the premature deaths families across America were suffering. Either way, the child was adamant: she was not going to the funeral; she was not going out with Harley ever again, not anywhere, not for any reason.

She kept her word, too. Mother and daughter were done. It wasn't for lack of trying on Harley's part, however, as she continued to look for a way through Wendy's armor. She took a ninety-day leave from her job in order to be there for Wendy. Having her mother around the house all day only served to enrage the daughter even more, Harley discovered. Her ninety-day leave was abandoned after only eleven days of trying. She had finally given up. The daughter she adored was simply lost to her. Two years went slowly by while the mother-daughter war continued. It was a time of few words, a time of loss and senseless silence by both.

Then a tiny spark ignited in Wendy's dark world. She joined drama club at school when a boy she liked had joined. She tried out for plays and built scenery and whispered dropped lines to actors from offstage. Her freshman year, she tried out for drama club and landed the female lead in *South Pacific*. It brought mother and daughter together. The joy of being in such an important musical lit all the dark corners in the Ellis household. After the play was over, however, the old doldrums and distance set back in again and there was open hostility.

Wendy wanted more. She begged her mom to allow her to try out for the movies. Wendy had listened to audience praise for her part in the musical and she had taken it in, deciding that she was special on the stage and that she really did have a future in film and stage. "That's why we're living in LA," she claimed. "Other girls aren't so lucky to be this close to the studios."

Harley said no film tryouts. She held firm against the idea. She told Wendy she was too young, and she had to graduate high school first. The cold war between mother and daughter came roaring back. Doors were routinely slammed, and days went by without words. Harley was beside herself then, after speaking with the psychiatrist, who said it would be a waste of money for Wendy to keep coming to see her. So, Harley gave in, even knowing that the movies might be a horrible experience for a fourteen-year-old who was troubled far beyond what the psychiatrist said was curable by talk therapy.

She took Wendy to her first screen test.

4

The marine layer hung low in the air, but the fog was thinning. A mischievous sailor tossed a bag of chips onto the beach and seagulls covered the sand, while just above the breakers a pod of pelicans skimmed for fish. A typical Monday at Santa Monica Pier. Skaters clacked by on the sidewalk at the end of the pier and bodybuilders lifted weights in the grass beyond the sidewalk.

The clock tower had just bonged noon. A swirl of activity meant it was the first day of the movie shoot of Ira J. Spielman's latest creation, *At Last, At Last*, a 1955 detective flick starring Martha Z. Gelb and Tag Zastrow, the older woman, the younger man. Him, a post-teen heartthrob whose costumes just did cover the tattoos plastered along both forearms—definitely not your Fifties look for Fifties police detectives. Her, fifty going for thirty-six; the makeup artist would be up for an Oscar if Ms. Gelb passed for mid-thirties.

Ira J. Spielman was there, wearing cordovan shoes, gray slacks, a double-breasted navy jacket with heavy gold buttons, a navy vest, and a scarlet ascot. His face was red as his neck cloth. His eyes were wide with rage. He was beyond shocked. "What do you mean the actors won't come onto the pier for the scene?" he barked at an assistant. "We're losing five-thousand dollars an hour for this?" He looked almost frightened as he shouted at his AD from among an expensive array of lights, cameras, dollies, grips, other AD's, and a dozen additional hands waiting for the shoot to continue. Everyone was looking at everyone else for an answer; finally, all eyes came to rest on Ira J. Spielman, the man in charge of making the movie for Capitol Films.

On the last bong of noon, precisely—a prearranged deadline with the Screen Actors' Guild—the entire cast of actors, including two dozen extras, had suddenly walked off the set, walked off the pier, and refused to participate any longer in the day's shoot. Then they had taken up picket signs and placards and were giving press interviews at the pier's entrance, explaining why they'd gone out on strike.

Martha Gelb—the female lead—wearing a stylish high-waisted suit, had the largest clutch of reporters gathered around her. She accepted a canteen of water from an AD and inhaled a withering drag from her long, black cigarette.

She cooed, "You darlings must know that Ira J. Spielman refused to meet Screen Actors' Guild's demand for a raise in salaries for the little people on the film. I mean, everybody knows he told SAG they could go fuck off."

Handheld recorders jockeyed even closer to her face. She raised a hand. "I mean, it's no secret that Ira's a total Jew asshole, is it?"

It was rhetorical. She was rich and in huge demand, therefore could say anything about anybody and it was always "Just like Martha" to say that. Gelb tossed her head back and chugged down one-fourth of the canteen. She wiped her mouth with the sleeve of her costume. A wardrobe assistant standing nearby rolled his eyes. There went a wasted hour—if shooting ever resumed—trying to get the lipstick stain out of the sleeve.

When the reality of the SAG strike had thoroughly wormed its way into Spielman's brain, he suddenly took off in a run for a payphone across from the pier. He dialed Reuben Ignacio Ordañez in Juarez. He waited impatiently, kicking his glossy half-boot against a surf store baseboard, as the phone beeped and beeped, waiting for the other end to pick up.

A heavily accented voice came on the line.

"Mr. Ordañez, Ira J. Spielman calling."

"Señor Spielman. I just heard the strike went ahead."

Spielman swore softly into the phone, casting a look back over his shoulder to make sure he was alone before he continued. General Security Services had the set on lockdown, and he hadn't been followed.

"I thought you told me you had leverage with SAG? You told me the strike wouldn't go off, General!"

"We do have that leverage. I will take care of this without delay."

"What do you plan to do?" asked Spielman, then, as fast as he could form the words, he shouted into the phone, "No, wait! Wait! Don't tell me. I don't want to know what you're doing."

Spielman was certain all phones were bugged. In fact, he saw bugs everywhere, especially the non-existent ones in pay phones.

Reuben Ordañez laughed sharply. "I was only going to say we're going to send our man to talk to the SAG and make a cash offer to settle the strike."

"How much will you offer?"

"Two million dollars." Spielman smiled. It was 1955 and it was a treasure.

"Where—where do you get that kind of money?"

"Oh, we have our benefactor."

"And who might that be?" Spielman asked, allowing his curiosity to overcome his request that he be left in the dark as to the how's and why's of Reuben Ordañez' derailing the SAG strike.

"He's a real estate developer out in the Valley. He's our best hope. Mickey Loden."

"Mickey Loden? What the hell kind of name is that?"

"Same as you, Ira, same as you."

"He's friendly?"

"They tell me he's friendly enough," Ordañez chuckled.

"You know what I mean. The money is washed?"

"It's coming out of his personal account. He's had it for years."

"Um, why's he loaning the money at all?"

"Oh, he hasn't agreed yet. But neither do we have his daughter for safekeeping yet, either."

"General, I asked you not to give me details! Call my other phone tonight!"

Spielman drew back his right arm and slammed the phone down hard enough to break it. He couldn't wait even another second and allow that call to be traced. If it were, he could go to prison for many, many years. He turned and headed back to the movie set.

Back across the street he could see the entire entourage of actors and extras gathered at this end of the pier. More press had arrived; there were TV cameras and microphones jammed in the face of anyone in costume who would talk.

Spielman took all this in and sadly shook his head as he approached. His large Ray-Ban Aviators were tight on his face, hiding the fury and hatred in his eyes that he was feeling toward SAG just then. He would have murdered Sir Lawrence Goolsby, the SAG president, were he anywhere near. The hourly production costs were horrific and were continuing to accrue even while everyone had walked off. Their studio contract called for a continuation in pay should SAG call a strike. It didn't even need to be a legal strike, according to the contract terms. Any old strike would do and Spielman—really Capitol Films—had to pay. Of course, in the end Spielman was actually on the hook for it, because he had to keep his shareholders happy. Without their support and majority vote in his favor he'd been out on his ear, left with non-voting shares of common stock that amounted to less than one-percent of the issued stock. It was a lot of money that he owned in stock shares, granted. But in the scheme of the total value of the outstanding stock, what he owned was a pittance. Which meant his power was based on a popularity contest that would nosedive when, at five o'clock that afternoon, the TV news screens jumped to life and newspapers hit the front porches. The SAG strike would be the top story and not more than two or three lines into the story, his own name would appear, and he would be held up as the blue meany who refused to negotiate with the studio employees. Which was now resulting in a chain reaction across Hollywood—no, across the entire movie industry—as more and more workers learned they wouldn't be going to work tomorrow, not in the face of a SAG strike and its picket lines, which no one would cross. Meaning, no one would get paid a full day's pay from then until the strike ended—all thanks to Ira J. Spielman, the stingy little Jew over at Capitol Films.

That was exactly how it would roll and exactly how he would look to the stockholders whose shares would plummet in value as the strike wore on. He swore and called the SAG president every manner of obscenity he could come up with. Screen Actors' Guild had even voted to expel any member who refused to testify before HUAC, an extremely unpopular move. Spielman hated SAG for this.

More than ever, he needed to hear from Reuben Ordañez that night and learn the plan for ending the strike with the help of money to be supplied by a name just now known to Spielman, Mickey Loden. The guy would have money and plenty of it and the money would buy-off the SAG officers and spread a few bucks around the membership, which would end the strike. The money needed wasn't chump change, either. After all, this was LA, and Hollywood's stores were overflowing with ostrich coats and boa constrictor boots just waiting to grace all actors loaded with money. It would toll Spielman's demise at Capitol Films if the strike impacted sales on Rodeo Drive.

He checked his watch. It would be four hours until Reuben Ordañez called him. He shut his eyes and pulled the sunglasses off his face. He pinched his eyes with his thumb and forefinger and wiped away the day's collection of debris.

Four hours and change.

But he could do it; he'd done worse in his life.

He'd done much, much worse.

∼

HE ACTUALLY WAITED SIX HOURS. The call came in at 7:05 that night. Spielman had a deal with a phone company engineer that he'd be notified if his phones were ever tapped. So, he felt secure, taking the call over a home line.

"You're late," Spielman said when he answered. "What the hell?"

"It took longer than expected. The developer was in Palm Springs when we grabbed his daughter."

"You have her now?"

"We have her, and the father knows. He will have the money to SAG by Sunday night."

"Then you release the daughter?"

"Don't worry about her. We still have need of her."

"But she's going to be all right?"

"Of course, Señor, we're not animals."

"No, that's not what I meant. I didn't mean to imply that you were."

"She will remain in our custody until we're sure about her father. He has two other, younger daughters. He must know they can never be safe from us. He is getting that lesson now."

Spielman was inspired by the man's knowledge of pressure points. "Ordañez, I want to come to Juarez to meet with you. We can talk about more work."

"Impossible. You won't be safe here. Too many American agents. I will come to LA and we can talk."

"Come right away. I have many ideas about the movie industry. You can make millions here."

"As can you," said Ordañez.

Spielman hung up the phone and gleefully rubbed his hands together. God was in his heaven again and all was right with the world. Tomorrow would be another buffet of actresses coming in for screen tests and then shooting would resume the next.

Oh, joy, he said to the glass of scotch that followed the call.

Oh, joy.

5

Ira J. Spielman was old and toady while Wendy was young and trim. In the real world women no longer looked at him. But this wasn't the real world: this was Hollywood, California, where anything could happen. He happened to be the head of Capitol Films. Now, too many women looked at him for the wrong reasons —they wanted something he had. They wanted the dream he could make happen. And as for Spielman? Too many men think sexual conquest is the end when, for the woman, it's really only the beginning.

The terrible Korean War had left Americans wrung out. All of the death-dealing and daily threats of another world war and death by nuclear fission left people needing an escape. Wendy went to Capitol Films to provide that escape as a movie star.

Her mother dropped her just beyond the studio gate. Wendy walked up and poked her appointment letter through the guard's window. Her face said it was her turn to make America fall in love again. The guard waved her on through and down the sidewalk toward Spielman's private office.

Spielman was a 1939 German refugee who knew how lucky he was to be alive, much less the head of a sprawling Hollywood studio with its back lots, its stable of established Hollywood screen stars, and the endless curves of firm flesh begging for a screen test. It was this avalanche of eighteen-year-olds that was immediately welcomed into Spielman's office where acting careers could be pursued on his casting couch. Literally, Ira J. Spielman kept a casting couch in his walnut-paneled office. He was Spielman, she was Ellis, what could go wrong?

Plenty. She had lied about her age: she was only fourteen. She arrived clutching a folder crammed with headshots and a bag of garish cosmetics. She was the beneficiary of a smile that cheered up others, a girl who'd skipped fourth grade when it was discovered she was reading at a twelfth-grade level, complete with a pert nose à la Doris Day and a wasp-waist and wasp ethic. Nobody could say she didn't fit the mold; she did. It only remained to claim her spot on some soundstage and charm American moviegoers.

No challenge was too imposing for the young woman. After Wendy had starred in her school's production of *South Pacific*, she was encouraged by admirers to carve out a place for herself in the movies. The problem was, she took their encouragements seriously. Without having at hand the mathematical probability of success in Hollywood for a one-hit freshman actress, Wendy had succumbed to the roar of the greasepaint and wheedled at her mother until Harley had acquiesced to the screen test.

How Wendy got there was simple enough. Her drama coach knew someone in the studio who knew someone in Spielman's office who knew Spielman. That last someone, armed with pictures of a middlingly attractive Wendy, casually mentioned her interest to Spielman who, it must be said, had taken note of her photos and instructed his staff to call her right in.

Wendy paused just outside Spielman's office and twirled around as if to get her bearings. Or as if she were Mary Martin with her first taste of some enchanted evening.

Wendy had arrived.

WENDY SHOWED up in the mogul's office on the fourteenth day of March 1955. She was wearing a plain white dress with a string of paste pearls, black heels, and enough rouge and lipstick for a Marlene Dietrich matinee. Her bedroom-eyes and porcelain face, perfectly framed by her Lucille Ball poodle cut, wasn't lost on Ira J. Spielman. He ignored the high-heel wobbling runway walk. It only added to her innocence.

She nervously twisted a small hanky and tried to smile at the appropriate moments as Spielman recited for her the studio's roster of movies currently being created as well as female roles that might be just what the aspirant prayed for. Spielman was overcome. Ever so meticulously he sunk the hook deeper and deeper into the fish's mouth until, when he paused to consider what else he could tell her, she was vibrating like a tuning fork, ready for the screen test she was certain must be coming. Maybe in his next sentence.

But his next sentence had nothing to do with a screen test. In fact, it had nothing to do with anything, as far as Wendy could see.

"Why don't you disrobe for me and let me see what you're made of," Spielman suggested in a thick voice.

Wendy recoiled. Had he been speaking to her? She turned to look, to be sure it was just the two of them in the room. It was.

"Uh-uh," she uttered.

"Oh, it's all right. This is standard fare in Hollywood. All studio heads want to see their starlets in the flesh—it's mandatory we know going in just what they will ultimately reveal in movie number five, typically, when the shirt comes off maybe in a beach scene or maybe in a hotel room. I need to know you've got the goods ahead of time, before I spend millions on your career and your persona."

Did that sound reasonable she asked herself. Then she thought of her mother, the police detective. My God, she would be mortified. But Wendy blamed her mother for her father's death. Besides, she knew nothing about Hollywood and its ways. While a full disrobe was a crime by mother's standards, Wendy was convinced by Spielman's casual invitation to do as he asked. Off came the clothes.

When she was nude, he suddenly lifted her from the floor, and set her upon his casting couch. Then he held her down. When he was finished, he rolled to the side and slipped to his knees. He rested his head in her lap.

"Stroke my hair, please," he asked.

"No, Mr. Spielman! Let me up!"

"You should know, Wendy, I think you've earned the junior female lead in my next film."

"What lead?" she whispered. Her face was grim. Tears were staining her cheeks.

The Gayle Howard role."

"I don't think I better take the part, Mr. Spielman," she at last said. "We shouldn't have done that."

"You don't want the part of Gayle Howard, a cub reporter on the newspaper?"

"What newspaper?"

"*The Los Angeles Gazette*."

"*The Los Angeles Gazette*? Is that a real newspaper?"

He smiled at her as a father would smile at a child who'd just cleaned her room. "Dear girl," he muttered. "Dear girl."

Wendy's racing thoughts caught up to her in the moment. "I think you just raped me, Mr. Spielman." Tears overflowed her eyes and she wept. Her hands shook as she tried to wipe away his saliva from her mouth.

"Of course not, Annie."

"Wendy. Yes, you did. You raped me. I'm only fourteen."

Spielman's face whitened beneath his sallow skin. "You'll mention it to no one! And if you do, I'll just say you seduced me, dear girl. I'm a well-known businessman, the head of a huge corporation, and you're—you're—you're Annie Nobody! Who will they believe?"

"My name is Wendy. If they won't believe me then I'll get a gun and shoot you."

"Wait. *Shoot me*? Where does that kind of talk come from?"

"From the US Navy. My dad's a sailor."

"Let's leave mom and dad out of this, please."

"I'll be expecting you to call about Gayle Howard in the next day or two, Mr. Spielman. You shouldn't have called me a nobody. Now I want the role."

Without comment, Spielman chased Wendy from his office. His secretary took over for him with all the usual promises about telephone calls to come, *have your agent call our office*, and all the rest of the roadblocks that would arise in front of Wendy until, in three or four months, her savings ran out and she would flee Hollywood and return to wherever the hell she'd come from.

Wendy found herself ushered out of Capitol Films' administrative offices, outside into the blinding Hollywood sun, where the female escort walked her to the studio entrance and waved her off as Wendy passed through the iron gate only to hear it groaning closed behind her.

Her mind was reeling backward over what just happened. At that moment, another young woman came up behind her. "Hey," she said. "I was in there before you. Got a minute?"

Wendy spun around. "A minute?"

"That guy in there, Spielman. Did he tell you there's a part for you?"

"Gayle Howard. I want it so bad."

The young woman's face fell. "I know. He told me I might have it, too. I want it just as bad. I can't get work and I need the part to get my kid back from foster care."

"The state took away your baby?"

"Yeah, she's four. She cries for me every night. I'm dying. Mr. Spielman said I have the exact looks for Gayle Howard."

"I sort of heard the same thing. Which is really crummy."

"I know. Hey, want to get coffee?"

"Sure."

"Number 11 bus will be here in about three minutes. We can ride it ten blocks and there's a cafe. Let's go talk."

"All right. What's your name?"

"Annalee Johnson. What's yours?"

"Wendy Ellis. I'm from Long Beach."

"Yeah, I live in Toluca Lake."

They caught the next bus and went up to the Morning Glory cafe. Coffee was ordered—no sweets, both were watching their waist-lines. They talked for several minutes, then more coffee came. Wendy then excused herself to go the bathroom.

"Watch my purse?"

"Sure. I'll be right here," said Annalee.

Wendy was crying in the bathroom as she tried to clean herself up. She urinated, washed and dried her hands, then broke down weeping even harder. She cried and cried, then dried her eyes. She then returned to the table. She noticed her purse had been moved. *Probably the waitress clearing the table*, she thought.

"Can I tell you something, Annalee?" she said when she sat back down.

"Sure."

"He raped me. I was crying in the bathroom."

"He tried it with me. I bit him so hard he lost his boner. You should call the police if he raped you."

"No, my mom's a detective. We don't get along. I don't want to have to explain anything to her. I'm just stupid for going in there alone with him. Then he called me a nobody. Now I want Gayle Howard to prove to him I'm somebody. I could kill him, though."

"Me, too, for you."

Wendy's mind raced. She deserved that role: she had earned it. Had she given him the correct number at home? For just a moment, she panicked. But then she said her number to herself. She had given it correctly. "He raped me, Annalee. Doesn't that mean he has to give me the part? But I know you need it for your little girl. This is terrible. I'm very frightened he would try it again anyway."

"I do need it. But you deserve it."

"I'm going to call and get a ride home. Do you want my mom to take you, too?"

"No, I'm too far. There's a bus."

Wendy stayed and had a cherry Coke after Annalee left for the next bus. She had called dispatch and dispatch radioed Harley. It happened all the time. She sipped on the sugary drink, thinking, nursing the soda while she waited for her mom.

She finished her drink and went out and looked up and down Hollywood Boulevard. Her mother's car was slowing to pick her up. She stared at the sunlight glinting up from her patent leathers. She couldn't have known, of course, that the innocence of youth was the customary currency for screen tests. She wouldn't fully understand the price that had just been taken from her. Still, tears wet her cheeks. There was something horribly wrong about what had happened. The Vice detective pulled over and told her to jump in. She asked what was wrong.

"Nothing." Wendy sniffed.

With Wendy beside her on the front seat, the detective gave her a sidelong look and shook her head. "Something bad happened with him, am I right?"

"Mr. Spielman said I might get a part. I'm crying happy."

"What part?"

"The Gayle Howard part."

The detective sighed. She was made up like a prostitute as she was still working Vice. She two-fingered a Camel out of her breast pocket and swept a sulfur match across the radio speaker cover. It flared, she lit up, then blew a long plume of smoke sufficient to snuff the match.

"Well," she said. "I'm sure you earned it."

Wendy cried again.

"Hey, kid, brighten up! You're gonna be in the movies!"

"It doesn't feel like I thought it would feel. I feel let down."

"Everyone who comes to the movie lots says that."

"Everyone?"

The detective waved her hand at the Hollywood stretching out beyond her windshield.

"Just ask around. Everyone."

TWO WEEKS LATER, Ira J. Spielman, was found slouched on his casting couch, a metal letter opener inserted into his right ear clear up to its hilt.

"I'm guessing fatso here punched some starlet's dance card and she punched him back. With an Oscar and a letter opener. 'Ding-dong, special delivery Mr. Spielman.'"

The speaker was LAPD Detective Danny Sullivan, who had just stepped into the mogul's office.

His partner, Lionel Black, peered down at the slumped figure of the movie maker and simply shook his head. "It wasn't special delivery and it wasn't some irate starlet. I'm putting my money on the wife getting fed up with him and putting his life insurance in play. She's probably already filed the death notice with Allstate."

"I like that," Sullivan said. He retrieved a cigarette and a small box of wooden matches from his pants pocket. The match flared and he sucked down a lungful of blue smoke. "Tell you what, Lio," he said to his partner, "How about you send a uniform over to their house and grab a copy of the life insurance policy? We'll run it past Allstate for claims made."

Lionel Black waved a uniformed police officer over and told him what Sullivan wanted done. The uniform immediately turned on his heel and headed for the door.

"Lio, check this out," Sullivan said. He had unbuttoned the top three buttons of Spielman's Hawaiian floral shirt.

Lionel leaned down to see. Claw marks raked the dead man's chest.

"Someone told him no and he had his way with her anyhow," said Lionel.

"He was dicking some lady against her will. Whether she stabbed his head just after he assaulted her or whether she returned later, we don't know. But the claw marks look old—there's some scabbing beginning to form. I'm putting my money on a return to the scene of her assault. She went home, stewed for a day or two, then returned and shivved Mr. Dead Asshole with the letter opener."

Lionel smiled. "You already hate the guy, Sully. Keep that on the down-low."

Sullivan shot a look around the office. Several crime scene techs and two grunts from the medical examiner's office were present but very busy with their work. He wasn't concerned about his feelings toward the so-called victim. He was most likely a rapist and the killer was the real victim. At least that was how he'd decided he would play it.

So, it began for Detective Danny Sullivan, Los Angeles Police Department, Hollywood Division.

6

Spielman had raped her but so what? she asked herself. Well, she felt dirty, like she had done something wrong. If her mother found out there would be hell to pay. And she wouldn't get to try out for the movies again any time soon. Probably never. Wendy imagined her mother would blame her, probably ground her, maybe lay a hand on her, Wendy didn't know. Her mother had never hit her before, but she'd never been raped before. She felt like she was at fault. She could've stopped it before it got so far along, couldn't she have? Well, why didn't she put her foot down and say no? Was it because she wanted the part so bad? Now she had to get away. She had to take her shame somewhere and bury it.

Wendy watched from the bus window as Hollywood Boulevard went by. *The Robe* was playing at the Iris. Long lines all the way down the block. Then came Rexall, Safeway, Thrifty, Lerner's, Kress, Admiral Theatre, Royal Rooms, Shoe City, Vermillion Hotel, FW Woolworth, and JJ Newberry at Hollywood Boulevard and Whitley. Stretched across the Boulevard were the red and white banners of the Red Cross with the words "On the Job!" Then came the Ford plant and long lines of brand new 1955 Fords. The freeway was all but empty of cars. She finally turned away from the window. She turned inside herself.

She had brought along a duffel stuffed with shorts and underwear and T-shirts and photographs of her dad and many of his letters.

The bus was crowded, for a midday. Her seat was halfway back, on the aisle. The bus exited the freeway and made a stop. She quickly scooted across the bench seat and turned her face to the glass. She did everything she could do not to make eye contact with the other loading passengers as they streamed down the aisle on her left. A sauntering figure, wearing a black cowboy hat and shades, paused next to her seat. "Ma'am?" he said. "This seat taken?"

"No."

"Fine, then I'll just help myself."

He sat down and let out a long sigh. "Man, it does feel good to let them doggies rest. I ain't never been so lost as I've been in LA."

She didn't reply; only kept staring out the window at the passengers yet waiting in line to board. Then they rejoined the freeway, heading northeast toward Vegas.

"So," he said. "Name's Robert Ray Miller. How about you?"

She turned slightly. "My dad was named Robert."

"Was? He ain't no more?"

"No, he died in the war."

"Now there's a frigging shame. I'm sorry for your loss, ma'am."

"Yes. He was a great man."

"Tell me what you liked best about him."

"He loved me. I was his only child and he adored me."

"Yeah? What else? Did he do lots of stuff with you?"

She felt a twinge of loss and her lip trembled. "He did everything with me. We went everywhere in Vallejo. Then he went in the GD Navy."

"Did he get bombed on a ship?"

"No one knows. He was on a whaleboat in the Inchon Harbor. That's all the Navy ever told us. I think it means they don't know what happened."

"I was in the Navy. Got out on a medical."

"Did you get hurt, Robert Ray?"

"No." He touched the side of his head. "Up here."

"That's too bad."

"I wanted to have it be my career. But not no more. They don't want me, piss on 'em. What's your name, anyway?"

"Wendy."

"Like Peter Pan. My sister read me that when I was very little. I remember wanting to fly. I wanted to fly in the Navy, but oh, no." Again, he touched the side of his head and this time winked. Wendy nodded and winked back. "Where you headed?"

"My ticket's to Las Vegas."

"Me, too. I'm gonna find a job there and eventually buy a house. Hey, where you staying? Your family there?"

"No, I don't know yet. I just decided this morning."

"Good for you. You can stay with me until you decide, then."

"Where do you live?"

"Well, first a motel, then when I get first and last month's rent saved up, I get a studio apartment. Then go from there. Do you work? You look young."

"I can do house cleaning and babysitting. I'm very good at both."

"Then you'll be fine. There's lots of that wherever you go."

"That's good to know."

"How old are you, Wendy?"

"Eighteen."

"So, you don't need parents' consent to get married or join the army. That's good."

"Don't worry. I'm not doing either one. I'm getting a place that's all my own and having my own life now."

"Well, the offer's always open. You can stay with me until you decide."

"What do you do?"

"I'm a helluva bus boy and car washer. Plenty of experience there."

"Do those pay well?"

"Hell, no. But I'm just getting started. That's why I'm going to Las Vegas. They've got a school that teaches you how to fly. That's my goal is to be an airline pilot. Hey, want a nip?"

She turned and looked. He had pulled from the pocket of his leather vest a half-pint of Old Grandad. He unscrewed the cap and took a draw.

Wendy shook her head. "Hate that stuff. It makes me want to throw up."

"I was that way at first, too. You'll get used to it if you stay with me. I party just about every night."

"When do you study for flying?"

"Oh, that's at the school. Don't worry your pretty head, Wendy. I've gotta save up for that first. It costs three-thousand dollars to get your license. I'm short by two-thousand-eight-hundred."

"You have two-hundred dollars?"

"To my name. What about you?"

"I've got five-hundred minus my ticket."

"Why don't we do this. Why don't we marry our property and money and go from there? That way we have a fighting chance."

"You mean put our money together?"

"I do."

"What do you have to put in the pot?"

He opened his backpack. "Two shirts," he said, pulling out two wrinkled T-shirts, three boxers, and Saltine crackers. "Plus, I got a folding knife I got in the Navy, a letter opener—why I have that is self-defense. It's metal. Do you carry anything for self-defense?"

"No. Do I need to?"

He retrieved the letter opener from his pack and passed it to her. "Here, take this. It'll fit in your purse. Anyone attacks you, strike back. What do you have to put in?"

She absently slipped the letter opener into her purse.

"I have my money, some clothes, a hairbrush, toothbrush, my dad's picture and a scarf he gave me before he went to the war. It has my initials. I did have two, but one got lost. That's about it, though."

"It ain't much."

She looked out the window. The bus was running into heavy traffic. "I don't know. I have twice what you have in money."

"That's just it. I'll work the first two weeks, so you don't have to. You can take your time finding the right job."

"That sounds about right. Tell you what, Robert Ray, you just got yourself a roommate."

"Damn, girl! Put her there!"

They shook hands then leaned back and stared out Wendy's window.

"This is pretty exciting," he said. "We can join forces and it has to work."

"Did they tell you what was wrong with—with your head?"

"The Navy? They called it sociopath. It means I'm very social."

"That sounds about right. I am too."

"I pushed a guy off our ship. They had a court martial and all. It wasn't my fault; the fool wouldn't shut up about my back."

"What's wrong with your back?"

"Here." He turned in the seat and lifted his shirt and vest. His back was covered in long, white scars. "Pretty sight, huh?"

"Who did that?"

"My old man. He thought I was a dog. It made me very social, the Navy shrinks told me."

"Figures. My dad would never do that."

"You had a good one, Missy. Don't crow. Luck of the draw."

"I'm sorry you're a sociopath. That must be hard."

"Just makes me want to do stuff sometimes. Stuff I ain't proud of."

"Like what?"

"I'm very protective. You'll be very safe with me. I take care of my people. Especially if they're good to me."

"That sounds about right. My dad was that way."

"I'm thirty-two, Wendy. I'm almost old enough to be your dad."

"I really miss him." She began crying. He took out a handkerchief and dabbed her tears.

"There, there. I'd kill the commies who killed your dad. Honest I would."

"That's very nice. Very kind."

"I wouldn't mind killing a commie right now."

"Don't be silly, Robert Ray. I'm hungry."

"Here." He reached inside a waist pocket and removed a pack of Hostess Sno Balls. He split them evenly, the pink one for Wendy, the white for himself. "Now, don't say I never gave you nothing. See there? I'm providing already. Just like a good daddy would."

"My daddy always fed me. He made my breakfast and my supper when my mom was working."

"What's she do?"

"She's a police woman."

"Oh, hello. You sure you're eighteen?"

"Positive. Want to see my ID?"

"Ain't necessary. Why would you lie to me, Wendy? You wouldn't."

"I don't lie."

"Me, neither."

The bus pulled beyond the Los Angeles city limits and headed northeast for Las Vegas at sixty-five miles an hour. There would be many stops. Wendy was excited. She'd already made a friend and had a place to stay—if she wanted. She decided to see what it looked like in Las Vegas before she decided. They were scheduled to arrive just after midnight.

The bus rumbled on across the desert. Windows were lowered and canteens were opened. It was very hot and there was no air conditioning.

Wendy and Robert Ray alternated between talking and making plans and dozing off.

"I'm tired. But I'm thinking I'll be staying with you the first week. At least."

"You could do worse, girl."

"I could, couldn't I?"

It would do for a start. She had made another decision that day. She was going to get set up in Vegas and then she was coming back to LA to confront Spielman. He had raped her and now she deserved the part.

She would return. Like Robert Ray said, she could do worse.

7

H arley slipped into the second row of Courtroom 1109, Hon. Joshua H. Bretherd. Judge Bretherd looked her up and down as she took her seat. Harley had appeared in his court before and there had been friction. Happily, the judge turned his attention back to the witness testifying. Harley just could see the lawyer at the lectern: Marcia Meriwether. She was medium height, with shoulder length brown hair from the rear. When she turned and scanned the crowd at one point, Harley could see bright red lipstick and wide-set eyes that appeared dark blue in color. She was all business, neither smiling nor frowning, when she turned and went back to her notes. Thanks to the Student Practice Rule for law students Marcia could appear in court under supervision and conduct arguments and witness examinations. She was paused, looking at her notes. Harley crossed her legs and leaned forward.

"Mr. Kleinschmidt," Marcia began. "You testified that when the officer pulled you over on July 29th you'd had two drinks over the course of about four hours?"

"That's right. I wasn't even feeling them."

"Why so few drinks? I mean, it was a wedding and weddings are pretty much drink-alongs, aren't they?"

"I knew I was driving my family home. You can have fun but not too much. Not when your family's in your hands."

"So, when you ran the stop sign and hit Jerry McQuade on his motorcycle, you are telling the jury the alcohol had nothing to do with that?"

"It was very dark out and he had no lights on the side of his motorcycle. I slowed but my brakes didn't grab."

"The police mechanics tested your brakes after the accident. The report says they were working one-hundred percent. Does that sound like faulty brakes?"

"I can't explain it. They didn't catch and the next thing I knew, this motorcycle comes shooting into the intersection at a very high rate of speed."

"Really? The reconstructionist who studied the skid marks said you were doing forty-five at the moment of collision. Would you agree that you were also traveling at a very high rate of speed?"

"Like I said, it was very dark, the speed zone was twenty-five, but it just had been forty-five and my brakes didn't grab. How fast did your expert say *McQuade* was going?"

Harley was relieved when Marcia ignored the question from the witness. Lawyers are never to answer questions posed by witnesses or the examination is instantly lost.

"I'm asking the questions. Let me repeat, would you deny that your skid marks indicate you were doing forty-five miles per hour at impact?"

"No, I don't deny. My brakes—"

"And you don't deny the hospital blood test that shows a blood alcohol reading of point-two-three? Far above the legal limit of blood alcohol?"

"They drew my blood. I have no way of checking how good their test was. My lawyer says—"

"No, not your lawyer. You need to answer: isn't it true you were over twice the legal limit?"

"That's what the hospital report said. But I wasn't feeling it at all."

"And when you opened your door to take the field sobriety tests you had to hang on to your door for support, correct?"

"It was slippery that night."

"Again, you had to hang onto your door?"

"I might have. But it was raining."

"Mr. Kleinschmidt, have you seen the accident report where the officer checked the box that says the road surface was dry?"

"I know it rained that night at some point. I don't deny that."

Marcia halted her examination. "Your Honor, I believe that is all."

"Thank you, counsel," said the judge. "We'll take our morning recess now."

As the court began to clear, Harley approached Marcia at counsel table.

She touched the law student on the shoulder and said, "Hello, partner."

Marcia turned. "Hey, Harley! I guess we're the new team."

"We are. If you're finished up, I'm hoping we can head somewhere quiet and get acquainted a little better."

"Yes, my part's done. Let me tell Mr. Reinhart I'm leaving."

Harley stepped back behind the bar. She watched Marcia speak with her supervising attorney, they shook hands, and then Marcia headed Harley's way.

"I'm good to go. Where to?"

"I've got my unmarked out front. How about Green Door?"

It was a lawyers' hangout two blocks west.

"Perfect. I can't wait to compare notes."

They climbed into the unmarked 1955 Ford. It was roomy inside, with a huge steering wheel that required two hands except when shifting. The dashboard was wide and sparsely populated with gauges and speedometer that rose up in a semi-circle. In the center was the Motorola police radio and a hand mike with a large button for broadcasting. There were no seatbelts and no head-rests, just a broad bench seat. They pulled out of police parking and into traffic on Wilcox.

Ten minutes later, they were settling into a window booth. Harley was wearing her usual navy slacks and white shirt and dark jacket, while Marcia was still dressed in courtroom attire consisting of a tweed suit and pink shirt with a turquoise brooch, a smiling alliga-tor. *Fair warning to whoever she's going to cross-examine*, Harley thought. Alligator alert.

"So, what's better, law or law enforcement?"

"You know, I don't even know why I stay in law school. I guess because my dad's a lawyer. I much prefer chasing burglars to cross-examining drunk drivers. It's just more adrenaline out in the streets."

"Will you eventually practice law?"

"Eh, hard to say. The money's definitely better but I like being a cop. It makes me feel good about myself. Hey, what do you think about the Unsolved Crimes assignment?"

Harley ordered coffee and an English muffin; Marcia said double that.

"What do I think of UC? It ain't Robbery-Homicide but it ain't bad checks or Vice, either. I just did two years of Vice. No thank you, ma'am. Boring. But with Unsolved Crimes we get everything, including homicides. So that's kind of pre-school for RHD, the way I see it," Harley said. "I think it's going to be whatever we make of it. By the way, we snagged the Spielman murder case today. Seems Sullivan and Black pissed off the widow and she called and complained."

"We scored Spielman? I say congratulations to us! Wait, why didn't someone else in Homicide get it?"

"They need cheerleaders. That's us."

They raised water glasses and clinked.

"Hey, excuse me if it's a bad time to ask, but how are you doing with your daughter's case?"

Harley winced. "Not good. I think about it day and night. I'm worried sick, I obsess. It's an endless nightmare. Don't let me talk your arm off about it. I can get pretty gloomy."

"Who wouldn't? I wonder if we can somehow work it in, I mean looking for her. Just know that I'm up for that if we can do some looking around every day. You probably know her haunts."

"Someone called and said she's in Las Vegas now. But I don't really know." She surveyed the restaurant crowd, then added, "I'll let you in on my big secret. Wendy was in Spielman's office about two weeks before he was murdered. She tried out for a part in one of his movies."

"My God, that's random."

"I know. I just wonder if he did something to her. It's driving me nuts to think."

"He wasn't the great old guy the papers have him. I've heard stories too."

"Yes, unwanted pregnancies in some pretty young women, illegal abortions, Tijuana back alley hack jobs, ruining careers where girls refuse to put out. I don't know what I was thinking, letting Wendy go there alone for a screen test. Same thing when I let her get the damn tattoo. It had been rough between us. I let my need to win her heart override my better judgment. I went along with the tattoo then the screen test all because I love her so much. Tell me I'm not a terrible mom for it. So now she's gone. And so is Spielman. I'm wired like a time-bomb waiting to explode."

"Hey, tell you what, Harley. We're going to find your daughter and bring her home. What is she, seventeen? Eighteen?"

"Going on fifteen this month."

"Oh. Well."

Their coffee and muffins arrived. Jam was spread and the toasty muffins were crunched as they chewed in silence just like all the other working stiffs around them. Give a working man—or woman—something to eat and all conversation ceases, Harley thought as she looked around the room. It was maybe going to be okay, she was thinking, being teamed with Marcia. She was willing to spend some time helping look around for Wendy, too. That spoke volumes to Harley.

Marcia broke the long silence. "So, you catch the rumor there's some real estate mogul in the Valley who wanted Spielman dead? I've heard that."

"Haven't heard that. What's the guy's name?"

"Mickey Loden."

"Who is he?"

Marcia explained, "He's from Long Island in New York. Huge developer there until all the sand was used up. Now he's moved west where we don't run out of sand. Least not in his lifetime."

"What does Mickey Loden have against Ira J. Spielman?"

"They've been at odds. I think Loden had a daughter who wanted a shot at the movies and Spielman tried to bang her. Bad blood, very bad blood. Anyway, it's just a rumor. I'm sure Spielman had beaucoup other enemies, too."

"Oh, yes. He's been hanging around LA with too much money for too long. He's bound to make somebody mad."

"Like Twentieth-Century Fox, Metro-Goldwyn-Mayer, and—get in line. Capitol Films is the top draw and it's all because Spielman has a choke hold on the Screen Actors Guild. He says 'jump!' and they ask how high."

"Where does that come from? I thought the unions controlled the companies nowadays?"

Marcia knew her recent history. "Not since the House Un-American Activities Committee and McCarthy blacklisted so many actors, writers, and directors. Spielman picked up where

McCarthy left off. He's got a personal blacklist as long as your arm. SAG lives in fear of him."

"Then what's all this stuff in the papers about SAG striking? How is that afraid of Spielman?"

"I know. Somebody got cross-wired against our victim. Told him to take his movie and shove it. Then Loden's daughter gets kidnapped and Spielman's suddenly back in business. Wonder who had something against Spielman after that? I know where I want to start the investigation."

"Interview Mickey Loden?"

"Let's work over the murder book. He definitely belongs on our interview list somewhere."

"I'm liking this already," said Harley. She felt the case held the key to Wendy's disappearance. Working on it took away some of the helpless feeling she normally felt anymore. It could be good, going into partnership with Marcia.

It could be just the thing.

8

Harley turned to Marcia in the squad room. It was months after the SAG strike suddenly ended and all the studios went back to work. The story had made the front page of the *Times* back then, along with several questions the writer had. He said it seemed like the strike was over even before it began. Harley had just now read the piece and then passed the clipping to Marcia.

"Check that out about the SAG strike?" Harley asked.

Marcia took a swallow of her coffee. "They weren't out a full week, and someone paid them off. They were back to work the next day."

"Paid who off?" asked Harley."

"Someone paid off the SAG management and the strikers caved in. They were back on the set the same week all over town."

"How do you know this?"

Marcia shrugged. "What else could it be? Someone's palm got greased."

"You gotta love them. That's the kind of stuff keeps us afloat in killer cases."

"So, SAG went away. My contact at the FBI said Mickey Loden's daughter was kidnapped and Dad coughed up the ransom money, which was then used to buy off the SAG. Then Mickey had Spielman murdered for kidnapping her. This is the FBI's unofficial take on it."

"I'm liking your idea of starting with Loden first. Makes the most sense to go to the guy with the biggest axe to grind."

"It won't be easy. He's lawyered-up and circled the wagons. But at least we can let him know he's under the microscope."

"I'm sure he's insulated better than a Frigidaire."

"Sure, he is. But somebody'll snitch. They always do."

Harley said, "Tell you what. I'm paging through the murder book. Let's grab coffee and go over all the witnesses. Then we'll know what order to put them. That way, we can build the story by getting this one to agree to what that one just said and so on."

"Makes sense."

"I also think we're going to have to have a sit-down with Danny Sullivan. He didn't want to turn the murder book over to me. We need to let him know we really have replaced him and that he needs to let it go. I know LT talked to him, but I want to face him down, too. It's tough, being a high visibility case and good for any detective's career, and I get that. But Sullivan is just going to have to walk away and not keep punching at it with the hope he might score a big win."

After coffee, Harley and Marcia opened the murder book on Ira J. Spielman. The murder book was a three-ring binder containing, among other things, a chronology, a victim section, coroner reports, and witness summaries. Crime scene photos were also found there. They took the book to a small conference room and opened it to the first page. The lead detective, Danny Sullivan had made and initialed all entries in the book, as required.

"Let's just start with the chronology," said Harley. "Sit beside me and let's see how two minds are greater than one. Ready?"

"Ready," said Marcia with a smile. "I'm starting now."

The first entry was the callout. The entry stated that on April 1, 1955, Sullivan and Black received a call from dispatch reference a call from the offices of Capitol Films. They rolled on the call, along with the crime scene unit and members of the coroner's office. The call had come at 9:23 a.m. and they arrived at Capitol Films at 10:02 a.m. They went directly to Spielman's office and found the two patrol officers who were first on the scene. They'd secured the inner office where the body had been found by Spielman's secretary. She'd prepared his morning coffee and, after knocking and receiving no answer she'd entered the office. She'd found him seated on the leather couch, right side, slumped toward the center of the couch.

Harley and Marcia figured he had lured someone onto the couch and, as they began whatever they were there to do, that same someone had inserted a metal opener into his left ear and slammed it home. According to the coroner's report, the metal tip of the letter opener actually sliced through the sinus cavity and pierced the brain, causing a massive cerebral hemorrhage. The bleed was listed as the official cause of death.

"It took quite a bit of force," said Harley. "Whoever did this was pretty damn strong."

"Agree," said Marcia. "I don't want to come across as sexist, but I wonder if most women could kill like this. He was overpowered *and* stabbed."

"You're thinking another man?"

Marcia only shrugged. "Let's keep going."

The chrono went on to describe what the crime scene investigators did, including all areas searched and items marked as evidence. It also described what the medical personnel did while there, the gross anatomy investigation and the preparation of the body—with the letter opener in place—for transport to the coroner's on Mission Street. The detectives spoke with all possible witnesses from that morning, including the temp secretary, Malencia Hines, and the roving secretary, Helen Bates. Hines and Bates described Spielman's mood that morning as "chipper" and stated unequivocally that he seemed free of worry.

Sullivan and Black had canvassed the building, finding no one who claimed to have any information. They then moved to the front gates.

The gate guards consulted their visitor diary for the morning of the murder. They reported that two young women passed through the front gate within three minutes of each other. They were Annalee Johnson and Wendy Ellis. Both presented letters confirming appointments, which allowed them to pass through the first level of security. Wendy Ellis arrived at the gate first. The guard watched her and could confirm she followed his directions to Spielman's office. Next through was Annalee Johnson, who was given the same directions. She was last seen entering Spielman's office as well. Both young women had previously met with Spielman, according to the front gate registry book. Annalee Johnson's letter, received by the front gate and kept, was a call-back. Wendy Ellis' letter was not a callback. In fact, it was a letter stating that she hadn't been selected for the role of Gayle Howard and thanking her for auditioning. The letter also said she could return at any time for a second screen test. The guard said that language was why he had passed her through. Evidently, she had convinced the guard that she was in fact there to test again. Both letters were retrieved from the guards by the detectives. They were then marked and placed into the evidence box.

There were other visitors that morning as well. In particular, there was a grounds crew that entered—the crew was from a company previously unused by Capitol Films. They were there to trim the public-facing palm trees. The names of the crew members were not recorded as they were "All Mexicans, probably illegals there just for a day's pay," said the senior guard.

There was also a telephone company crew, two of them in two separate vehicles, there to install new service in a new administrative building that was apart from the building where Spielman had his office. Again, single names weren't taken down.

The detectives had gone on to contact both the tree trimming company and the telephone company and obtained full lists of all workers who'd entered the grounds that day. Many were no longer in their employ and some had even returned to Mexico. After checking with the Border Patrol, it was determined that those same members of the tree trimming crew who were Mexican citizens had actually not crossed into the U.S. since the day of the murder. They had previously crossed, two of them on the same morning as the murder, coming across at San Ysidro, fifteen miles south of San Diego.

All entries in the murder book were signed off with the initials DS for Danny Sullivan, senior detective.

The two secretaries presented Harley and Marcia an interesting conundrum. They had been in the office when the young ladies arrived. The young ladies had come in and taken seats, yet, when the police arrived, after Hines discovered the body, neither young woman was on the lot any longer. The puzzling part was that both secretaries reported they were momentarily gone from their work area when the visitors left. The guard station didn't record departures per its habit, and so the investigators were unable to pin down who had left when. At any rate, neither young woman came up on the radar again that day.

The documents section of the report—a sub-report within the evidence section—contained one startling finding. A letter was found inside Spielman's personal correspondence folder in his locked desk drawer. The letter was signed by Wendy Ellis. Upon reading it, Harley's heartbeat doubled, and she had to stand up and move about for a full minute, slowing her breathing before reading it again. It seemed that Wendy's letter to Spielman was a cry for help: she was terrified she'd gotten pregnant when he raped her. She wanted to know if he'd help support his baby if it came to that? Or would he pay for an abortion and tell her where to go? Or what else should she consider? The letter was written in the unmistakable childish scrawl of her daughter's hand, Harley could see. She sat back down, breathing hard. After a third reading, she again leapt to her feet and stomped around the room, breathing deeply and moaning to Marcia half-sentences about her daughter's plight.

Finally, Harley sat back down and was able to say, "This letter is old. Maybe I'm the mother of a girl who had an abortion. It rips my guts out."

"Excuse me and I hate to say this, but there's also another possibility for you and Wendy."

"What's that?"

"You might soon be a grandmother."

"I couldn't bring myself to even say that!"

"Sorry."

"We need to count months and start checking hospital births."

"And we need to check records for known abortionists. I don't know how to do that since abortion is illegal. But we'll find a way."

"I've been working Vice. I think I know them all."

"Let's start there."

"Sweet Jesus!" cried Harley. "Take me someplace, Marcia, I need to settle down!"

They left, then, taking the murder book with them.

TWENTY MINUTES later they were situated in a booth at the Family Cafe, two blocks away from Hollywood Station on Homewood. The waitress brought iced tea and apple pie. She didn't seem to notice her customers were sitting side-by-side in the booth, a large book opened and spread out before them.

The two detectives turned two pages, viewing color crime scene photos of Spielman. Then they came to a transcription of his wire-tapped phone call with Reuben Ignacio Ordañez. There were also notes about a certain engineer at the phone company being fired when it was learned he was tipping-off Spielman about phone taps. They read about Mickey Loden in the Valley, read about his daughter, and found out Spielman and Ordañez had been involved in a very serious plot involving the Screen Actors' Guild.

"Let's get this straight," Harley began, slowly chewing an apple slice. "SAG went out on strike. Capitol Films was shooting, Ira J. Spielman was on location. Maybe directing, producing, it's hard to say. SAG suddenly leaves and later that night, this Ordañez calls Spielman at home."

"So far so good," Marcia agreed. "From what I gather, twenty-thousand-foot view, it was cheaper for the film industry if the SAG management took a bribe than it was to actually enter new contracts with the SAG's thousand members."

"Right. So, they needed lots of money to bribe the SAG officials, money Spielman didn't have. And it wasn't like he could go around to all the movie companies and take up a collection. So, he turned to Ordañez for help."

"Ordañez somehow knew about a real estate developer out in the valley. Guy by the name of Mickey Loden. It seems Loden's daughter had done a screen test with Spielman."

"How do we know that?"

"I read it in Sullivan's earlier notes."

"So Ordañez kidnaps Loden's daughter and sets her ransom at two million, which Loden pays to get his daughter back. He gets her back, and everybody's happy. Especially the SAG president: he took in one million himself."

"Everybody's happy except Mickey Loden. He knows Spielman screen tested his daughter and tried to get in her pants. He also knows Spielman's Capitol Films was hardest hit by the strike. Spielman had the most to gain from getting the cast returned to work. At least around LA. So, Loden's going to suspect Spielman in the kidnapping. We know Loden is connected. Has been since New York and Long Island. It's a short jump from his connections to him bumping off Spielman as payback for the kidnapping. It also sends a message."

Harley half-smiled. Marcia was relieved to see her settling back down. "Wonder if Loden's daughter is still trying to get into the movies?"

Marcia shook her head. "Unknown."

"So, let me see if I have this straight. We've got conspiracy against Spielman and Ordañez. We've got kidnapping against Ordañez. And we've got possible murder against Loden. What about Ordañez, any reason for him to bump off Spielman?"

"I don't think so. I'm guessing Loden. Or—or—"

"Wendy Ellis," Harley said in a small voice. "The girl who had a reason to kill the guy who raped her and got her pregnant. It's okay, Marcia, go ahead and say it."

"I didn't want to say it. But we have to look at all the possibilities. I'm sorry, Harls. Truly sorry."

Harley shrugged. "More reason to find Wendy. If she's still alive. It's also occurring to me that Spielman had a damn good reason to get rid of Wendy. She was an embarrassment and could get him divorced. Or even removed as head of Capitol Films on a morals beef. She was a huge threat."

"It's a possibility. We have to follow up."

"So, let's make a list."

They wrote it all out, in order of who they'd contact:

1. Mrs. Spielman - see what she knows about enemies of husband.

1. Reuben Ordañez - see what he'll say about Spielman and Loden

2. Mickey Loden - did he report the kidnapping? Contact with Spielman? Convos with Ordañez?

3. Wendy Ellis - Role?

4. Annalee Johnson - Role?

5. Loden's daughter - Role?

6. Tree trimmers - contact all names in truck that day

7. Telephone company - contact all crew

After they made their list, they continued to talk. It was decided they would try to work the interviews together. One to talk and one for safety. Some of the people on the list were dangerous, especially Ordañez and Loden. They weren't afraid but they were cautious. They knew Lieutenant Chall would back them on that.

9

Danny Sullivan stayed late Thursday night. He waited until the RHD room was cleared out, then opened the murder book on the Spielman homicide.

Danny was a Notre Dame grad and was deeply religious. He was rigid in how he viewed his cases. Everything was either black or white to him, much like he saw his church. A thing was either right or wrong, no grays, no ambiguities. So, when he was pulled off the Ira J. Spielman case, he was angry, yes, but even more, he was determined not to be left holding the bag. He still planned to find out who killed Spielman and bring that person to justice. It was unthinkable that Ellis and Meriwether should make the arrest. The file still belonged to Sullivan—as far as Sullivan's thinking would allow. Thus, he checked the case book every night for any new information that might inform what steps he might take next, what rocks he might turn over.

At just after nine that Thursday night, Sullivan poured himself a fresh cup of coffee and started in reading the Spielman file updates. Then the name of Annalee Johnson caught his eye and held him there. Where had that entry come from? He read the file entry again, a statement by a traffic officer. The entry read, "Stopped cruiser and gave a ride to a citizen I saw running in high heels outside Capitol Films. Her name was Annalee Johnson. She climbed in my vehicle and I asked what was wrong. She said she'd just been assaulted by Ira J. Spielman. I suggested she might want to press charges. She said no, she said she doesn't press charges. She said she gets even. I asked if he raped her and she said no, but he, "Tried like hell, grabbing me all over." I took her up to the next bus stop, where she demanded to get out of my unit. That was the last I've seen of her." There were then a couple of follow-on notes, to the effect that Ellis-Meriwether calls had been made to the telephone company searching for a number for Annalee Johnson. They were unsuccessful.

Danny Sullivan wrote down the girl's name and the date of the contact. He was astonished that more hadn't been done. Here was someone who had made a threat— "she gets even"—and had motive to murder Spielman as he had just physically assaulted her. Why wasn't the entire city out looking for her? Surely there would be a note at Capitol Films where the girl had to make an appointment in the first place? Had that call been chased down? What other possible links might be found in and around Spielman's own office? Sullivan wasn't sure, but he did plan on being at Capitol Films front gate first thing in the morning.

AT SEVEN A.M. FRIDAY MORNING, Sullivan and Black were there at the gate. They badged the gatekeeper and were waved on through. They knew exactly where to go as they'd been there previously.

Spielman's inner sanctum was closed by two double doors at the end of the first hall. His name was yet on the door: *Ira J. Spielman,*

Producer & Director. They pushed through the doors and found themselves in his outer office. An old woman wearing horn-rimmed glasses and her hair in a bun was pounding a typewriter. She wore a headset and appeared to be transcribing. Sullivan approached and laid his huge paw on her desk.

"Excuse me, are you Mr. Spielman's secretary?"

She swept the headphones off her ears. "I'm his receptionist. He had several secretaries, except we call them associates."

Sullivan laid his badge on her desk. "LAPD, ma'am. We need to find out whether you have a telephone number. We're looking for a call that came in about a week, maybe two, before Mr. Spielman died. The caller's first name was Annalee."

"Sure, I've got it right here. I wondered why no one came around looking for it. Her name's Annalee Johnson and she had an appointment with Mr. Spielman just before he was murdered. She was looking for a role. Aren't they all?"

Sullivan's pulse quickened. This was too easy.

"Do you have a number for Annalee Johnson? A callback number?"

"I sure do. Write this down."

She turned to a page in her call diary and turned it upside down for Sullivan to read. He scribbled the number in his notepad. Had no one even called her yet? he wondered.

"You're sure no one's been around from LAPD looking for this number before?"

"Not while I've been here."

"How long have you been here?"

"One week. I'm a temp. Denise Calloway is out on maternity leave."

"Was Denise the regular?"

"Was, is. She'll be back in three months. I'm just filling in."

"Is it possible Denise gave out the number to someone else?"

"Entirely possible. But she was only here two days after the murder. I think the murder is what made her water break. But I'm no doctor, Detective."

"Is it possible I might get hold of Denise?"

"Can I have her call you? I mean with a new baby and all—"

"Give her my card, or ask her to call my number, please. I only have a couple questions for her. It won't take but a minute."

"Okey doke. Anything else I can do for you gentlemen?"

"Well, have you come up with any other ideas? Or talked to anyone else who has?"

She waved air at her face. "Goodness, ideas about what, officer?"

"Ideas about who might've killed Spielman."

"Oh, we talk all the time about that. You can't go to lunch with anyone here that you won't hear another theory. This place has more theories than Einstein."

"That's a novel way of putting it," Sullivan said. He turned his head and smiled at Lionel Black. Black shrugged and smiled gratuitously. They were being as friendly as two jaded homicide detectives knew how to be, hoping some new morsel might be tossed their way, even by accident. That she might say something that might lead to something that might—that was the idea. But she cooled right down, then, and took on a look and body language that told them she was ready to return to her work.

"All right, then," Sullivan finally said, "we'll run along and call this Annalee and see what turns up. Thank you."

"By the way," said Black, his time arriving, "do you have a phone we could use?"

She turned and swiveled her head as if looking for a free telephone.

Then she stopped short. "I guess you could use the phone in Mr. Spielman's office. I don't see what that would hurt, you being the police and all."

She then led them into Spielman's dark office and switched on a light. Sullivan stepped behind the desk and sat down. He smiled at the woman until she realized he was waiting for her to leave them alone in there. Which she did.

Spielman then dialed Annalee's phone number. It rang once, twice, then it was picked up. A slow, sleepy voice—it was now seven-thirty—came on the line. "Hullo?"

"Annalee Johnson?"

"That's me. Who's calling?"

"My name is Danny Sullivan. I'm with the LAPD."

"Again? The lady cop already talked to me. I don't want to do it again. Do I have to?"

"What was the lady cop's name?"

"You know, Halsey, like the motorcycle?"

"Oh, you mean Harley?"

"I'm dumb. Harley, yes."

"What did she ask you?"

"She asked me if I remembered the police officer who gave me a ride. Heck yes, I remembered. He saved my life after butthole tried to rape me."

"Whoa, slow down. Who tried to rape you, Annalee?"

"Ira J. Spielman. He came after me on the couch in his office."

Two sets of eyes turned to the three-cushion leather couch. A movie camera on a tripod overlooked it as well. Then Sullivan turned his attention back to his call.

"How did it happen he came after you?"

"Because he could. I wanted a role so bad in one of his movies. To be honest, I let him get to first base and didn't stop him. Then he suddenly got to second base and I tried pushing him away. I didn't want his hands there. But he wouldn't stop and then he pushed me down on the couch and tried to force me. I resisted. I'm strong cause I'm a lathe operator."

"Did you call out?"

"I don't remember. I needed the Gayle Howard part. Probably I didn't yell."

"Were you crying?"

"I don't remember."

"Did you tell the police?"

"I did. I told Harley that day she called me. She said why didn't I press charges."

"What did you say."

"I said I didn't want to. I never wanted to have to see him again. Which isn't true. I had to have the part. But it turned out he lied to me."

"Did you ever see him again?"

"Never."

"Did you kill him?"

"Did I what?"

"Did you kill Ira J. Spielman?"

"No, but I wish I had. It would have felt so good to stick that letter opener in his ear. Yes, I read the papers about that. I almost wet my pants I laughed so hard."

"You're sure you never saw him again?"

"You already asked me that once," she said, a note of alarm in her voice. "Hey, are you thinking I know who did it?"

"No, I'm not thinking you might know who did it."

"Are you thinking it might've been me?"

"Not really. I'm just calling to see what you know. Do you mind if we come by and talk to you in person?"

"Who's we?"

"Detective Lionel Black and me."

"And what's your name again?"

"Danny Sullivan. We're both homicide detectives and we'd like to take you downtown for more questions, if that's all right. Where can we swing by and say hello?"

"I'm in Toluca Lake at a friend's house."

"Would this morning be all right?"

"I guess. I should probably talk to my folks first. They're in Flagstaff."

"No need for that. I've got daughters. It would be fine with me if the police needed to swing by and see if they could help. All we want is your help. We know he wasn't a nice man at all."

"I'll say. I'm sure I wasn't his first victim."

"Tell you what. Give me your street address and we'll swing by."

"1667 N. Latham, unit eleven. It's a double-wide. My room is here."

"Can we come by in an hour?"

"I guess. I'll take a shower first."

"All right. We'll bring coffee and donuts."

"Suit yourself."

"We're on our way, Annalee."

"Okay, bye, now."

Sullivan hung up Spielman's phone. Black was grinning and clapping his hands. "Perfect."

"Know what that is over there, Lio?"

"I do. That's Spielman's casting couch."

"Do you think the camera's for filming the girls?"

"Course it is. Pervo, Sully. A real pervo on our hands."

"Wonder why Harley's report doesn't mention any casting couch?"

"I dunno. Oversight?"

"No, she left it out on purpose. But I can't say why. The photographs show it. Oh well, I'll think about that."

Just then, the temp came into Spielman's office. She was holding a telephone call message, the part below the carbon paper in the call book. "I just remembered we have this," she said, and passed the copy of the telephone call to Detective Sullivan. He read it and passed it to Black.

Sullivan said to the temp, "The name is Wendy Ellis. Same as the guard shack. Did she actually get in to visit with Mr. Spielman?"

"She did, on March 14, 1955."

"Do you know how long they were together?"

"About forty-five minutes, give or take. I remember I was writing letters to cast members and I made it through the leading characters by the time she came out."

"What state was she in?"

"What do you mean?"

"I mean was she flustered? Were her clothes in disarray? Was her lipstick smeared."

"My goodness, you do go right to it, don't you?"

"Please answer my question."

"The answer is yes. All of those."

"She was flustered?"

"Yes, in a great hurry and she had been crying."

"Clothes were in disarray?"

"You know, those things are really none of my business as I'm just a typist. But yes, she looked like she had disrobed because two buttons on her blouse were unbuttoned."

"Lipstick smeared?"

She sighed. "Yes. She arrived wearing a huge amount of rose-colored lipstick. It was all but rubbed off."

"Did she say anything as she left?"

"Not a word. Just hurried out the door."

"What did you think?"

"I thought she was in a hurry. I didn't want to think about why. That was none of my business and I need this work. If I get a bad rating on my temp job performance, then I don't get more calls with my agency and my kids don't eat. See? That's how it works in the real world of today's Fifties' woman, detective."

She sounded sour on the entire event, obviously. Sullivan decided to back off. She would always be available for follow-up later, if necessary.

"All right. We're leaving now."

It was an uncomfortable few minutes in the detectives' unmarked car as they set out for Annalee's. They knew Harley and knew she had the case, now. Talking to another detective's witness was a no-no. They had no business driving to her home and having a conversation. But Danny didn't give up easily. He drove and Black looked out his passenger's window. Their eyes didn't meet.

Sullivan kicked himself for screwing things up with the widow. He still wanted the case. So did Lionel Black. So, off they went, headed for Toluca Lake.

10

Harley and Marcia were stepping from their car on Santa
Barbara, near Crenshaw, when their radio erupted. Code
211 at a liquor store at the corner. They were closest, so they
jumped back inside and headed down Santa Barbara toward
Crenshaw half a mile south. Running Code 3, lights and sirens,
they wheeled up in front of the liquor store, where a crowd was
gathered on the sidewalk. The crowd was formed in a circle. On its
outer edges, pedestrians who were the uncurious stepped around
and didn't bother to look. They didn't bother to catch a glimpse of
the bloody newspaper spread over a dead body.

But Harley and Marcia were interested and more. Harley jotted
down their time of arrival. They climbed out and pushed through
the crowd. Harley knelt down by the dead man's head and peeled
back the front page so she could see his throat. He was wearing a
stocking over his head. She laid two fingers on his carotid and
waited. She thought at first she felt something. Maybe it had been
a muscle relaxing its grip on life, because after that she felt
nothing and felt nothing again for another minute. When she was

sure there was no hurry, she waited for the uniforms to arrive and surround the scene to keep people away. They came just minutes later and hopped to it.

Harley went to her car and called for the coroner. Then she joined Marcia inside the store.

Things seemed normal enough. There were several patrons browsing the shelves of the liquor store. The owner stood behind the counter, at the cash register, a twelve-gauge shotgun displayed atop the rubber counter. He looked like nothing was unusual or out-of-place, as if that man-killer gun was always there on the counter in front of God and everyone.

Harley approached. She was wearing her shield on her belt. *Make no mistake*, her shield said, *the LAPD is here.*

"I'm Detective Ellis. What happened here?"

The Korean man behind the counter frowned. "What happened? He robbed me so I shot him." The man was wearing khaki slacks, a blue shirt and a white apron tied around the middle. The store was obviously his.

"Tell me how that worked, sir."

"He was just another customer until I turned, and he had a stocking over his face. He jammed a gun in my face and demanded the cash from my register. I opened it and scooped up the bills. He wanted them in a plain paper bag. And he wanted a pint of Seagram, and a pack of Chesterfields. I even threw in a book of matches from the Brown Derby. My own matches, Detective. I'm trying to explain I did nothing except play along.

"So, he had my bag and my cash and my whiskey and my cigarettes—all free. I handed it over. He jammed his pistol in his waistband and turned his back on me and headed for the door. I reached under the counter and came up with my shotgun. I always got one jacked in the chamber. It's a semi-auto so I just flicked the safety and pointed it at his back. Then I pulled the trigger. You found him out there where he went down when I nailed him. I did go out and get my bag back. I put my own newspaper over his head. I've had it with these people, Detective. I can't stay open if I keep getting hit every week."

Behind Harley, Marcia said, "Sounds to me like a justifiable homicide, partner. Let's clear it and write it."

Harley turned to her partner. Then she pulled her ten feet away from the counter. "You cannot be serious. This was a cold-blooded shotgun slaying of a man with his back turned. A man who threatened no one because he had put his gun away. It wasn't self-defense, if that's what you're thinking, detective. It wasn't a killing done to protect another. Listen again: the man was threatening no one when he was shot and killed by this man here."

"That's pure bullshit, de*tec*tive," Marcia all-but-shouted in reply. "I say our liquor store man gets a medal for doing our job for us. You say he goes to prison. Hey folks!" Marcia called to the crowd gathered around the dead body. She shouted again, "Do we give this guy a medal or take him to jail?"

"Medal!" shouted a mother holding a small child's hand.

"Medal!" shouted a man in a crisp business suit. He shifted his briefcase hand-to-hand as he shouted, again, "Medal times two!"

"Jail!" shouted a black man wearing a summer straw hat.

"Medal!"

"He gets the keys to the city!"

"Jail" shouted a youngish woman in a bikini with a towel wrapped around her waist. "The guy was leaving, and he wasn't hurting anyone.

Marcia turned to Harley. "There's your jury, Chief. You sure you want to take this one to trial?"

Harley ignored the crowd, then turned back to Marcia. "No, I don't want to take this case to trial." She turned her attention to the proprietor. "Sir, I'm going to write you up for discharging a firearm in the city limits. You can pay a fine for that and you're done. But I'm not going to ask for an arrest or an indictment. It's your lucky day for killing a man over fifty bucks and a pint. Your *big*, lucky day."

"Sorry, I just wasted your time."

Harley walked back to the soft drink cooler. She selected a Coca-Cola and shouted back to Marcia, "Want anything?"

"Yep, same as you."

Two Cokes between four fingers, Harley walked back up to the counter and laid two one-dollar bills across the shotgun. She stared at the Korean's eyes. "Keep the change."

Then she walked outside, Marcia two steps behind. They circled the crowd that clustered around the police officers guarding the scene.

"Have the body removed," Harley said to the uniform in charge.

"No case, Sergeant?"

She shook her head. "None that we could sell. Remove him on my say-so."

"Right, Sergeant. What do I tell the homicide dicks when they arrive?"

Harley paused and nodded. "Tell them the jury's already voted and came back hung."

"Hung jury. Right, Sergeant."

They continued on to their ride, climbed inside, retrieved the bottle opener from the glove box. Marcia popped both caps and passed a sweaty, cold bottle of Coke back to Harley.

Harley took a long swallow. "I'm glad we took a vote."

"It's the only way, case like that."

She radioed in and cleared the case.

Harley turned the key and tucked the bottle down between her thighs as she wheeled the unmarked car into traffic on Santa Barbara.

She shook her head. "The only way. Even the Lieutenant will understand why no charges."

"Even the Lieutenant."

11

H arley dropped Marcia back at Division and went for a
     sandwich. She then returned and completed her report on
the liquor store slaying. She then drove home at the end of her
watch.

Marcia went to the Property Office and signed out the evidence
box on the Ira J. Spielman case. She went into a fenced-in carrel,
still within the confines of the evidence room in order to safeguard
the chain-of-custody for courtroom proceedings. There, she
unsealed the evidence box. The yellow label said it was last
opened by Danny Sullivan himself.

She removed the lid. Immediately on the top, marked in individual evidence bags with the CSI officer's signature, were the
letter opener, clothes, keys, wallet, eyeglasses, and miscellaneous
objects from his office which were found to have "other than"
fingerprints. "Other than" fingerprints were just that: items with
fingerprints on them other than the victim's own.

She began with the letter opener. Interesting, long metal, silver, with an angled handle. Along the blade, partially covered in blood, she could make out the lettering: *Wang's Hardware, Las Vegas.*

Marcia was going through the items of evidence to see whether there was any item there that could conceivably be something left behind or touched by Wendy Ellis. In part, she wished to do this outside of her partner's vision. Not because she was trying to hide anything from Harley; rather, because she wanted to spare Harley the heart-wrenching job of perhaps seeking evidence against her own daughter, the daughter whom she adored.

The typical items, contained in plastic bags, such as keys, wallets, eyeglasses, and so on were lifted out and set to the side on the metal table of the evidence carrel. She then reached beneath the folded shirt, slacks, and tie worn by Spielman on the day he was murdered. Down below, was a white scarf. Marcia's breath snapped in her throat. The scarf was monogrammed "WE."

Wendy Ellis.

She lifted the scarf, white with black borders, and gingerly sorted it through her fingers. *Why on earth?*

She read the tag clipped to the scarf: "Found on the victim's sofa, hanging across the left arm of the sofa, half on and half off." The tag was initialed "LF"—the initials of the CSI tech who had chosen to seize, tag, and box the item.

Now what? thought Marcia. *If I tell Harley, she might go off the deep end. But if I don't tell her, we don't give enough weight to a possible lead.*

Then she admitted to herself what she'd known from the first moment she laid eyes on the piece of evidence: she had no choice but to bring it to Harley's attention and discuss it with her. She then spent the next thirty minutes going through each piece of evidence in the box and checking it against the list in the murder book. She was making sure that (1) every item in the murder book could be found inside the box, and, (2) that each item inside the box had actually made it into the murder book.

Finally, there was a letter Addressed to Ira J. Spielman. Signed by Wendy Ellis. She was afraid she was pregnant and might need money for an abortion. Abortions were illegal but here was a fourteen-year-old ready to deal with this and figure it out on her own. Would she have killed Spielman over it? Marcia returned the letter to the box. Her hand was shaking as she realized this could turn the case a whole new direction.

She then checked the sign-out sheet on the evidence box. It appeared that Sullivan had been back to the box on two other occasions previous to the last. He had spent approximately two minutes with the box on each of those two visits. Marcia stopped and read the sign-out sheet again.

Two minutes each time? Only two minutes?

She quickly inventoried the items in the box a second time and rechecked them against the murder book. All was "in," and all that was "in" checked out against the book. So why had Sullivan been here twice for just two minutes each time? What could he possibly have been looking for among the inventory that brought him back three times?

She sat thoughtfully and stared at the welded mesh wall of the carrell. What would he be looking for? Possible fingerprints? She was certain the crime lab had dusted and lifted all prints. Blood stains? There were none except for those on the left collar and left shoulder of Spielman's white shirt. Gloves? A second weapon? What was Sullivan after?

Seeing no obvious answer, she knew she'd discuss her findings with Harley. Maybe it was something as simple as Sullivan had been interrupted on each of those two previous times and had had to prematurely break off his review of the items of evidence. That, she decided, was possibly as close to any explanation as she was going to get just then.

But then another thought occurred to her. Ask Sullivan himself. She stood and went out to the first officer's desk. "Use your phone?" she asked.

"Sure."

She dialed the detective bureau.

"Cindy, it's Marcia. Is Detective Sullivan around this afternoon?"

"He's signed out downtown. Off to see a witness. Do you need the address where he's gone?"

"No, thanks. I'll let you go."

She then dialed Harley's number.

"Hey, Harley, Marcia. I've found a very disturbing item in the evidence box I want to give you a heads-up about."

"Heads-up? That stuff has been in the box for months. What could suddenly deserve my heads-up?"

"I found a scarf in the box. It's a white silk scarf maybe thirty-six inches long and six inches wide. It's white with a black border. On the bottom of the end is the monogram WE. It's done very properly and, of course, was added to the scarf as an after-purchase personalization. Do you have any recall of such a scarf in your house?"

"Yes, we gave Wendy a personalized scarf on her ninth birthday. It was to wear at her dance recital. It's white with a knobby stitch?"

"That's how I would describe it, yes."

"And it's in the murder box?"

"It is."

"Oh, my God. Where was it found."

"Next to the victim on the leather couch in his office. As you stand facing the couch, it's on the right-hand arm, half-on and half-off."

"Any blood or characteristics to connect it to the killing itself?"

"Nope. It was seized by CSI so I'm sure it's been to the crime lab and back."

"So, nothing to indicate it was worn by Wendy, or taken in there by Wendy, at the time of the murder?"

"Not that I can tell. It could've been lying on the couch for a week. Or a month, before the murder."

"Sullivan knew about Wendy's letter, correct?"

Marcia nodded. "That's correct."

"And he knew her initials were WE, correct?"

"Correct."

"So, he has a pretty strong lead, someone he really must talk to, named Wendy Ellis."

"Correct."

"Then answer me this. Why in God's name wouldn't he come to me and ask me about Wendy? Every detective in Hollywood Division knows my daughter's name. Hell, they even know about her tattoo on her belly. I've gone to great pains to make sure everyone knows. So, I ask again, why would Sullivan let this drag on for months and not come to me?" Harley was furious: whether it was anger at Spielman or Sullivan or both, Marcia couldn't say.

"I don't get it either. I put in a call to him to ask that same thing. He's out on a statement."

"Put a note on his desk, okay? Tell him we'd like to meet with him first thing in the morning. Oh my God, I need a drink. This just keeps getting more bizarre, Marcia. When does it end? Did my daughter actually kill this guy? I can't even conjure up a mental image of her doing something like that. I can tell you right now I'm one-hundred-percent sure she didn't do it, but I'm also one-hundred-percent sure we have to track her down and take her statement and totally investigate her alibi. If she even has an alibi. Oh, dear Jesus. I'm afraid I'm going to lose it. I've got to hang up. I need a drink."

"Make it just one, partner, okay? Then get to bed early and try to get a good night's sleep. We'll pounce all over Sullivan in the morning. I have my own questions for him, too."

"Copy that. I'm out."

"Out."

12

———

Harley and Marcia cornered Danny Sullivan at his desk in the detectives' bureau early the next morning. Detective Black was off to the side at his own desk, his head canted toward the conversation. Even the watch sergeant was quiet and probably listening.

Marcia led off. "Danny, I was in Property and opened the Spielman box. Remember the case?"

Sullivan shot a look at Harley, then looked back at Marcia. "Sure, I remember. What's up?"

"Two things. First, why would you check the property box out and keep it for two minutes each time then check it back in? I'm asking because I'm wondering if I maybe missed something there."

"Why would I—I did? Twice? Come back to that. Let me try to remember. What else do you have for me?"

Marcia had earlier told Harley about the letter. The blood had drained from her partner's face. She was too stunned even to speak. Instead, she had gone into the bathroom for a good ten minutes. When she returned, her eyes were swollen and red.

"What else do I have for you? The elephant in the room. The pregnancy letter from Harley's daughter to Spielman and the scarf with Harley's daughter's initials. Why didn't you ever confront Harley about her kid?"

The color drained out of Sullivan's face, then just as quickly returned. Now he was red-faced and looked like he might sputter when he spoke.

But he didn't. "I didn't confront Harley because I didn't trust her. I trusted her to be a good mother before a good copper. Look, if I went to Harley and tipped her off about our evidence, I was leery that she might tip off her daughter and run hide her." He sneered at Harley then and added, "Truth be told, I'm not so sure she didn't. The kid went missing right after the murder. What do you say, Detective Ellis? You have anything to do with her going missing? You're not hiding her out from LAPD, are you?"

Harley's fists clenched. She slammed down her coffee cup hard enough that dark brew spilled over the side onto Sullivan's desk. It puddled next to a stack of yellow notepad papers, wetting the edges. "Goddam, lady!" cried Sullivan. "Somebody hand me a paper towel."

"Shit," said Harley under her breath as she reached to her desk and grabbed tissues. "I'm sorry, Danny. Don't mean to be so goddam dramatic."

She mopped up the spilt coffee and pitched the soggy Kleenex into Danny's wastebasket.

After a minute of trying to get her emotions in check, she cleared her throat. "No, Detective Sullivan, you know as much about my daughter's whereabouts as I do. I only wish you had come to me. I would have joined right into your search for her. As it is, if it turns out she's involved in the case, I'll be the first one to turn her in. That's what a good mother does."

Danny scowled. "I know, I know. It's a bitch, ladies. The kid might be in, might be out. I probably shoulda spoke up. Lio wanted me to approach you, but I called him off."

All eyes went to Detective Black. He appeared to be genuinely busy with a file on his desk. He didn't look up, at least.

"So, what did you make of the scarf?" asked Harley.

"I think it's very suspicious, based on it was on the couch. On the other hand, there's no blood. I had it tested twice for blood spatters. Nothing. So, I put it on the back burner at that point. If Wendy stabbed the guy and she was wearing the scarf like they're usually worn around the throat or shoulders, I guess, there shoulda been blood spatters. Maybe not visible to the naked eye but visible to the purple lights. But it came up nada."

"What about her letter to Spielman?" asked Marcia. "That seems like strong evidence of motive to kill the guy."

Sullivan shrugged. "Maybe yes, maybe no. I gave the kid the benefit of the doubt on that one. I figured Spielman probably bought her off and she went away quietly. The other thing was the kid's young age. I checked with her school. She's only fourteen, she's a great student, had a good attendance record, comes from a good home. Not the type of perp we ordinarily run into. My idea of the real killer is someone who had some major beef with Spielman. Someone like Mickey Loden. Someone like Reuben Ordañez. Ordañez kidnaps Loden's kid, Loden puts two and two together and figures it was all brought about by Spielman so Loden hires someone to punch Spielman's dance card. That makes more sense to me than some teenager who got herself knocked up. No offense meant there, Harley. I'm just talking here."

"None taken," Harley said with the slightest smile. It was obvious from the slump of her shoulders that she was relieved Danny Sullivan had turned his sights on Loden or Ordañez and away from Wendy. It also, in all the honesty she could muster, agreed with her own thinking. Wendy might have been in a rage, but Wendy wasn't a killer. Ordañez...he was a killer. Loden, with his mob connections, might be too. Which is why she was going to move the case in that direction first chance she got.

"So," Danny said, looking from Harley to Marcia and back to Harley. "Are we good here?"

"Yes, except for my first question. Why go into the box twice for only two minutes?"

"That," said Sullivan, "shall remain my secret. You're both pretty good dicks. Let's see if you can find what I found."

"Come on and come clean," Marcia persisted. "This is serious."

"Alright, look in Spielman's Rolodex. His address and phone numbers."

"Okay, and?"

"He's got the phone numbers there of some pretty famous actresses and actors."

"And?"

Sullivan sighed. He ran his hand across the back of his head. Then he said, quietly, almost meekly, "A certain gossip columnist pays twenty-five bucks for a name. I was making out."

Marcia's eyes widened. "You were selling famous phone numbers?"

"I guess so."

"Sullivan, you're off the case."

"Son of a bitch," said Harley. "And you didn't think you could trust me? Ha!"

The foursome went to breakfast, then, and made their peace and got their ducks in line for the next portion of the investigation. Sullivan and Black wouldn't be involved, but everyone was all square by the time the bill came.

Harley paid. She felt like she owed, and nobody fought her for the ticket.

13

Friday night, payday, found Harley arriving home again after five. The bank was extra hard-hit because it was Labor Day weekend and families needed money for the parties and cookouts and adventures of the three-day holiday.

She was sitting on her couch, enjoying her latest record, the Firehouse Five Plus Two, and having her first vodka, when she noticed.

In the center of Harley's coffee table sat a large, round amber ashtray. It was a deep amber, and striations could be seen deep within the glass, running concentrically around the bottommost bevel. A cheap thing, she remembered, thinking maybe seventy-nine cents at FedMart. As she stubbed her first cigarette in the receptacle, Harley, leaning near, at first saw what she thought to be her own image reflected dimly in the glass. But then she looked again. She looked again because, deep in the amber interior, when she moved her eyes up and back, she realized the face she was seeing wasn't her face at all. It was Wendy's. Wendy's image was fixed deep within her ashtray.

Shocked and on edge, Harley stood straight up from the couch and took her drink into the kitchen. She turned on the tap and poured her drink down the drain, standing there and watching it swirl and disappear down the pipe while her heart pounded. Then she set the glass aside, bent down, and splashed water on her face with cupped hands. "I must be dreaming. Or that's a triple-strength drink." It was a new brand of vodka, one she'd never tried before. So, she was ready to ascribe the image to an extra-strength drink that she hadn't seen coming.

Harley spent the next five minutes brewing a strong cup of coffee. She watched, mesmerized, as the pale brown liquid began spouting up inside the glass bulb on the top of the pot. Then it quit percolating. She poured a Navy mug. She skipped adding a dollop of cream in favor of the strongest caffeinated drink possible. She dropped in an ice cube and drank the black stuff down. Then she poured another out of the silver percolator. This time, no ice cube. And she did settle it down with a quick spiff of canned milk.

Back to the couch. She lit another Camel and sat there, thinking. Her hands had stopped shaking as a result of the earlier vision. This time she didn't look in the ashtray. She laughed, even, and scoffed at herself for imagining she saw Wendy's face in the glass. She puffed again and again, flicking her ash into the amber glass. All the while, she was thinking about Wendy, wondering what she was doing just then.

The phone rang. She reached to the end table and lifted the receiver.

"Ellis," Harley said, half-expecting it to be a call from Division.

Marcia spoke up. "Harley, did you happen to notice the two-for-one happy hour at the Brown Derby tonight?"

"No, I haven't opened the paper. Just got back after the bank. What a mess!"

"Yes, well, I think we should change into something slinky and chase on down to the Derby and see what's cooking."

"You know, that doesn't sound half-bad. What do I have to wear?"

"LBD with your gold locket. The one with the S on it."

Harley knew the one Marcia meant. Inside, was a picture of Robert, his boot camp graduation picture. It was done in touched-up color.

"I could do that. What are you thinking?"

"Same thing. Little black dress. With my mom's pearls. I don't think I'll get so drunk I break them and watch them roll all over the Derby while I'm down on my hands and knees chasing them like marbles. You won't let me have that much fun, right?"

"No, you'll be fine, Marce. Me get you or you get me?"

"Right, only one car. I'll come for you. Thirty minutes good?"

Harley took the last drag on her cigarette and then stubbed it out. Without thinking, she leaned over the amber ashtray to kill the coal and, when she did, she looked deep inside. She jumped to her feet. She slowly leaned forward and looked again.

Wendy. This time the image was almost as clear as a photograph, though limned within the glass. She looked harder, straining her eyes. Wendy's mouth moved. She was speaking.

"Uh, gotta go, Marcia. See you in thirty."

"S'long."

She grabbed the ashtray, brushed aside the contents onto the coffee table, and held it in front of the light. There it was—her mouth was moving. But was she saying something or was she crying? Then the image faded, and Harley found herself looking through the glass of the ashtray at her hands on either side, holding the receptacle up to the light. "Jesus," she said. "Oh, Jesus."

She remembered the time. Marcia was coming to pick her up.

AN HOUR later they'd finally been seated at the Brown Derby. A small bandstand was set up along one wall and a band with guitar and sax was warming up. "Friday night dance," Marcia said through cupped hands, as the noise was deafening. "Let's dance together. We'll get seen that way."

"Okay," Harley shouted back. "Jitterbug."

"Right."

The band finally reached its point of no return and began playing. First up: Bill Hailey's *Rock Around the Clock.* Halfway through, Harley realized that, for the first time in years, she was actually laughing. She was enjoying the freedom of moving her body in time to the music immensely. There was nothing purposeful about what they were doing, unlike the rest of her life. She could just let go and feel without thinking. She smiled, she beamed. A sailor walked up and began dancing at her side, facing her. She turned away from Marcia and let him cut in. But she didn't totally freeze Marcia out, either. Friends don't do that to friends. The song ended and the sailor encircled her waist with his arm and walked her back to her table. She allowed it. His hand on the small of her back felt like a miracle. She hadn't been touched by a man in—

what, years? It was so innocent because nobody took it seriously. It was just what happened on dance floors.

"Can I sit down?"

"Sure," said Harley. Marcia slid forward in her chair and beamed at him. "Got a friend?"

"I do," the sailor said with a laugh. "I've got lots of friends. Some good, some not-so-good. What's your type?"

"Oh," said Marcia, "successful, secure in himself, maybe thinking about settling down some day." It was her turn to laugh. Her lilting laughter said it was all in fun.

"What's your name?" the sailor asked Harley.

"Harley. And my friend is Marcia."

"Well I'm Bill Appleton. I'm from Arlington, Illinois and I enlisted at Great Lakes. Now I'm in California while our ship is retrofitted. We're headed for Korea."

Harley cringed: oh, no! Another American sailor bound for that hell hole. She couldn't stand to look at him for several minutes. In her mind's eye, he was lost to her already. "Excuse me," she said. "Ladies room." She stood and got her bearings then saw the neon "Ladies" and "Gents" signs on the back wall. Off she went.

Inside the ladies' she worked her way through the mob up to the powder bar. She pulled her compact out of her purse and checked the back of her hair with the large mirror behind her and the compact in front. She smiled and rubbed a finger across her teeth. She took out a tissue and dabbed lipstick from the corner of her mouth. Then she snapped the compact shut. Then she froze. Just as she was putting the compact away—she slowly reopened it. She stared deep into the mirror. There was Wendy's silhouette. The nose was a giveaway. It was Wendy, for sure. Harley closed the compact ever so carefully and settled it in the bottom of her purse. *Oh my God*, she thought, *what is happening to me? Am I losing my mind? Can I tell Marcia to look?* Her thoughts raced. Then her hand jumped inside her purse and grabbed the compact and she flipped it open again. This time there was nothing.

"Hey," said a voice behind, "can you let someone else have a chance at the mirror? You're playing with your compact up there, girl."

Harley's face reddened and she looked down at the floor as she made her way out of the ladies'. *What in God's name was going on?* She made her way back to the table. Both Marcia and Bill were gone. She spun around. Of course, there they were, dancing, a slow dance, "*Some Enchanted Evening.*"

When the song was over, the new couple—it looked very coupling-like to Harley—returned and sat down beside each other.

"Tell you what," Harley said, "I got sick in there. I'm going to catch a cab home. Call me later, toots," she said to Marcia. Marcia decided to protest but Harley shook her head violently. "No way," she said, "I don't need a ride and you, young lady, need to dance. Have fun. Nice to meet you, Bill. Best of luck in Korea."

"Good night, Harley," they said in unison.

Harley picked her way to the entrance. A whole row of cabs waited with their engines idling. She opened the door of a first cab in line. It was cool for Labor Day, sea breeze cool, and she pulled her wrap around her shoulders once she was settled in the back seat of the green and yellow cab. She gave the driver her address and sat back. She shut her eyes against the bright lights of the oncoming traffic.

She could hardly wait to get home to her ashtray.

It was all that mattered.

14

Ira J. Spielman's estate, set back from Bel-Air Road, was a shining mansion upon a hill. All the lights were burning when Harley and Marcia arrived just after eight p.m. The family had buried the studio head only a few months ago and then gone silent. But now, Spielman's widow had agreed to speak with the new detectives after getting Sullivan and Black tossed from the case. Sullivan and Black had told her some song and dance about Ira bedding young starlets. She was expecting the new detective crew to respect Ira's memory and avoid all such theories. There was a need for a new release of information on the case, and fast. Lieutenant Chall had made it clear he wanted a favorable story in the *Times* and fast.

The murder had been exceptionally violent, and the press had been running away with the story and the fact the LAPD had no comments. Which meant, the reporters reminded Los Angelenos, they had zero leads. "*Is LAPD Losing its Edge?*" asked one headline in the *Times*. The detectives' intention was to deflate that rag with a quick arrest.

Harley and Marcia pulled up to the gate and badged the guard. He was standing just far enough back in the guard house that Harley, at the wheel, couldn't get a good look at the guy, though she wanted to. At this point, everyone was a suspect. The guard said something unintelligible and the gate parted at the center and rolled back on either side. Harley let out on the Ford's clutch and rolled on through. They wound up to the circle drive. They parked and Harley radioed their twenty. She then wrote down the time of arrival on her notepad. They exited the unmarked car. Marcia stretched. They went up to the front door, where a maid in a black dress with a doily apron answered and stood aside to allow them to come on inside. "She's in the study," said the woman. "She's expecting you."

The widow was a fifty-five-year-old woman. She was dressed smartly in a black suit. Her mourning hat with attached veil lay at her side on the huge couch. She had evidently just arrived home from who knew where, just in time to accommodate the detectives. She was a pretty woman, thought Harley, and the clear sclera of her eyes gave away the fact she hadn't been crying all that much.

The widow began talking almost immediately after introductions.

"Everybody loved Ira. He was a shining light in the dark city known as LA. Ira did good. He hosted an annual fund-raiser for inner city kids. Kids who never got birthday presents. He set up a trust that guaranteed they would all be remembered and gifted on their birthdays. He helped with finding lodging for some of the city's destitute. People living on the streets. It was very common for Ira to have his driver pull over and assist some street person with a child and get them set up to live someplace. He was just like that."

"It's always the good ones die young," Marcia commented. She was

standing at the far end of the couch, looking for an ashtray. Ordinarily, LAPD policy forbade officers smoking inside anyone's
house. But it had been a long day and Marcia needed a smoke.
She was hoping the hostess would realize her need and make
provision. So far, she had not.

Harley was making her notes as the widow continued. She cleared
her throat and asked, "If he was so very kind, why would someone
want him dead? That's the part I'm not seeing."

Mrs. Spielman spread her hands. "I think he must've been robbed.
I think he had money or valuables around that the intruder knew
about. I think he was killed over them."

"But such a twisted death? Have you seen the police reports?"

"About the letter opener? I saw that. Terrible and heartbreaking."

"Mrs. Spielman, somebody jammed a letter opener down your
husband's ear canal into his brain. Someone was very piss—angry.
Does that make you think there's something very odd going on?"

"You had to know Ira. The man had no enemies. It must have been
a deranged person who killed him. Willing to do anything and did.
No worse than being shot with a gun, I mean, dead is dead. Poor
Ira."

She sniffled and pulled several tissues out of her Kleenex box. She
blew her nose and dabbed her eyes. "Damn whoever did this to
hell! I'm not so nice. I would like to see them gassed at San
Quentin and hope I live to see it."

"We're going to try to help make justice happen," Marcia said.
Marcia was still standing at the end of the couch, holding a
cigarette pack and her Zippo and hoping the widow got the hint.
She still had not. Marcia appeared to have been only half-listening
to what Mrs. Spielman was telling Harley about her husband. But

looks could be deceiving; maybe she'd heard every word. Harley couldn't be sure.

"Yes," Harley agreed with her partner, "we're giving this case special attention because we all want to see speedy justice get done here. Can you tell me, Mrs. Spielman, did Ira ever interview young people for different roles? I can guess what your answer will be."

"Of course, he did. Boys and girls."

"Do you know if he was ever alone with young men or women in his office?"

"I'm not sure what you're getting at. I'm sure all studio heads inter-view boys and girls together and separately at times. Why does this matter?"

"I don't know that it does, frankly. But I'm trying to think of how it might happen that someone could have been enraged enough to kill him with a letter opener. What would make someone do that? They were sure angry about something."

Marcia turned from the table. She was ready for bluntness, ready to get the key question on the table and see where it went. "Was he ever alone in his office with teeny-boppers? You know, young women he might've made a move on. Or, hell, even boys, now that I think about it. Did that happen?"

"I would never in a million years think Ira acted inappropriately around a young person. Or even an old person. That just wasn't who he was, Detective Meriwether."

"Okay, I had to ask. Is there an ashtray? Would you mind?"

"I do mind. I hate cigarette smoke."

Harley redirected her attention to the case. "Did your husband ever go out with young women or men for dinner, drinks, anything like that? Did you ever feel a twinge of jealousy?"

"Did he go alone with someone? Never. He was too smart to let himself be alone with someone who might try to blackmail him with a phony claim. Ira was nobody's fool, Detectives."

"Did he ever disappear overnight, where you didn't know his whereabouts?"

"He stayed away some nights on business. Maybe San Francisco or Las Vegas. But he always called to say goodnight to me. I always knew exactly where he was."

"Did you always know who he was with?"

She sniffed and wiped a tissue under her nostrils. "I resent that implication—if that's what it is. Tell me, Detective Ellis: what is it you get out of painting my husband to be some kind of sex monster with young people? Why would you even think that? Are you meaning to indict his memory?"

Harley sat up on the couch; she arched her back. "In fact, I'm trying to catch his killer. There are many questions I need to ask. Not only questions of just you, either, Mrs. Spielman. I can assure you of that."

"I just hope your questions out in the world don't bring Ira into some kind of disrepute. That's unnecessary and it would be unfair."

The widow sat back in her chair and lifted her coffee cup. It was the finest of fine china, complete with all the right names and delicate flutes. She pressed the rim to her lips and appeared to sip. Harley, watching closely while appearing not to, would've been hard-pressed to know whether the woman's lips actually engaged liquid or not. It might have been just a moment to gather her thoughts. Or appear at ease. But why would she need that? Harley wondered. Clearly the woman had as much need to find her husband's killer as anyone else needed to solve the case. It was her guy, after all. Her man. Her Ira.

Still, Harley couldn't help feeling the right questions had gone begging for too long. A letter opener? Down the ear canal? That was rage, more than she'd ever heard the old-timers recount.

"I knows what I see," she told Marcia once they were driving through the gate, leaving the dead studio head's estate. "And I see someone who's mighty fucking pissed at our man, Ira."

"Pretty simple, you ask me," said Marcia, ever the pragmatist. "Ira seduced some young thing. He promised her a starring role in one of his movies in exchange for a few times in the hay. Then he reneged. And the role never materialized. She never got the studio call. So, she returned and stabbed the bastard in the brain. Case solved, what else you got for me to look at? Other cases at all?"

Harley laughed. She hit the steering wheel with the flat of her hand. "That's good. My friend, Marcia, doesn't mince words. That's what I like most about you, partner, is you've never much cared for finesse. The bull in the china shop. Dr. Watson would be proud."

"What's that make you? Sherlock?"

"That makes me perplexed. I think we've yet to ask the right question, that's all."

Marcia tapped her Marlboros against the back of her hand and then opened the new pack. She tapped the opening against the meat of her hand and shook one free. Then came the cigarette lighter shooting out of the dashboard, its coil glowing. A touch of coil to tobacco and she was inhaling like she'd been deprived of oxygen for too long. Harley wondered that her head didn't cave in

—an old joke a boyfriend new in town, from Myrtle Beach, told her after she'd taught him to surf one Sunday afternoon. "Suck any harder on that cancer stick and you're gonna cave your head in, girl." Happier times, times of freedom and joy in the sun. No cares, no missing children, no long line of battered prostitutes visiting her sleep and asking whether she'd found their pimp yet. Yes, she had those dreams and, more often than not, had to say no, the perp hadn't been caught yet. Those dream victims then faded out and another would step forward with the same question. At other times she dreamed of Wendy. The daughter more alive in the dreams than the victims had ever been in real life. Just because. Because it was Harley's dream and Harley, being one of the true tough ones, didn't have to explain her dreams to any goddam person on earth. There you were.

"Like I say, I think he fucked the wrong girl—or boy—and got offed for it. No big mystery, Harls. Simple and sweet, in one ear and out the other. No, not quite, but it might as well have been."

"Ouch. There's an image. How about coffee?"

"How about a shake at Bob's Big Boy? We're almost in Burbank."

"Done. I'm famished, now that you mention it."

"Why don't we sit down with a shake and a burger and check our list of people we want to shake down. Let's start with Ira's secretary. And his lawyer. Surely his lawyer has some black facts to disgorge to us. Some dark matter."

"We need to talk with his directors, too. See if any of them wound up with a young actor or actress they didn't expect, orders of Ira J. Spielman. I think if we do just that we'll have some names to chase down."

"Credit card receipts. We'll get those from accounting at Capitol

Films. We're looking for hotels, motels, fancy restaurants. Especially where he's registered in a room on a weeknight—something mama wouldn't question too closely. Weeknights are great for recreational fornication because he can always say it was business and mama believes him. Oh, I feel a chocolate shake coming on!"

They pulled into the Bob's parking lot and parked. Both doors swung open simultaneously and they were hit with the sounds of *Autumn Leaves*, the day's most popular song, over the outdoor loudspeakers.

They went inside and ordered.

15

After their watch updates on Monday, Harley and Marcia called Mrs. Spielman and obtained the name of Mr. Spielman's lawyer. His name was Benjamin Sercease and he worked from a downtown office. They drove to South Olive Street and parked in long-term at Sercease's building, Mercantile Trade Center. Up to the fifteenth floor they went, where they were seated in the reception area and were provided fresh coffee as they waited for Mr. Sercease to finish up with a client.

Twenty minutes later, his secretary came, apologizing for keeping them waiting past the time of the appointment they had set with her. Harley told her not to worry, that the *Life* magazine article on Midwestern women was engrossing.

Benjamin Sercease was olive-skinned, black hair graying on the wings, and wore a three-piece suit with a Phi Beta Kappa chain on his vest. He was intent on charming the detectives from the gate.

"Detectives, my office is open to you to help you in any way I can with Ira's death. You have questions? I just might have your answers, so please, ask away."

Harley led off with, "As his lawyer, you will probably know who was pissed enough at Mr. Spielman they'd want him dead. Can you help us with names?"

"For openers, I can't offer any specificity that I know as fact. I'm thinking Mickey Loden out in the Valley might be on your list. Also, there was a Reuben Ordañez in Mexico that qualifies."

"What part of Mexico?"

"Juarez, I believe. I know that Ira met him when the man contacted Capitol Films about a daughter who wanted to screen-test. As I understand, she was a sultry, big-busted Latino who came to Hollywood and who couldn't speak a word of English, Ira found. So, it went nowhere, but Ira and this Ordañez did talk about Ordañez perhaps financing a film or two where there might be a role for a Mexican princess who speaks only Spanish. Something to that effect. But be careful: I also understand Ordañez is a very dangerous man and that his business might not be on the up and up. In fact, I'm of the opinion he trafficked in narcotics, though I only surmised that after a few strange incidents. I have no other proof than that. But be careful, nonetheless."

"Did the film or films ever get cast with the Ordañez daughter taking a role?"

"No, I can tell you they did not. As Ira's lawyer, I see all studio contracts. In fact, I write ninety percent of them. I saw nothing involving an Ordañez at any time."

Harley asked, "Can you give me this Ordañez' phone number? I just might want to talk further with him."

"Sure, I'll have Natalie write it down when you leave here. Just, please, be careful."

"How did Ira get along with the missus?" Marcia asked. "Any troubles on the home front?"

"Never. I think Mrs. Spielman was forbearing and knew enough to turn her head and ignore certain things."

"Such as?"

"Well, I'd be lying to you if I said there hadn't been times when Ira would find himself needing to pay money to a young actress. This didn't happen that often, but it happened. I always supplied the necessary cash to buy someone's silence. I also contacted a doctor I know in Tijuana more than once. You know, for certain procedures illegal in the States."

"Abortion," said Harley. It wasn't a question.

"Exactly that. There were times when Ira wasn't entirely careful with his seed-sowing. Sometimes, things got out of hand."

"No pun intended," said Harley.

The man smiled. "Exactly."

"Would Mrs. Spielman ever be angry enough to murder her husband, at least that you knew?"

"I'm not going to lie and say she never came storming in here, demanding explanations. Or demanding he stop his philandering as it was embarrassing to her at one time or another. She was social and the last thing she wanted was to see Ira's name mentioned by Hedda Hopper or one of the movie rags. She's insisted on buying someone's peace herself at a time or two when she was contacted by some irate wannabe or, worse, the wannabe's parents."

"So, she might have had some very strong feelings about Mr. Spielman now and then?"

"Oh, I'm sure," said Sercease.

"Anything specific you can help us with."

Sercease frowned. "Well, there has been a sort of a nagging problem. That would be Tag Zastrow."

"The teenage heartthrob," Marcia said.

"Yes, Tag threatened to expose his relationship with Ira on several occasions. He was paid off. In fact, his apartment in Malibu is well-known to Ira. They had a thing."

"A homosexual assignation," Marcia said.

Sercease nodded. "It always seemed rather pointless, to me. Mr. Spielman didn't prefer men at all. In fact, Tag seemed to be a one-time thing. It never happened again—at least not where my services were needed. It seems to have just been Tag, poor fellow."

"Why poor fellow?" Harley asked.

"His promised role never materialized. It was supposed to be a beach blanket teenage romance movie. But by the time it came around for casting, Tag was too old for the part. He threatened to sue, I threw money at the problem, and it went away. Tag just needed someone to take care of him."

"So," Harley said, "we have the wife who at one time or another was in a rage at him. We have various starlets who might've been angry. We have Tag Zastrow—was Tag capable of violence?"

"Well, if you call missing a feeding of his calico cat violence, when Tag stayed out late, then he was. But no, Tag was sweet and charming. Violence wouldn't be something he was capable of."

"What about the Screen Actors Guild?" Harley asked. "I know there was the famous one-week strike. What was Mr. Spielman's role in all that?"

"That was outside my office. You know as much or more about it than I know. But I did hear a rumor Ordañez helped end the strike. How that would've worked or what he might have done, I don't have any idea. But, if you can do it long distance, he's a man for you to talk to. For God's sakes, don't go to Juarez. The life expectancy for a white American in that city is fifteen minutes. Very unsafe."

"Anyone else we've not asked about?"

He sighed. "Not that I can think of. But in case something comes up, please leave your card."

Harley dropped a business card on his desk. He handed it back. "Please leave it with my secretary when you pick up Reuben Ordañez's phone number. Is that it for now?"

The detectives stood and Harley nodded. "Yes, for now. You've been very helpful. Oh, yes, any directors or producers at the studio? Anyone who might've been on the outs with Mr. Spielman?"

"Hmm, not that I can think of right off-hand. I'll call you if a name comes to me."

"Can't ask for more than that," Marcia said with a smile. She shook his hand. "Thank you, Mr. Sercease."

"Yes," Harley said, "thanks so much." She shook hands as well.

They were then shown out by the same secretary, who passed a note containing Reuben Ordañez's phone number in Juarez. Harley left a business card with her, and they left the office.

"Helpful," Marcia said in the elevator."

"I think he's a pretty straight shooter," Harley added.

"Yes."

"What's next"

"Tag Zastrow? I say we buttonhole him."

"Agree. Ready now?"

"Let's go."

16

Harley took a recorder into Property and played the tape of the Spielman-Ordañez wiretap several times. She thought about her next move. Mickey Loden's daughter was returned home before Spielman's death. The LAPD had run down literally thousands of calls with supposed information about her, none of which had panned out, until one day a Chevy coupe pulled up to her father's front gate and pushed her out. She was shaken up, but alive and quite well, considering. Harley immediately understood what had happened. She made a time for the next day to speak with Lieutenant Chall. She was going to tell him she knew who murdered Spielman, and it wasn't Annalee Johnson. Far from it, in fact.

At last, she knew what she had to do.

~

AFTER HARLEY UNLOADED her thoughts and plans on her lieu-tenant, Chall was anything but convinced. After all, Harley's presentation was pure speculation whereas Detective Sullivan had investigated Annalee Johnson and felt good about her guilt. There would be hell to pay if the LAPD backed off Annalee, reversed course, and went after someone else. Harley could see that wasn't going to happen—at least not without a lot of convincing and hard evidence. But one thing she did manage to convince the lieutenant was that she be allowed to follow-up on the kidnapping and ransom of Mickey Loden's daughter by Reuben Ordañez. For that, Lieutenant Chall grudgingly signed off on Harley making a trip to Chula Vista to lay a trap for Ordañez. It was decided, after much discussion, that Harley would make the trip undercover, posing as an associate of Spielman who wanted muscle in order to capitalize some of the schemes Spielman had raised up to Ordañez. She was going to give Ordañez the chance to make some easy money.

"But you're risking your ass, Sergeant Ellis," Lieutenant Chall needlessly reminded Harley.

"I guess it depends on how good an actress I am," Harley replied. "But after posing as prostitutes for two years in Vice, I can tell you I know how to entice men. Ordañez won't be a pushover but he won't be invulnerable, either. Buy me a ticket and stand back, LT."

"A prostitute, you're going as a prostitute?"

"Union official. That's my official title. I need a driver's license with a new identity and business cards. I'll provide the rest."

"I'm unconvinced, Harley. I think we need to forget the whole talk we're having."

"I can't do that, Lieutenant. The wrong person could die if I just drop it. It's a first-degree murder case. I can't just watch some Annalee Johnson die when I know she's innocent. Let me say it this way. Ordañez kidnapped Mickey Loden's daughter. That's a federal rap but it's a state rap too. It wouldn't look so odd to anyone to find out the LAPD is working up that case because it happened in Los Angeles. There's your justification for allowing me run down to Chula Vista and get an admission. I'm simply going undercover for a single operation. Besides, who knows what else I might turn up? It's cheap and I'm quite good at hustling men after two years in Vice. Let me do this, LT."

"Well—"

"I can handle myself."

"I don't doubt that. Up to a point. But I would want to send another officer with you just in case you get whacked. I can't have you there without backup."

"Not Marcia. You're not thinking Marcia?"

"I'm thinking of Noel Ithaca. An undercover officer. He'll go along as your backup."

"Perfect! When can we leave?"

"As soon as Ordañez will see you. Let's suit up and get it done and over just that fast."

"Done and done!"

Later that afternoon, Harley dialed the number that Spielman's lawyer, Benjamin Sercease, had given her for Reuben Ordañez. A non-English speaking person answered but Harley was able to make him understand she wanted to speak to Ordañez and pronto. It was urgent.

Ordañez picked up. "Si?"

"Señor Ordañez, my name is Constance Spielman. I am Ira Spielman's daughter-in-law. I'm calling to say I think you and I might have some things in common."

"Oh?"

"Yes, there's money to be made in Hollywood. Evidently, you've got a knack for making money and I know some whales."

"What's this?"

"You know, whales. People with lots of money. Rich, stupid people."

"How can I do this?"

"I don't trust the phones. Will you come to Chula Vista and meet me to talk?"

"I don't think so. I think I prefer Juarez. It's okay."

Harley hesitated. She didn't have clearance for Juarez. But he was waiting and it was her chance to meet with him. She then made a snap judgment, determined to expand what authority she did have. "All right. I can do that. Tell me where and when."

They talked and traded information and addresses and hung up. She was shook; Chall hadn't approved an out-of-the country excursion. She immediately went in and told him what had happened. He exploded at her for promising without authority, but she managed to calm him down and even got him to approve, since it was already done.

And so it began, with Harley taking a day inside the LAPD bureaucracy assembling the fake ID and other items she would need for the bit. At first, she didn't even tell Marcia what was happening. Only that they were going to take a trip and that Marcia would be a key actor in it. She didn't tell her any more than that.

"How do I dress?"

"Like you always dress."

"Slacks or a dress?"

"Either is fine."

"Slacks, then. I travel better in slacks."

"Marcia, we'll be gone and back the same day. It really won't make that much difference."

"Okay. Yes, I know. I know. But I'm wearing slacks."

"Good, then so will I."

THEN DANNY SULLIVAN did the unthinkable: he arrested a witness in Harley-Marcia's Spielman case. The *LA Times* evening edition carried the exclusive story: LAPD had arrested the woman who murdered Ira J. Spielman. She was in jail, she had motive, she had admitted wanting to kill him, and she had opportunity. When the reporter asked Detective Sullivan if there was a confession he only smiled and said, "Stay tuned." Other area newspapers repeated the same or similar story in their morning editions. Then the TV picked it up and the wire service. It was a national story by Saturday noon and international by nightfall.

Annalee Johnson was being held without bail. Her father, a plumbing contractor from Flagstaff, Arizona, told the papers the family would be hiring a lawyer to defend Annalee. That announcement would come soon.

HARLEY CALLED MARCIA THAT NIGHT. They were enraged over the

arrest, which neither had seen coming and which neither had been consulted about. "Sullivan's head is on the block, far as I'm concerned," said Harley.

"How's that work?" Marcia replied. "He's made an arrest and that's what LAPD wanted. He's the good guy right now and we're the non-producers."

"Never mind. We're going to Juarez regardless."

"Agree. We can sell that to the LT if we need to because we were never consulted about the arrest."

They then commiserated over Annalee's problems and the fact she was as innocent of the crime as Sullivan himself. Sullivan and Black had already spoken with her at length, their interview was in transcription waiting to be typed, and the file would soon be updated with their comments to the effect that Annalee was clearly innocent. They believed her when she said that murder just wasn't who she was.

Besides, Harley herself had moved on down the road and had caught a glimpse into Spielman's real problems, beginning with the strike and walkout foisted on him by the Screen Actors Guild. She was sure the case was much bigger than one Annalee Johnson, a nice but gentle young woman who wasn't the type to commit a violent murder.

THE FOLLOWING MORNING, Harley demanded a three-way meeting with Lieutenant Chall, Danny Sullivan and Marcia and herself. She was steaming when they met in the lieutenant's office at seven-thirty a.m. Chall indicated she should have first say.

"This is incredibly wrong," she began as evenly as she could muster, given her rage. "This is our case, LT, and Sullivan has over-stepped all bounds of propriety. He should have at least consulted Marcia and me before arresting one of our witnesses and making a big splash in the newspapers."

Chall looked at Sullivan. "Well? Can't say I disagree, Detective Sullivan."

"I tried to consult. Unfortunately, Harley's been unavailable. Every time I turned around she was running off someplace, making arrangements to meet with her Mexican suspect. I believe she's dead wrong about her suspicions there and I was getting pressure from another source to make an arrest."

Chall looked at him, puzzled. "Pressure from where, Detective? Not from me."

"Pressure from the mayor's office. My contact there said the mayor wanted it to get to me that he needed an arrest without further delay. I was only making his Honor, the Mayor, happy. Harley, I'm sorry for it, but you just weren't around."

Harley didn't have an answer. Her Juarez preparations had kept her out of the office the past two days with efforts being directed at getting a phony driver's license out of the state and a phony set of Social Security and official state ID made as well. She was finding it hard to contradict Sullivan about that.

"You could've left a message and I would've gotten back," she said, but everyone knew the protocol wasn't enough to delay the arrest on a major homicide case. Sullivan's judgment was given the highest confidence rating just because detectives were autonomous and their judgments mostly beyond reproach.

"I'm going to tell everyone to get back to work as you were and let's see where this goes. Harley, I'm now especially interested in your investigation, given Danny's arrest of Ms. Johnson. Do we still need that follow-up?"

"More than ever," Harley said. "More than ever before."

"Very well. That's it for now. We'll talk again when Harley reports back to me on one more aspect of the case that doesn't involve you, Detective Sullivan. Dismissed."

Chall was declaring the complaint shelved for the time being. Harley could only step back and continue with her Juarez preparations. Besides, Christmas Eve was tomorrow and thoughts were elsewhere just then. She sighed and left the office.

Once alone with Marcia, Harley cursed Sullivan and Marcia cursed Sullivan, then they split up and welcomed the holiday with some last-minute Christmas shopping.

17

C hristmas Eve, 1955 and colored lights stitched LA east to west and north to south; mock snow-flocked Christmas trees created a spotty forest along Wilshire Boulevard. Whiskey Bill Parker, LAPD's alcoholic but genius Chief of Police, was half in the bag as he dressed up as Santa Claus at LAPD's Christmas party for underprivileged kids and, just as they were ready to roll for the party to help serve Pepsi and cake, Harley reached for the mike as a call-out came into the squad car. Marcia, riding shotgun, jerked her makeup mirror up to catch the trailing car's headlights as she applied lipstick for the party. Ordinarily, no cosmetics on duty, but what the hell, Marcia told Harley, it wasn't official police business to serve Pepsi and punch to a bunch of adorable little kids.

Harley scooped up the mike and acknowledged the call. They were closest to 6724 Hollywood Boulevard and rolled on the assignment. The crime: 288a P.C. - Forced Oral Copulation.

"Motherfucker," Marcia cried, "sticking his joint down some bird's throat. He'll be lucky I don't shoot him in the pecker."

"You know," Harley said, "it's just another rapey, raper, sexual assaulter, take your pick. No need to get invested yourself, Marce. This is the third time we've heard a 288a call tonight."

Two marked cars and four uniforms were already on the scene. They double-parked, hit the emergency lights, and headed for the sidewalk. A dozen large stars of the Hollywood Walk of Fame spread to the right and left as they crossed the sidewalk and went inside the building. Harley and Marcia produced their shields and headed upstairs to the sixth floor of the apartment house. One of the uniforms stopped them before they entered the victim's apartment. "It looks like he actually jumped up to a light fixture and swung himself up to the fire escape. So maybe it's a monkey we're looking for. He managed to pull open the single pane bathroom window, and somehow get his skinny-ass creepy body inside. She was asleep in the bed and he held a knife at her throat while she blew him."

"That's disgusting," said Marcia. "But it ain't the first time for her, right?"

"Jesus, Marcia," Harley said. "Keep it down. Poor girl's inside, probably freaked out of her mind. Okay? Stuff it."

"She's pretty upset, detective," the police officer agreed. "You can still hear her crying. She's only nineteen. Came from East LA to get a job making costumes. That's all she's ever wanted to do is be a movie seamstress. She'll tell you. Her name's Angelina Sosa."

The two detectives proceeded into the apartment. Harley told the inside copper that she and Marcia would take over. He stepped back but didn't leave the room. Harley turned her attention to the weeping young woman. She was Hispanic, looked to be a young nineteen, and was wrapped in a terrycloth bathrobe. She wore bunny slippers on her feet. An open bottle of mouthwash was balanced on the arm of the wooden chair where she sat at the kitchen table. She took a mouthful as Harley watched, swished it around, and then spit it into a cereal bowl. Marcia's jaw tightened at the display of post-coital hygiene.

"I'm Detective Ellis and this is Detective Meriwether. We were close by and took the call although Sex Crimes isn't our usual beat. If you want, we can call in the normal unit and let them handle your case or we can take it from here on. The other team is two men. We're the only women you'll get a chance at. So, what do you say, do you want us to take the case?"

"Uh-huh. I want women. I don't wanna tell any men nothing. My dad is going to kill this guy. My brother's a pachuco and runs with ten other pachucos. They're gonna catch him and chop his dick off, I promise you. So maybe you better find the guy fast for his own safety, rotten bastard."

The tears hadn't stopped flowing. She spoke between the ebb and flow. Another shot of mouthwash; another spray into the bowl. "I'll swallow the next one. I already vomited everything I had. Even the shrimp I had for dinner came up. Sorry."

"Can you give us a description?" asked Marcia. She pulled out her notepad and poised her ballpoint.

"Mexican guy, maybe sixteen or seventeen. He was tall but very skinny. I don't know how he got in through the bathroom window. I only keep it open for air. I have smokers on both sides and the fumes make me sick every day when I get home from work."

"Where do you work?"

"Car wash. I'm the cashier just off Wilshire and Tower. I also help detail the chrome. It don't pay much but I don't need much. I've got a roommate but she's out tonight with her boyfriend, probably won't be back."

"Had you ever seen the intruder before?" Harley asked.

"Never. But it's funny, I really only got a good look at his chin and mouth. He made me look up at him while I...."

The crying came roaring to life again. She pressed a damp washcloth over her eyes and held it there for a minute until the weeping subsided enough to talk. "What do I do if he had the clap?"

"There's medicine, we can direct you," Harley said. "What color were his eyes?"

"Brown."

"Hair?"

"Black."

"Any identifying marks or scars?"

"He wasn't circumcised. I had to skin it back. And it was very red, like he'd been rubbing it too much."

"Anything else? Something about his face or arms?"

"He had the pachuco sign on that part of his hand—the cross and dots thingy."

"Every Mexican guy under thirty has that," Marcia ventured. "We could run our legs off if we chased down every pachuco with that sign."

"It could help," Harley said to the girl, ignoring her partner.

Marcia turned away and wandered out onto the fire escape. She randomly shouted back inside, "This perv-o is scurvy and skinny.

It's a tight-ass fit through the window. I can look out west and see the Hollywood Theater marquee. Used to spend my Saturdays there, Harley. Nothing much else to be seen but a neon jungle where the animals lurk. God, I hate this part of town." She returned inside. Harley was still speaking with the victim, jotting down information in her notebook.

"Do you have anyone to spend the night with you?" Harley asked.

"My oldest brother is coming from Camp Pendleton. He had to get emergency leave. He's gonna find this guy and de-nut him."

"Seriously? Do you really expect this guy to be found, Señora?" Marcia broke in. "Alls you can tell us he's a young Mexican guy who's a pachuco with brown eyes and black hair. You just described half the city of LA. Which is useless. You need to put your thinking cap on and try again. Give us something useable, *por favor*."

Stunned, Harley used all available restraint to keep from dragging her partner outside and tossing her off the fire escape. She immediately tried to repair the breach.

"What Marcia means, Angelina, is that it's very difficult for any police officer to even know where to begin without something more. What I'd like you to do is take a day or two and think back about whether you'd seen the perp before. Maybe in line at the car wash? Maybe he served you your lunch today?"

"I buy tacos off the truck."

"Well, maybe he was behind the window in the truck taking orders? Just take a day or so and let your mind wander back over things. Maybe you'll hit on something and you can give me a call. I'm leaving my card with you—here it is. We can wait for your brother to arrive, too. I don't want to see him do anything foolish."

"Wait a minute. I did see him before."

"Oh?"

"He goes to my church. He's an altar boy. Now I remember him!"

"Can you give us a name?"

"No, but Father Canberra can, I'm sure. You should call him."

"Which church?"

"Our Lady of Wilshire Boulevard," said the girl. "That's what we call it to joke. The real name is Blessed Sacrament. On Sunset. It's not far."

"Let me write that down. Spell the priest's name?"

"C-A-N-B-E-R-R-A. Father Canberra."

"When's the last time you saw this kid?"

"He's not a kid anymore. He's a man now. I think I saw him Sunday. I think he was with some other young boys in the back. He smiled at me when I left after mass."

"Did you smile back" asked Marcia.

"I think I did."

"Now we're getting somewhere."

"I know what you're thinking, Detective," said Angelina. "But it wasn't like that. I smile at lots of people. I'm very friendly."

"When your brother gets here, we'll need to take you to the hospital for an examination. They'll probably have medicine, too," Harley said.

"Probably penicillin," Marcia offered. "That way you won't get the clap."

The weeping erupted again. Another slug of mouthwash followed, this time swallowed down. Harley took the washcloth to the sink and ran warm water over it. She squeezed it out then ran just enough for it to be slightly damp when she handed it back to Angelina. The girl clutched the cloth to her eyes and cried sound-lessly for a full minute. Then she withdrew the cloth and placed her forehead in her hand and tried to calm herself down. Harley reached and touched her shoulder. She lightly massaged her shoulder and the back of her neck. The girl seemed to relax. She slumped forward and put both elbows on the table. The shivering that racked her every couple of minutes seemed to lessen in its violence.

"Herman will take me to the hospital. It would be best if you left and let me explain to him. He's going to be in a rage and seeing police officers won't help. If you go, I can probably calm him down and he'll take me."

"We'll call admitting and alert them you're coming. We'll tell Admissions what we need. So, we'll take you up on that," Harley said. "If you think you can manage now."

"I can manage. I have a long butcher knife in that drawer."

"He won't be back," Harley said. "He knows we'll be watching. But just to be sure, I'm going to leave a marked car downstairs. That will keep him at bay until Herman arrives, just in case he's one of the crazy ones who decides to come back. Which I highly doubt. These guys are usually fifty miles away by now, the real sick ones. Hard to catch because they don't ever strike the same area twice. Anyway, that's neither here nor there. You have my card, call me with anything. And feel free to have Herman call me too, if he wants. I can deal with him, no problem."

Angelina reached and touched Harley's hand just before the

detective removed it from the girl's shoulder. "Thank you. I'll call if there's anything."

"We'll update you after we contact the boy. I'm sure we'll track him down and take him in for questioning. We'll also do a lineup but that's later."

"All right. Thank you. You should go now and take the rest of them with you."

"Done and done. Good night."

"Night."

Back inside the squad car, before turning the key, Harley withdrew her hands from the wheel. She turned in the seat to face Marcia. "Jesus Christ, Marcia! Do you feel nothing for these people?"

"What would I feel?"

"Let's try compassion. You come across like they're wasting your precious time. If you ever pull that crap again, I'm going to clock you. So just watch for it. I swear to God, I'll knock your cold ass straight down on the floor."

Marcia removed her compact from her shirt pocket. She opened it and lifted it to catch the headlights bouncing in the interior. "There. Just enough lipstick to look alive. Not so much as to get a write-up. Sharesies?"

Harley dropped her arms and slouched back against the seat. She was out of words. It was what it was.

"No," she said, "I don't want lipstick. I want to go home. I need to do Christmas Eve alone in my bed."

"Fuck that! I'm stepping up to the plate tonight. I might even go dancing later with Chief Parker."

"Lord, help me find my way home to bed."

"C'mon, we hit the kids' party and I'll catch a ride home with someone else. You can stay a half hour then boogie. It'll be fun."

"Seriously? After what we just saw up inside that apartment? There's still fun to be had?"

"Hey, she took it in the mouth, not me."

"Marcia, I—I—"

"I know. I'm cold and immature. But you know what, Harley? I sleep at night. Like a baby. How about you?"

Harley remembered coming awake too many nights, tangled in the bedsheets, wet all down her back. "A half hour at the party. Then I'm gone."

"Suit yourself."

"If only. Besides."

"Besides what?"

"Wendy might call. Christmas Eve and all."

Marcia stopped with the lipstick. She snapped the compact shut. "Then you should go straight home. I'll drop you and take the squad. You don't want to miss her call."

"No, I don't. It could happen."

They drove to Harley's and Marcia dropped her.

"Get inside and I'll say a little prayer for the call."

"That would be good."

"Then I'm gonna kidnap Chief Parker. I'll call you tomorrow."

"Suit yourself."

"Now who's cold?"

"Yes, I take back what I said."

"It's all right. It's not like we're grief counselors. We're only cops."

"We're only cops. Good night."

"Night."

Harley didn't pause to watch the taillights drift away and disappear down the hill. Her step quickened.

It could happen, tonight of all nights. She entered her apartment and touched Wendy's picture where it sat in its frame atop the piecrust table.

It could happen.

18

C hristmas Day 1955

Harley had her husband's *Times* obituary memorized.

Robert Ellis was living in Long Beach, CA when he entered the service and served aboard the heavy cruiser USS SAINT PAUL (CA 73).

He and five other seamen were listed as Missing in Action, when the whaleboat they were in disappeared in Inchon Harbor, South Korea on June 11, 1952.

CPO Ellis was awarded the Purple Heart, the Combat Action Ribbon, the Korean Service Medal, the United Nations Service Medal, the National Defense Service Medal, the Korean Presidential Unit Citation and the Republic of Korea War Service Medal.

Ellis is survived by his widow, Harley Ellis, and their daughter, Wendell.

It was family custom that Harley and Wendy would share Christmas dinner with Bobby's parents. This year, however, both Robert and Wendy were gone, leaving only Harley to carry on the tradition.

Ralph Ellis, in his middle fifties, greeted Harley at the door. The father-in-law embraced Harley. She pressed her face against his; the Old Spice aftershave was the same Bobby wore every day. They pulled apart and stared into each other's eyes. She knew she was looking into the face of the man Bobby would have become: father and son looked almost like brothers. Then she looked away. He turned and led her into the kitchen. "Charmaine, Harley's here."

Bobby's mother closed the oven door. The sweet smell of Christmas ham hung throughout the house. She turned, setting aside the oven mitt then wiping her hands on her apron. She held out her arms and gave Harley a hug. "Anything?" she asked in reference to the missing Wendy.

"Not a word. No sightings, no calls. Just gone."

"How's work?" asked Ralph. "Got some new cases to share with us?"

He was a lifelong barber, a man who loved to cut hair and gab, a man who kept the *Daily Racing Form* in his barber shop and had plastered on his shop walls pictures of Derby and Triple Crown winners. He smoked a briar pipe, which he filled now with Prince Albert and ignited with a kitchen match. He sucked and puffed until half the kitchen was caught up in the velvety odor of ham mingled with pipe smoke. Then he led Harley into the family room, where Bobby's younger brother and sister were playing Hearts. They invited Harley to join the game, so she sat down at the small table and unbuttoned the top button of her shirt. Her green Christmas sweater was full enough to blouse over the service weapon she wore concealed. "What did you guys get me for Christmas?" she kidded.

"A partridge in a pear tree," said James, who was Harley's age.

"How's Navy?" Harley always called him "Navy." Everyone did. He was on his third tour.

James said, "We did Japan last year, Hong Kong and Singapore. Then back to Pearl and home."

"Any secret war stuff we should know about?" Harley kidded.

"Only that Ike hasn't seen fit to invade China yet."

"There's a win."

"Harley," said her father-in-law. "We got the presents you left with Mattie. We all went in and got you one present this year." He proudly handed her a small box about the size of a teaspoon. "Open it!"

"No," said Mrs. Ellis, "After we eat. Then we can get pictures. Dinner's ready now or never."

Dinner was served. Baked ham, mashed potatoes and gravy, candied yams, cranberries, green beans with bacon, hot rolls and real butter, and fig jam. Everyone dug in.

Mary Ellen, Bobby's sister, the youngest of the three kids, studied Harley closely. "Is it okay to ask about Wendy?" she finally asked.

"Not much to tell," Harley told her. "I haven't heard a word since she disappeared. But you've grown up and out. College looks good on you."

"I'm working on my dissertation. It's tedious and boring."

"Topic?"

"I'm embarrassed to say. Mating habits of sea lions."

"Sea lions? That doesn't sound boring. Or tedious. Sounds like it might be pretty interesting," Harley said.

"Compared to what you do every day, it's pretty boring," Mary Ellen insisted. "Can you tell us about any interesting cases?"

"I've got the Ira J. Spielman case. That's keeping me jumping."

"I read about the girl's arrest. Anything new?" asked Ralph.

"No. The widow thinks he died of natural causes, the way she sees it. I've tried to get her to open up and acknowledge it was a very violent, mean death. But she refuses to see it that way. So, she's been zero help. We're working our way through movie directors now, looking for some out-of-sorts actor or actress, someone Spielman might have angered."

"Any leads there?" asked her mother-in-law.

"We've got one or two we're looking at. Not much, though, not really."

"I wonder what Wendy's thinking today, knowing we're all here without her," Mary Ellen said in the manner of one much younger than her years. In retrospect, Harley would almost think the girl was just speaking her thoughts out loud without realizing how painful the topic was for Harley.

"That's—that's—"

"She's probably enjoying a meal with friends," said Bobby's mother, Charmaine. "She's probably doing very well. I'm imagining she's working some place."

"Thanks for that," Harley said, resignation in her voice. "That's much better than the thoughts I have about her. I worry nonstop."

"We all do," said Ralph Ellis. "Our only granddaughter. I can't help but think she's just angry about losing her father. I think that's what's got her going."

"She hated me the last two years," Harley said. "She told me her dad would still be alive if I'd put my foot down and not let him join the Navy. Maybe she was right."

"Not at all," Ralph said. "Nobody could stop him from joining up for Korea. Besides, it wasn't your job. He knew he had a family to take care of. He knew better than to run off and get himself killed in Inchon Harbor."

"Ralph," said Charmaine, "let's change the subject. Bobby had only love for any of us. He joined up because he thought it was his duty."

"Thank you," Harley said. "It's been so long now I can't even remember it anymore."

"Five years?" her sister-in-law mumbled. "Five years is so long?"

"I mean it's all become a jumble in my mind. I don't know. I guess it really hasn't been that long.'"

"I think he was still pissed about Mare Island in 1943," said Navy. "They made him keep working there and wouldn't let him enlist for the war. I'd have been plenty pissed too."

"Maybe so," Harley agreed. "Maybe that was it. I only know I—I miss him so damn much."

Tears clouded her eyes. It was terribly difficult to come and be around his family without him. Which was why she only agreed to it once a year. It always ended with her in tears, too, or so it seemed.

"So, who did kill Mr. Spielman? That girl they arrested?" Charmaine asked, changing the subject.

Harley could only shake her head. She dabbed at her eyes with her paper napkin. "That's the sixty-four-thousand-dollar question.

Like I said, I've got my money on someone other than some budding actress he took advantage of. That wasn't my arrest."

"He was such a philanthropist," the mother-in-law continued on her end of the conversation. "Seems hard to believe he would use his position like that."

"Not so hard from where I sit," Harley said.

"You're jaded," Mary Ellen said with a smile. "You're a cop."

"Guilty," Harley acknowledged. "Jaded is my middle name."

Dinner finished, the hostess, with Mary Ellen's help, served an apple torte and peach cobbler. Whipped cream was homemade. Then came coffee and small talk.

"Okay," Ralph finally said, "let's see you open our gift, Harley."

She pulled the small box from her sweater pocket and began unwrapping. Then she saw: it was a US Navy issued fountain pen, emblazoned on the side, *USS SAINT PAUL (CA 73)*. "Bobby's ship," was all she could manage to say. She then cleared her throat and added, "This is the best present ever. Thank you all *so* much."

"They have them for all the ships. The Navy signs off on them. It's made out of real gold."

"All right, Ralph," Charmaine scolded, "Harley can see it's a nice pen."

She again fought back the tears. For a moment she had the feeling her husband was there, among them, smiling at his family and his wife. Then she blinked hard, twice, three times, and the moment passed. She was back. "I do see what it is, Ralph. I cannot thank all of you enough. This pen will go everyplace with me. That's a promise. A piece of Bobby."

"That's what we thought," her father-in-law agreed. "A memento of him. But just let me add, Harley, it's been five years now. Charmaine and I were talking about you. We kind of hoped you'd take up with someone new by now. Bobby would want that for you."

Harley reached and placed her hand on Ralph's. "That's extremely kind of you. But you know what? Until this thing with Wendy is resolved—until she comes home—I'm not going to be much good for anyone else. A piece of my heart is out there walking around without me right now. Until I get it back, I can't give it away again. So, I'm kind of in no-man's land right now."

"I understand that," Charmaine said. "Just know that you have our blessing when Mr. Right does come along."

"I love you guys for that," Harley said. "I really do. But even when it happens, I expect you to be there right alongside of me. Even with any new guy. I'd never leave my family behind. So, know you'll always be right here in my heart. Right beside my new fountain pen," she added with a laugh. "Now if I can just figure out how to use it so I don't have ink stains on my police outfits."

"Well, it's a cartridge pen, so there shouldn't be much chance of ink spills and bleed-throughs," Ralph said. "Just plug in the cartridge and you're good to go."

"How about a game of Hearts, everyone?" said Navy. "Family tradition time."

"I get to deal first," Harley said. "And I'm dealing off the bottom, just so you know."

They laughed. The Hearts game got underway after everyone had carried their plates into the kitchen and scraped and rinsed and loaded into the dishwasher—the only one in the neighborhood,

Ralph proudly pointed out to Harley. The food was put away, loosely covered so leftovers could be quickly grabbed for supper.

Harley went out and climbed into her Ford Fairlane at eight-thirty. She drove home without the radio. Halfway home she opened her glove box and pulled out an old pack of Salem's. She lit one, inhaled, broke into a coughing spasm from the menthol and cracked a window so she could flick it into the slipstream. "Nothing's going to take the edge off tonight," she reminded herself.

Once inside her apartment she checked her answer machine. "No messages," the voice told her.

So, she turned on the TV and sat nursing a cup of decaf before bed.

She remembered the nib pen in her pocket, then. She hadn't had the heart to tell the family that every piece of paperwork they processed in a day was done with at least four copies—which required a heavy hand and a ballpoint pen. The fountain pen would go into her jewelry box with her other special items.

She would have to remember to carry it the next Christmas when they visited again. It was her final memory of him.

19

They pulled into Blessed Sacrament on Sunset and parked. Inside the church, they told the receptionist they were looking for Father Canberra. She asked to see ID so both detectives displayed shields and ID cards. Satisfied with their credentials, the receptionist took them into a small office and told them to wait there.

Harley looked around as they waited. Two walls were bookcases, filled with hundreds of tomes, most of which were theology books. Whatever else they had, the priests had a great place to study and access to a huge number of books, Harley decided.

They sat facing the back wall, which had two tall windows looking out on the parking lot and alley beyond that. It was sunny outside, and Harley knew the light from the windows would make it difficult to see the priest's expressions. She'd just have to do what she could to make it work.

Five minutes later, a young man dressed in priestly garb and white collar came into the room and warmly introduced himself, shaking hands with both detectives and putting them at ease. He sat down behind the desk with the sun at his back and asked how he could help.

"We're here about an altar boy," Harley began. "An altar boy who could be in a lot of trouble."

"What do they say he did?"

"Forced oral copulation," Marcia replied. "Stuck his you-know-what down a girl's throat."

"Oh, my word! And she thinks he's from this church?"

"That's right," Harley said. "She saw him here last Sunday during mass."

"How did she describe him?"

"Mexican boy, sixteen or seventeen, tall and skinny, pachuco sign on his hand."

"That must be Guernica Aguilar. He's one of our longest-serving altar boys. Comes from a good home, his father's a bricklayer and his mother's a cook at Naome's Cafe. He has two older brothers and three sisters. I know the family well. His older brothers also served as altar boys and one is an acolyte."

"Does he have the pachuco sign on his hand?"

"Oh, yes, I see it when he is serving especially. He also owns a zoot suit but he is not allowed to wear that to church. His parents hate it and I've talked to him a few times about his appearance. But he's very impressionable. I don't know that he would ever be able to do the crime you're asking about. Never in a hundred years would I expect that out of him."

"We need his address," Harley said. "Can your secretary help us?"

"He lives two blocks down on Tower. The small pink house with the Spanish dagger plant in the front yard. Be careful what time of day you go—his mother works nights and sleeps in the day."

"All right, Father," said Marcia. "Duly noted."

After leaving Father Canberra the detectives jumped into their car. Turning south, they looked for the setback pink house in block two. It was easy enough to find, with several Spanish dagger plants in the front yard. A sagging gate protected the premises.

The gate opened easily, and Harley and Marcia made their way up onto the porch. Harley rapped her knuckles on the outer door. No answer. She knocked again, harder this time, rattling the door in its frame. A girl of twelve cracked open the door and looked out at them from behind the screen.

"We need to talk to Guernica," Harley explained. "Is he here?"

"I don't know. He's always in his room."

"Can you go look, please?"

"Okay." She disappeared, leaving the door open and the detectives standing on the other side, waiting.

Then a young man of about seventeen walked into view. He was wearing Levi's and a white T-shirt, huaraches on his feet. Harley stole a quick glance and saw that, indeed, he had the pachuco cross and rays on the web between thumb and forefinger.

The detectives displayed their badges and the young man's color drained from his face.

"I know her. She invited me in," he immediately said.

"She says you snuck in through the bathroom and forced her to take your penis in her mouth," said Harley,

"No way. She asked me to come over Christmas Eve and listen to her Elvis Presley record."

"Really? What record?"

"'I Forgot to Remember to Forget,' or something like that. It's country and western, kind of. But we listened to it ten times and danced. Then she asked me to kiss her. She said her roommate was out with her boyfriend and her brother wouldn't be there until tomorrow and so she told me to take my clothes off."

"What did you do?"

"I—I pulled down my pants and she had me put it in her."

"Did you put it in her mouth?"

"No way. It was my first time inside a girl. Am I going to go to jail for that? My mom and dad will kill me."

Harley looked at Marcia, who only shrugged.

"She told us you forced her to suck you."

"Not true! She made me put it in her. Well, didn't make me but you know what I mean. She's lots older than me and I didn't know what to do."

"How old are you?" asked Harley.

"I'm almost seventeen."

"So, you're a minor?"

"I'm a freshman in high school."

"Did you get held back?"

"Two years I got held back. But there's nothing wrong with me."

"The sex was her idea?"

"I don't want to blame her or anything. We were always friends. I thought."

"Why would she claim you forced her?" asked Marcia.

"I don't know. Maybe cause I didn't use a rubber?"

"No rubber? You're thinking she did it because she's afraid she might be pregnant?" asked Harley.

"I don't know. I thought we were friends."

"Well, is there anything else you want to tell us?"

"No."

"Are you planning on moving or leaving the state?"

"No, ma'am."

"Will you call my number on this card if you do decide to leave California?"

"I will."

"We'll probably want more statements from you, but for now we're not going to take you to jail," Harley said. "It looks like it's her word against your word. Plus, you're a minor. If you can prove she had sex with you voluntarily on her part that would be statutory rape of a male minor. My guess is, she wouldn't want to go there."

"My folks will kill me for that."

"For now, I don't want to talk to your folks. I'm going to go back and talk to the complainant first."

"What's her name?"

"Angelina."

"That's the one."

"Have you ever talked to her before that night?"

"No. I wanted to, but—I was afraid."

"Let us talk to her again and see what else we can find out."

"Okay, thank you."

"Thank you for cooperating. Remember, don't leave the state."

"I won't. I promise."

THEY CLIMBED in their unmarked cruiser and pulled into traffic. Marcia was pensive. She looked out the passenger window and wouldn't draw her gaze back inside. At long last, she said, "You treated him almost pleasantly. Now, why can't you be that way with me instead of jumping me when I'm insensitive?"

"What are you talking about?"

Marcia leaned away. "The other night with Angelina. I was talking about downtown Hollywood and you got pissed. You jumped me for being insensitive. You even threatened to *clock* me. Why can't you be as patient with me as you were with that boy back there?"

"That's what you're thinking? That I should let off of you?"

"Hey, you don't see me busting your chops."

"No, but if you think that's what I'm doing to you, you're wrong. I'm just verbalizing my feelings."

"I think you owe me an apology for all the times you've been short with me."

"All right. I apologize for all the times I've been short with you."

"You didn't mean it!"

Harley sighed. "You could've drawn a much easier partner to tool around town with than me. Too much on my plate and I don't handle it well."

Marcia looked at the side of Harley's face. Then, "It's all right. If they keep us together long enough the shoe will be on the other foot and I'll be asking you for patience. I don't mind. I feel heard."

"Good. I'm so sorry."

"Okay."

20

Marcia Meriwether accompanied Harley on the flight to Juarez. She would remain with the plane and provide security to the chartered DC-3. They strapped in and the plane began taxiing.

Before takeoff, Marcia sat across the aisle from Harley, foot tapping in time to a staticky Count Basie on her transistor radio. Marcia removed her Ray-Bans and leaned across the aisle, catching Harley's attention.

"Here's something else, Harls. If you're American, you have no business ever going to Juarez, Mexico. The average lifespan of an American citizen is less than eighteen minutes, according to Russ Hinckley over at the FBI."

"I'd heard something like that," Harley responded. "But we're at a stalemate. Sullivan arrested Annalee. There's no damn case, but some cowboy in the mayor's office is after her for political reasons. That hasn't really left us an alternative, right? Besides, Ordañez is next on our list. We agreed."

"Right. I'm just saying, better to find some other place than Juarez for a meetup."

Harley knew these things even as the plane landed at Abraham González International Airport. But she had a security pass this time: she'd called Reuben Ignacio Ordañez a second time and arranged a face-to-face. He agreed to guarantee Harley's safe passage *to* the meet. Not after. Harley had enrolled Noel Ithaca, an LAPD undercover operator, on the passenger manifest to help with the leaving Juarez part of the journey.

The plane taxied to a large hanger and stopped. The engines were cut and quickly stopped fanning the air.

Harley arose from her leather seat but held back so Noel could proceed first down the aisle. Noel—thirty-eight, black, gold eyeglass frames, dark liquid eyes and full beard—grabbed his satchel and headed for the exit. He had a spring in his step; Harley saw the guy actually loved the kind of tension Harley was feeling. There were no other passengers; the cabin crew stood just inside the front of the plane and watched as Harley and Noel hurried down the stairway. Marcia remained seated, fanning herself with the front section of the *Times*.

The sun was boiling on the tarmac. Harley put on sunglasses. She touched Noel's shoulder. "Hey, let's talk just a second."

Noel paused and turned back. "Sure, boss."

"We're going to have the taxi deliver us to 4332 Simon Bolivar Avenue. When we step inside, I go first. I want them to immediately identify me rather than be confused by who you are. I didn't tell them I was bringing anyone along so I'm first through the door. Understand me?"

"Sure, boss. You go first."

"Next thing is, let me do all the talking. Don't you say a word, even if they speak to you. Always let me be the one to answer even if it's you they want to hear from. That way we won't risk crossing any wires. I know where and how I want this to do. You don't."

"Sure, boss, but--"

"But what?"

"What did you bring me along for if I'm not security and I don't talk?"

Harley smiled. "If they kill me, I want you to kill every damn one of them. You're SWAT. You know how that goes."

"How do I do that? I don't have a gun."

"That, my man, will be up to you to figure out. I'll do everything I can to get a gunman close to you, so you've at least got a chance at a takeaway. That much I promise."

"So, my commission is to kill them all if they kill you?"

"Right. Kill them all, take their money—anything you can carry out, you take."

"And where do I go? They know about our plane ever since we touched down five minutes ago."

"You're right. They do know about the plane, know how many of us are coming, know our gender and race, and are trying to decide whether we're armed. So right now, let's remove our suit coats and let them see for themselves. No waistband holsters, no bulges, no shoulder holsters. Ready? Now."

The detectives removed their coats. They were wearing white shirts. But it was clear they weren't armed, as they slowly turned around and around. Harley felt certain that somewhere nearby someone was studying them. Maybe through binoculars, hell, maybe even through a high-powered rifle scope with orders to shoot if anything was even one hair off. But it couldn't be helped. Right then, she held their lives in her hands. There was nothing to do but proceed. "All right, Noel, let's find that taxi."

They passed through the small, dirty terminal then out to the passenger loading zone. Several taxicabs waited in line. Drivers reading the afternoon papers, tapping their heads in time to unseen signals, smoking, some talking, probably to *esposos*, on the pay phones. The first driver looked up and pointed at the two travelers then at himself. It was universal sign language: they belonged to him. So, they loaded, and Harley gave the driver their destination. Off they went, deep into the city. The driver studied them in the mirror. "Hey," he said, "you're sure you want that address? It's not safe there."

Harley smiled and nodded. "Yes."

The driver steered them out to Mexico 45, where they headed northwest for the next forty kilometers before exiting on Boulevard Oscar Flores. Behind a six-foot steel rod fence was a narrow, low building. The address matched with what Reuben Ignacio Ordañez had given Harley. They had the driver pull over and stop. Then they unloaded and Harley handed the driver a twenty-dollar bill. "Wait here," she said to the man, who nodded and smiled. He would definitely wait.

"I don't know, boss, this place is a dump."

"I'm sure he doesn't live here, Noel."

"I just don't like the looks of it. They're going to lock that fence behind us. That means they'll have to unlock before we can get away. That's a trap."

"It is. But we've come this far. Let's walk in like we own the place." With that, Harley grabbed the double chain holding the gate closed and began rattling the metal on metal and shouting for someone's attention.

She needn't have. Two armed men, looking like Special Forces warriors with battle webbing bearing a dozen magazines for their automatic weapons came outside the single building and strode up to the gate.

"ID, Señora," said the Mexican man with the handlebar mustache.

Harley and Noel flipped open their wallets and pressed their false driver's licenses against the bars. Handlebar Man studied them while his *compadre*, a very tall, very young man with a natural sneer, looked on bemused. Harley knew why: even the very young knew what a fine menu of walking dead gringos was coming inside. They were easy targets and at such great disadvantage that it was even amusing.

Harley went first through the open gate, followed by Noel.

Harley heard the gate bumping over the ground behind as it closed. Next, the chain was drawn across the opening. Then came the unmistakable *click* of the lock snapping shut.

Now they were locked inside.

The young man with his machine gun slipped in behind them. He quickly patted them down and reported finding no weapons. Then Handlebar led them inside the one-story building.

21

The building was nothing fancy, nothing like where Harley had imagined a Mexican *mafioso* would be holding court. Of course, that was just it. Reuben Ignacio Ordañez couldn't allow himself to be found inside palatial hotel rooms or sprawling villas. That's just where his enemies would be looking for him. So, he kept to the back alleys and the junkyards and the cement block buildings. "Hell of a way to live, Noel," Harley said as Noel stepped inside behind her. If the Mexican men understood any of what Harley had said, they didn't indicate such. Handlebar pushed through an interior door, stepped across a hallway, and knocked twice on a door where two more men guarded the entrance. "*¡Entrar!*" came the response. Handlebar turned and pushed the doorknob. Harley and Noel followed him into the interior room.

They found themselves staring straight ahead at a raised hot tub faced with vertical slats. At one side stood a middle-aged Mexican man wearing a salmon-colored suit with black brogans, who, Harley guessed, would be the interpreter. To the left side of the tub were two men dressed in rich three-piece pinstriped suits who, Harley also guessed, were Juarez *abogados* or maybe even American attorneys in place to judge the sense and substance of the financial services arrangement Harley was there to offer.

And there, in the tub itself, his head just showing above the tub edge, was Ordañez himself.

A voice from behind told them to proceed five steps nearer then stop. They complied.

Ordañez spoke from within the steamy water. His interpreter spooled and repeated his words.

"Constance Spielman, you are here for your dead father-in-law?"

"Yes, for Ira J. Spielman," Harley said.

"What do you have to offer me?"

"I've come here to offer my financial services. Which are significant assets. Also, if you will agree to two terms, I will work to overturn the conviction of your brother, Matin Ordañez. He is being held in San Quentin."

"You will work to do that? Can you guarantee his freedom?"

"There are no guarantees in law. I'm sure Señor Ordañez knows that."

"I've heard that. But I've never hired a lawyer without a guarantee."

"That's just it. I'm not a lawyer. I'm offering financial opportunities in Central California."

"Your dead father-in-law gave his guarantee that Matin would walk out from that courthouse a free man. He lied, as we now know. So, he had to die. Now you have something else for me? You want to change my mind about killing the rest of his family? Well, change it, Señora Spielman. I am waiting."

Harley's heart jumped in her chest. Her appraisal had been totally wrong. She was sure Mickey Loden had killed Spielman for kidnapping his daughter. Now, here was Ordañez saying flat out that he'd killed Spielman because his brother was in San Quentin? They'd had a deal, it appeared, where Spielman was to use his lawyers to spring the brother from San Quentin. That had evidently failed, and he was dead. Now Ordañez was expecting her, Harley, to offer the same legal service in order to secure his brother's release. She was totally unprepared for that.

She tried to back-pedal. "I can't make a guarantee." Realization dawned that she was Ordañez's best hope of freeing the brother.

"I understand. Maybe you should walk away. But your husband and children will die—before you die. And you will watch. Don't ever forget that, Señora Spielman."

That was the problem with going in without all the facts. She had misjudged. The only idea she had was to get the hell away and rethink everything. She saw Ordañez' face, then, suspended above the steaming water, the expression angry and mean. She knew, in that instant, that it was only a display of bravado that was going to walk them out of there alive. He had said he would kill her—and her child—if she did just walk away, which scared the hell out of her. Harley was never the type to scare easily and was collected even now. Still, she knew only that she had misjudged, and it was time to try a different tack. "I propose we work together so killing my family isn't necessary. I will do everything that can be done to free your brother. I will personally handle the case and make all influences myself. I will do this without pay. See? I've already saved you a million dollars and I just got here."

The man smiled when he heard the Spanish translation of Harley's words.

He broke into speaking perfect English.

"Yes and thank you for that one million dollars. I'll be careful not to spend it, however. But I am going to tell you something since you're here. I'm going to make you a counter-offer. You set my brother free and I will let your child live. The one you call Wendy. Oh, yes, Detective Ellis, we know all about you. I don't know who you people think you are dealing with up there in your shiny offices with your shiny badges and shiny houses. I have my sources and I know everything in Los Angeles. You are not the daughter-in-law of the very dead Ira J. Spielman. You are nothing but a detective from the LAPD and I think you are here to kill me. Let me say this again. If you fail to get my brother released, I will kill Wendy, kill your in-laws, and kill your mother. Do you doubt me, Señora?"

Harley gagged, her vision dimmed, and the room spun. She took another step forward. "¡Alto!" cried a voice from behind. She heard the distinct sound of an automatic weapon being cocked. No doubt several guns were aimed at her. Harley froze then slowly raised her arms, extending them out away from her body.

"I don't doubt you."

"Do you think we don't see your precious Wendy in Los Angeles? So close you've driven right past her and not seen?"

She was floored. Her head spun and her ears began ringing. She felt woozy and needed to sit down. But she resisted her body's fear and stayed upright and breathed evenly. Not a shred of fear could be shown to this man. She had to keep her cool or Wendy would die.

"Señor Ordañez, where I come from, we kill each other. Even now, harm even one hair on my head and my husband, an Army veteran with a Silver Star from Korea, will see your brother dead. And maybe your family. And maybe you too, Señor. So, let's not play that old game. Let's talk sensibly. I will oversee your brother's release. I will do everything humanly possible to get his conviction overturned and get him a new trial. While I am doing this, you will leave Wendy alone and unharmed. If I am successful, our business is done, and you will deliver Wendy to me. If I am unsuccessful, we will meet once more and further arrangements will be discussed."

Ordañez drove his fist into the water. "Señora, you do not dictate terms to me! I dictate terms to you. If you fail, your child dies. That is my last offer."

"And if I walk out?"

"They all die anyway. And surprise, there is no walking out today. Do not test me on this, Señora. It won't ever work."

Harley worked to suppress a shudder. It hadn't come so close to home ever before. The trouble was, Reuben Ordañez wasn't just one man sending one killer. He was an empire with the money and the power over people to send killer after killer until someone died. Then someone else, and on it would go. Until her family was all dead. She realized there, on that spot before that hot tub, that she had made a huge mistake coming here. Chall had warned her. It wasn't supposed to come to this. She resolved that she couldn't leave it like this, no matter what. So, she went one step further than before.

"Señor Ordañez, I will make my final offer. I will set your brother free or I will return here, and you can do with me as you will. But you will leave my family alone. I alone will pay the debt for your brother. An eye for an eye."

"I can agree to just thirty days for that."

"Sixty days," said Harley "plus enough time for a new trial." She had no idea in the world why the brother was doing a stretch in Q. No idea and so she had no idea how to bluff it.

"No, Señora Ellis. Thirty days, period. After that your family dies while you watch. It's only fair. Your LAPD put him there."

"He might need a new trial. Give me sixty days for the whole thing."

"Sixty days?" Ordañez looked at the two lawyers to his right. One of them blinked. It was almost imperceptible, but it was a blink. The deal was done.

"You have touched me with your daring, Detective Ellis. Very well, today is January 6. I will give you until March 6. Goodbye to you. We will make sure you arrive safely at the airport today. If you ever return here, there are no such guarantees. Do you understand my meaning?"

"I do. One more thing. Should I have to return here you will want to lock all the doors. Good day, sir."

"Adios, detective. Thank you for playing the game."

"The game? This was a game?"

"You were playing a game, detective. I was not. I meant every word I said."

"As did I. So, check your doors."

Harley and Noel were escorted to the front gate where, waiting for the chain to be released, she felt the muzzle of the young man's gun probe her kidneys.

Then the gate opened, and the taxi beckoned. He had waited. Harley blew out a sigh of relief and stumbled for the taxicab, her arms and legs weak with fear.

Yes, the man had scared her. But had she scared the man?

She seriously doubted it. She was one and they were dozens of insiders. Maybe even one hundred. She took her seat in the taxi and sat back, squinting against the harsh afternoon light until her eyes adjusted.

Then she could relax. She drew a deep breath as the driver pulled away. Beside her, Noel shivered.

"Shit," muttered Noel. "I was safer in Korea."

"You were," said Harley. "You were safer in Korea."

"Were you out of your mind? You're going to free his brother from Q? What's he in there for?"

"I have no idea."

"You're going to tell your lieutenant all that happened here?"

Harley turned and faced Noel. "I don't know yet. Do I have to tell him?"

"I didn't see or hear anything. I waited in the taxicab."

"You are a good man, Noel."

"I'm just glad I waited in the taxicab. I would've been scared shitless by those people in there."

"I was."

"I'm sure you were. What about your daughter, Wendy is it?"

"Yes."

"What's her story?"

"No story. She went missing months ago."

"How old is she?"

"Fifteen."

"Shit. You know, then."

"Know?"

"She's someone's old lady by now. She's probably hooked on heroin, too. They'll have her peddling her ass on Sunset. You were a Vice hooker."

"I was. I know all those things. But I cannot afford to let myself think them. I've decided she's been put away someplace safe until I can find her. It's easier than listening to rumors and Ordañez' words."

"Why do you think that?"

"Because I cannot stand to think anything else, Noel. It's just not possible to consider the alternatives. I would die by my own hand, and then where would she be?"

Noel turned and whistled softly. "Shit," he muttered at the window glass on his side. "For shit's sakes."

"That's right. Now I have to get that brother out of jail. Or trick Ordañez into coming to the US then arresting his ass. Or shooting him. Maybe shooting him is the best way."

"Look, Harley, I'm going to pretend you didn't say any of this stuff to me. You didn't say a word about shooting anyone. Now you need to button it."

"You're right. Thanks for that. I didn't say any of it, then."

"We had an uneventful trip down and back. That's all I know."

"I forgot what I was saying just now. I'm sorry, but I don't recall."

22

Upon landing at LAX, Harley and Noel and Marcia piled into Noel's unmarked and drove back to Hollywood Division. Without checking in at the Station, Harley went straight to her bank on Wilcox.

"How much in my account?" she asked the first teller, a young woman popping gum behind her Plexiglas.

"Let's see—um, that would be...$265.45."

"Thank you."

She walked across the lobby and took a seat in the waiting area. She was going to need much more than that to pull it off. There would have to be a trip to San Quentin on her own dime—on a personal leave day, too. San Quentin was eight hours by car, maybe more. Much longer by bus. And that was one way. But did she really need to visit Matin Ordañez? How much good would it do, really, except to show Reuben good faith? She decided against a visit and went home for the night.

The next day was Saturday. She got up early and dragged the city's known drug areas on her own time. There was always the chance she'd get a glimpse of Wendy. But she did not.

Early Monday morning, back at the Station, she checked out the Matin Ordañez file. *State of California v. Matin Ordañez*. Six convictions for possession of narcotics with intent to distribute. Great, not just one conviction or two—*six* convictions. Probably all good busts, too. She read further. Undercover narcotics officer named Halstead Miner made six purchases from Ordañez. He was in the case posing as a street vendor of the heroin he was purchasing from Ordañez. All sales were recorded in the same motel room and there was even film footage. Interesting side note: Matin's brother, Reuben Ordañez was Matin's supplier. This was according to Matin on the video. The case against Matin looked impossibly tight, perfectly tied up with a giant bow on top. Getting Matin Ordañez sprung from Q was looking bleaker and bleaker. The reality came crashing down on her: Wendy's continued existence depended on Harley pulling off the impossible and getting this guy out of prison. Or did it? Again, what about getting Reuben Ignacio Ordañez to come to the United States and arresting him? Or killing him? No—too much security, too many unknowns. So, that left bringing Ordañez into the country somehow and arresting. Some hook, some reason he would find irresistible to come here.

She read through the rest of the file and returned it to the clerk.

She poured herself a cup of coffee and returned to her desk. As Harley returned to her desk, Marcia looked up. Cops read their partners better than they read their spouses. Her frown said she knew something was up with Harley.

"Need to talk?"

Harley shrugged. "Not good, Marce."

"Let's go for coffee."

They checked out and headed for the Tiki Coffee Shop, a ten-minute drive west on Hollywood Boulevard.

"You wouldn't talk on the plane. What happened in Juarez?" Marcia asked after they were seated, and their coffee orders taken down.

"We were blown going in. At first, he pretended my cover was working. Then he cut the crap and nailed me. He knew my real name and my real job. He also knew about Wendy. He's going to kill her if I don't get his brother released from San Quentin in two months. I'm scared, Marcia, really scared."

"Can he do it? Can he find Wendy, I mean?"

"He says he already knows where she is. I can't chance that he's lying."

"No, you can't. What's his brother in Q for?"

"Narcotics beef. Six sales. Recorded. Airtight. He belongs there."

"Any thoughts on stopping Ordañez?"

"Short of killing him? None."

"What about killing the brother in prison. I mean, it's been known to happen. That removes the catalyst."

"Then I'm looking at Murder One."

"Well, there is that," Marcia said, attempting a small smile in the hope her partner would relax a click. But she did not.

"Sorry, I'm not doing so hot today."

"Hey," Marcia said, animated, "what if we found Wendy and moved her far, far away? Just took her out of the picture? Then he's got no one to kill?"

"He said he'd go after my in-laws and my own mom and dad."

"Your folks? I hope not."

"All I know is what he said if I didn't spring his brother. He said it was LAPD's fault that his brother was locked up. Probably there was some police entrapment going on, getting the guy to agree to sell and all. But that's legal, unfortunately for Ordañez."

"What about the *Sorrells* case? The majority opinion located the key to entrapment in the defendant's predisposition to commit the crime. Was entrapment even raised at trial in the Ordañez case?"

"God, Marce, I'm sure it was. Probably a high-priced lawyer from one of the best firms had the case, knowing Juarez and the bucks they have to burn."

"We need to find out."

"How? Call the defense lawyer?"

"I wouldn't do that," Marcia said. "Word would get out we're looking. How about we read the defense cross-examination of the arresting officer and the narc who made the buy. We can tell from the cross-examination whether they were going for entrapment. Plus, there's the jury instructions."

"Listen to my lawyer partner."

"Right. Only four more years of night school."

"Better than not. Okay, so where do we get the witness examinations? Court reporter?"

"You know what? If the case is up on appeal, and I'm sure it is, there's a whole record on appeal with it. That means all the testimony, motions, jury instructions—it's all right there in the court of appeals waiting for me to dig right in."

"God, that could be huge if they didn't try to use entrapment in the defense."

"It could be grounds for a new trial. That would buy you more time."

Harley scowled as she poured another cup out of the carafe. "But you know what? Here I am, a detective, trying to help a goddam convict get a new trial. How sick is that?"

"Put that aside. This is your kid we're talking about. None of the rest of that matters."

"That's more about me than about Wendy."

"Let's do this. You drop me at the court of appeals. Let me spend the day there, reading. You scurry back to the office and cover us. Tell Chall I'm following up with a witness or something. By the way, have you reported in to him since Friday?"

"No. I've got to get in there as soon as I get back. He'll be wondering what the hell happened."

"Then let's go."

AFTER DROPPING Marcia at the court of appeals, Second Appellate, Harley returned to her office and walked down the hall to Lieutenant Chall's office, where she stuck her head inside the open door.

"Been wondering where you went, Ellis," he growled from inside.

"Come on in and bring me up to speed. I take it you met with Ordañez?"

She took a seat and shook her head. "I saw him, but the undercover bit was a farce, LT. We've got a snitch in here."

"He knew you were LAPD?"

"He played along at first, then he sprung it on me. He knew everything. That I have a daughter who's on the street, he knew about my in-laws, my mom and dad, and he threatened to kill them all."

"Kill them all? Because you tried to run a play on him?"

"Yes. He's in a rage about his brother. Evidently we put him in Q."

"Who did?"

"LAPD. Drug bust, maybe an entrapment, maybe not. Anyway, Ordañez's brother is in San Quentin on six consecutive drug buys. He'll be in his eighties before he's eligible for parole. Ordañez wants him released."

"Or he'll kill Wendy. And your family. That was the risk, Harley. You chose to ignore it."

"I chose to try to find Spielman's killer, you mean." Harley felt her face go hot. She didn't appreciate how he'd said she chose to ignore the danger. "I was doing my job."

"Harley, your job was already done. Danny Sullivan already had an arrest on the case, remember? You thought it was a bad arrest and you wanted to go after Ordañez instead. Let's keep our facts straight, Sergeant."

She sighed. He was right. She had wanted to make an alternative arrest. Or at least investigate the possibility.

"So where are we with Mickey Loden in the Valley? Are you still thinking he nailed Spielman?"

"Yes, even though Reuben Ordañez made it clear that he killed Ira J. Spielman. Ordañez is lying about killing Spielman. Bastard."

"What about kidnapping of his daughter. Ordañez again?"

"Sure. All the way. The kidnapping case begins and ends with Ordañez. The murder case? I don't believe a thing Ordañez told me. I'm honestly thinking Loden did it as payback for Spielman getting Ordañez to kidnap Loden's daughter."

"God, I'd love to bust his nut. How do we get him to come into the US, Harley?"

"That is the sixty-four-thousand-dollar question, LT. But I'm working on it."

His eyes narrowed. "What about the brother at Q? You're not thinking about springing him, are you?"

Harley's face burned. It was a physical response that was involuntary, one that always happened when someone saw what was really going on with her. "No, I'm not thinking of springing him. Although I did wonder about entrapment on his case." There, she'd said it. No reason to keep it a secret at this point because she'd already told her lieutenant way more than she had ever intended, going in. He knew the whole deal now.

"Let me save you some time. Entrapment won't win you a new case in the Second Appellate, Harley. Appeals hates entrapment cases. They never have overturned an LAPD conviction for that alone. Never. So, if you're thinking of going with it as a way of getting this scumbag a new trial, my advice is that you forget it. That's also my order. So why don't you go on down to the court of appeals and bring Marcia back to the office? Yes, I know that's very likely where she is right this minute. Tell her I, for one, will be very happy when she gets her law degree and can practice legally, but now to get back to work and solve one of my unsolved cases. That is, let's remember, your bottom line. We're finished here, Harley."

"LT, what about my daughter? He's threatened her life. And the rest of my family."

"There's nothing I can do about that, Harley, since I don't know where she is, and you don't either. We can't save someone we can't find."

"Copy that, sir."

"Now go retrieve your partner and hit the streets. We have a thousand unsolveds waiting."

"LT, can I ask you something?"

"Sure. What?"

She cleared her throat and squared her shoulders. She'd been totally honest so far. Once more couldn't hurt. "Can you give me a few days out of the office to try to run her down?"

"Come again?"

"Wendy. My daughter. LT, she's all I have left. Her dad was—was—killed." Tears pricked her eyes. She rubbed her sleeve jacket across her face. She swallowed hard. "Now the bad part. She's also a person of interest in the Spielman case."

"Not possible. What the hell are you trying to say?"

"Long story short, Wendy tried out for a part in a Spielman movie. She was on the Capitol Films lot the day he was murdered. Her scarf was found in his office. Sullivan had tagged her in the murder book. I've got the case now and she needs to be interviewed."

"Conflict of interest?"

"You bet. But I can set it aside and do my job."

He sat back and rubbed his eyes. "Tell you what. You've got thirty days to find your kid. Take Marcia with you. Put out an APB again, whatever you need through Traffic. Same with Detectives. Now go find your kid. Don't come back in here and tell me you didn't. Understand me?"

"Yes, sir." Harley's heart was pounding. Now if she could only catch a break.

"And if you don't find her and get that interview, I'm taking the case away and putting someone else on it. They might not be as kind, if you read me."

"Yes, sir." He meant there was a possibility any other team would take precautions against Wendy as a threat to their safety. Who knew what might happen if they approached her?

"And when you find her, Sullivan interviews her, not you, not Marcia. Understood?"

"Understood. That sounds right."

"Good. I'm bending the rules for you. Do not let me down, Ellis."

"Nossir."

"Good. Go, then. Get out."

"Yessir."

"Thirty days or your kid belongs to me."

"Yessir."

23

Harley went to Angelina Sosa's apartment on Hollywood Boulevard. It was a Tuesday and rain made the streets glow a purple oil sheen under Harley's headlights as she pulled up in front of the girl's building.

She went upstairs and knocked. Harley was wearing Levi's and a black T-shirt. A light jacket covered the shirt—and her gun in its shoulder holster. The door opened and there stood Angelina, looking puzzled and frightened. "Did you catch him? Do I have to come look at him and say he's the one?"

"No," said Harley, "I don't need you to come look at him. And yes, we found him. I wonder if I can talk with you a little bit?"

"Am I in trouble cause I called the police that night?"

"No, no, no, nothing like that. I'd just like to get to know you better. That's all."

"Oh, so should I invite you inside or what? Gerri and her boyfriend are in her room and they're noisy, that's the only thing."

"Have you had supper?"

"Yes, I just boiled two eggs and ate them with salt and butter."

"What about coffee? Do you drink coffee?"

"I do."

"What do you say we go to The Family Beef a couple blocks up. You like that place?"

"They got great hamburgers. Some of us run there for lunch and bring everyone burgers. Not bad."

"I've got my car. Let's drive over there and have some coffee and let me pick your brain, okay?"

"Sure. Right now?"

"Sure, come on."

"Let me get my keys."

She reappeared after two minutes and they went downstairs and climbed into Harley's Ford.

"Is this your police car?"

"It is. I'm a detective so it's plain black."

"Has it got lights and a siren?"

"I can't show you, but yes, I've got lights and a siren. Sit back and let's slide into traffic—there we go, and up two blocks."

They parked at The Family Beef and Harley discovered it was a drive-in, so they pulled up for service by one of the waitresses on roller-skates. One came by, ducked her head down and took two coffee orders. She returned in minutes with two mugs of steaming coffee, sugar and cream. She placed it on Harley's tray and skated off.

Harley wasted no time.

"So, we found the boy who had sex with you. His name is Guernica Aguilar and he's seventeen. He's also the altar boy you saw at church. I asked him what happened, and he told me you had sex with him voluntarily."

"No way! He's lying!"

"Listen, Angelina, I've worked with a lot of young people. In fact, believe it or not, it wasn't so long ago I was your age. One thing I found out is sometimes people get scared and say things that are only partly true. Like maybe they're scared of being pregnant and so they say someone assaulted them and got them pregnant. I've seen that happen lots of times. And you know what? I don't hate the girl and I don't take her to jail. You know what it is? I feel sorry for her. I know how scary it must be to be young and pregnant and not be married. It must be horrible. And I'm wondering if that sounds like anything you might know about? Is there any chance that's what happened with the altar boy?"

"I didn't say he raped me. I said he forced his penis in my mouth."

"I know that, but I'm wondering if maybe you forgot the part about having sex the other way. I'm wondering if it's even a little bit possible he had sex with you and that you might have wanted him to. Has there been someone else before whose baby you might be carrying now?"

"That wasn't what happened. He forced me to—okay, we talked first. Okay, he came over to listen to records. Okay? So, I made up the part about him climbing in the window. He was there and I was there, and we started kissing. Then he pulled out his thing and made me—made me—he, I let him put it in me. Okay, so I'm going to hell for lying. Is that it? Do you take me to jail now?"

"Nobody's going to jail. Nobody's mad at you. Nobody's saying you're in trouble. At least I'm not. You know what I think? I think you need a friend. I think you need someone who can help you through a hard time. Like maybe help you make some decisions about being pregnant. How close am I?"

"I missed my period for three months. That's why I invited him over. I was going to say he raped me but he's too young to rape someone. So, I said he forced his penis in my mouth because I was going to tell my parents he's the same one who got me pregnant. They can't ever know I did something this bad. They'll disown me."

"I'll tell you what...why don't you let me talk to them?"

"You? Talk to my parents?" Her voice was incredulous. She seemed certain she was hearing things.

"Yes, I'd like to talk to your parents. I want to tell them what a great daughter you are and how you made a mistake and you're afraid of them. They need to hear it from your police detective."

"You'd do that for me?"

"I would."

"So, what's the catch?"

"No catch. You need help, I'm here to help."

"When would this happen?"

"If you give me their number, I'll call them tonight and make an appointment for tomorrow after work. Or as soon as they can meet."

"What if they say no?"

"Then we'll know that's one avenue that's not going to help you for right now. We'll do something else."

"Like what else?"

"Like get some money together for hospital and doctor expenses. Get some money together for formula, a diaper pail, diapers, all the stuff you're going to need."

"Why don't I just get an abortion? Because my church hates that?"

"I think you can think about that. But for the right now, this week or month, you need to work and save money. How much rent do you pay here?"

"Fifty a month."

"How much for food?"

"Seventy a month?"

"So, you need one-twenty to live on?"

"Yes."

"And how much do you earn?'

"Two-hundred a month."

"As a car wash cashier."

"That's right."

"How much does the doctor cost?"

"One-hundred."

"And the hospital?"

"Two hundred."

"See, that's three-hundred and I think you can save it up."

"How can I do that?"

"I've got an extra room at my house I'm going to rent you. Cheap. In fact, the room will be free. And you'll eat what I eat, so food won't cost. You'll keep working and save every penny. You'll find a job closer to my place in Long Beach. Somewhere that you can ride the bus there and back. Then we can start putting some things together for the baby. I'm thinking at first it can live with you in your room. Then we'll go from there."

"Wait, wait, wait. Why you do this for me?"

"Because sometimes we've got to reach out and give someone a hand. It never hurts to help someone who's having a hard time. There's only one catch to it. You've got to do something like it for another person before you die. It's not hard, and you will get that chance."

"I can't believe this."

"Believe it. Get your stuff packed up tomorrow. I'll swing by after work and pick you up."

"Then what do I do about the altar boy?"

"Nothing. We'll just do nothing for a while. You don't say any more about it and I won't say any more about it. Deal?"

"Deal. Can I bring Mira, my cat?"

"I'm allergic to cats," Harley said.

The girl's face fell. "Okay. I'll leave her."

"No, bring her. I've got a small patio and she can spend some of her day out there. Plus, I can get medicine for allergies. Please bring Mira."

"Okay, I'll bring her bowl and her box."

"Okay, then. Welcome aboard."

"I can't believe this."

"Mi casa es su casa."

"Gracias."

"Si."

24

Danny Sullivan arrived at five a.m. at Hollywood Station and went straight inside to his desk. He reached over to Harley's desk and began thumbing through the murder book. He was like a dog after a bone. It was obvious she was soon talking to Mickey Loden. Sullivan scoffed; Loden was way too heavy a character for Harley and Marcia. Sullivan determined that he and Black would hit up Loden first. Take his statement and rule him out.

He went for a cup of coffee, thinking. Another possibility to rule out, in order to protect his arrest, was Wendy Ellis, Detective Harley Ellis' pregnant daughter, who was trying to extort abortion money from the victim. Had Harley really taken a good look at her own kid? That was the problem when family was involved. Once the kid's letter had been found, Lieutenant Chall should've immediately kicked the case back to Sullivan and Black. No questions asked. So, Sullivan decided he was going to clear Loden then rule out Wendy Ellis. The mother wouldn't fight her on that. Then Annalee gets convicted without a hitch. It was important that he do these things so the defense lawyers for Annalee, at trial, couldn't claim the detectives had arrested the wrong person by not going after Loden and Ellis. He needed to plug those holes to protect his arrest. Not even the lieutenant would argue with his plan.

He grabbed Black as soon as he arrived at seven and they headed to the Valley and Loden's. They had no idea where they might find him on any given day, but stopping and asking around at a few development subdivisions should lead them right to the guy. He explained his thinking to Black. It's crazy, he said, but we're talking to Loden in order to clear Loden. We're looking for a reason he didn't kill Spielman so Annalee's lawyers couldn't use him at trial as another possible killer. Black understood; it wasn't his first dance, either.

It was a clear day, the sun was beating down, and the traffic was remarkably light outbound from the city. Sullivan was in a good mood and yet felt just a little over the line because here he was again, undermining Harley on her case.

"We're just gonna brace the guy and leave, right, Sully?" asked Black.

"Right. Just stand him up, ask a few questions about Spielman, and see what he has for us. Let me do the talking, here."

"No sweat," Black said. "I've got your back. What do we know about the guy's associates?"

"We know he was connected in New York. Which gives us every reason to think he's connected out here. We want to catch him at his subdivision office where other people are around. But you keep your eyes open. Get rid of any interference while I make my play."

"Roger that," said Black.

An hour later, they pulled into Merryland Subdivision outside Calabasas after stopping and asking directions and questions about Loden a half dozen times. Everyone agreed that Merryland was his baby.

They straightened their ties and went inside. The office was actually a model home located at the entrance to the subdivision. Inside, they found a makeshift telephone/coffee/conversation area around a table with kitchen chairs scattered around it. One of the salespeople said she thought Mr. Loden was in a back room on a call. She said she'd tell him they were there. And who were they? she wanted to know. They badged her and her face fell. "I'll make sure he knows you're waiting. Please sit down at the table and help yourselves to coffee and danish. It's all fresh."

Black helped himself to a cheese Danish while Sullivan lit a cigarette. Five minutes passed. The young woman returned but then left through the front entrance. Five minutes later, another man arrived, wearing a raincoat on a sunny day, which caused Sullivan to raise an eyebrow. He turned to see whether his partner had noticed, but Blackie was licking his fingers and looking for a napkin just then.

Raincoat Man stopped at their table. He was dark, early thirties, in need of a shave, and looked every bit the dullard, thought Sullivan when he looked up.

"Gentlemen," said Raincoat, "Mr. Loden is inspecting a new build. Why don't youse follow me in your car and I'll take youse to him."

Sullivan's face flushed. "The girl said he was in a back office. We'll wait here."

"He ain't here. She came to get me, and I came to get you. If youse don't want to talk with him, fine. I'll go tell him something came up."

"No, wait," Sullivan said with a glance at Black, who shrugged and looked like he was in complete control. "We'll follow you. All we need is five minutes of his time."

Raincoat Man climbed into a pickup truck and the detectives followed behind in their Ford. They drove to the end of the block, then right, then turned left on Taurus Lane. They followed him to the end, stopping at the last house on the right. Its roof was wood and was being shingled that morning. The day was still warm, and the birds were out—the detectives found themselves feeling like what they were doing was safe and open to public view.

Inside the door-less home they followed Raincoat. It took several seconds for their eyes to adjust from the bright sunshine to the dim, unlit interior. During these few moments, they felt two men move in behind him and place guns at their backs. Hammers were cocked. The detectives froze.

"Youse guys shouldn't-a come here without calling," said Raincoat. "Now we'll talk to Mr. Pultec and see how he wants to handle this."

A fourth man, wearing denim coveralls in brown with a brown utility shirt emerged from the dark. He was holding a .45 semi-automatic Colt and waved it back and forth between the detectives. Sullivan thought he looked comfortable enough with the firearm. He kept his arms raised and didn't resist when Raincoat reached inside his sport coat and disarmed him then turned to Blackie and did the same. Neither detective offered any resistance.

"What did you gentlemen want to see Mr. Loden about?" asked Denim Man.

"His daughter was kidnapped. We're trying to help solve that."

"Naw, you ain't," said Denim. "The FBI's got that case. Suppose you level and tell me why you're really here."

"We need five minutes of Mr. Loden's time," Sullivan said, much less confident now. "It is about his daughter, I can guarantee."

"I don't take guarantees from cops. Mr. Barkley," Denim said to the man wearing the raincoat, "I want you to take these men to Mr. Loden. Put them inside your truck and drive them there."

"Inside or in the bed?"

"In the bed. We'll have Gemmi and Jose ride with them."

The detectives were ushered back out into the sunshine. Every time they faltered, a gun muzzle pressed up against their backs, forcing them to move along.

Then they were forced to climb into Barkley's pickup, and shoved down with their backs against the sides. The two thugs kept guns trained on the detectives, and everyone lurched as they pulled away from the curb and went toward the cornfield that would fall next to the bulldozers as the subdivision spread like a disease upon the farmland.

Noontime in Hollywood Station reflected an undercurrent of worry. Danny Sullivan and Lionel Black hadn't called in since heading out to the Valley. Radio calls weren't answered, and deputies dispatched to the area had reported no visuals. By two p.m. the search party had been doubled. By four p.m. it had been doubled again and a full-scale Valley-wide search was underway. All leads were being followed. Families were questioned for any peculiarities, and, finding none, the canvass then turned to the partners' caseload, starting with any hardened perps roaming free. Not much could be done down that road, however, as no one was talking. Snitches were rolled out and they were cajoled and threatened by the LAPD en masse and still no actionable intelligence developed. No leads, no call-outs, absolutely nothing moving.

Harley and Marcia approached Lieutenant Chall with a question. It was known the missing detectives were headed to the Valley "to follow up a lead." But what if that lead was really Mickey Loden on the Spielman case? In other words, what if Sullivan and Black had been crossing the line and gone to Loden to shake him down?

"How would we know?" Chall asked the two detectives. "Loden isn't someone we can phone up and say "Hey, have you seen our two missing detectives?" It doesn't quite work like that.

"He's next on our list of interviews on the Spielman case," Harley said. "All I'm asking is that you let us make any approach on him so we're doing it and not some team unfamiliar with our case."

"Sounds fair to me," said Lieutenant Chall. "It's your baby. But let's not delay. Get on him like white on rice now."

The detectives said they would do that very thing.

25

Harley found Mickey Loden's number in the *Yellow Pages* and called for an appointment. His secretary said he wanted to know what the police wanted with him. Harley said to tell him it was in regard to his daughter's kidnapping, that she might have news. Grudgingly—it seemed—he finally agreed, though he specified he would have his lawyer present. A meeting was set for the next morning at a model home in the Valley. Harley had tried to force a meeting the same day Sullivan disappeared, but Loden refused. It was the next morning or nothing.

The search for Sullivan and Black continued overnight. There were no leads, no sightings, not even any false leads. The detective duo had simply vanished.

Harley and Marcia arrived at Loden's the next morning at nine sharp. It was agreed Harley would do the talking.

There was an office inside the model home, with a wall-plat for the subdivision underway. There were wide, curving streets and areas designated as "green areas." There was also ground allocated for a fire department and a police substation. Nice, she thought. Maybe at some point she'd look out here herself.

Mickey Loden was waiting with two other gentlemen. Hands were shaken all around as introductions were made. Then the detectives were asked to sit down.

Harley sized him up. Loden was probably in his middle forties, hair graying at the temples and combed back on the sides. A widow's peak created a sharp V on his low forehead, and his eyes were icy blue. At the moment, those peepers danced with what appeared to be alarm that the police were there to see him. He and the two others were on one side of a makeshift desk, which was actually a round kitchen table, obviously used for staging in the dining room but commandeered for the office. The man on his right spoke first. "I'm Racine Steerman, Mr. Loden's business lawyer. On my far left is Westervelt West, who you may have heard of from downtown?"

"I've heard of WW," said Harley of the famous criminal lawyer. "I know his work. My pleasure, gentlemen. There's no need for lawyers, however, we're just here to follow up on Dinah's kidnapping."

"How can we help with that?" Steerman asked.

"We're looking into the why of the kidnapping. We understand there was a sizable ransom paid, but any insights into why Mr. Loden was targeted would be helpful. Oftentimes there's a much larger criminal plot behind what we might consider an isolated event and that's what we're trying to track down."

Loden set down his lime green coffee cup that said "Merryland" on the side in curlicue lettering. "Plot? I don't know how there could be a plot. They wanted money, I paid up and—"

"Mr. Loden," WW broke in, "Why don't you let your attorneys answer these questions. With your approval, of course. Detective, what Mr. Loden is trying to say is that he has no knowledge of any plots. Will there be anything else? It seems a shame you drove all the way out here for one question."

"Yes, in fact, there is," Harley said. She drew a deep breath and continued. "I'd like to ask Mr. Loden about his relationship with Ira J. Spielman."

"There is—was—no relationship," the criminal lawyer quickly replied. "Mr. Loden never met Mr. Spielman."

"Is that right, Mr. Loden?" Harley said to the developer. "You never met him, not even when your daughter screen tested with him?"

Loden quickly shot back, "I don't see what the hell difference it matters if I knew him or not. Spielman didn't grab Dinah."

"Who did grab Dinah?"

"Bunch of tacos from TJ," the developer answered, again beating his lawyers to the gun. He was going to be quite a handful to control, Harley noted. Meanwhile the lawyers were all but apoplectic their client was refusing to shut the hell up. Eye rolls and long, impatient sighs were their contribution.

"You're telling me it was Mexicans? How do you know that?"

"Because I personally handed over a Samsonite suitcase containing two million in cash. I got a good look at the guy's face."

"How did it happen?"

"We met not a mile from here. His car was pointed west on Harmony Lane, my car was pointed east. He reached his hand out the window and I slid the suitcase through my window. At that moment, he said, *'Gracias Señor, tu hija estará aquí pronto.'* He was saying Dinah would be home soon. Then he drove west, and I went up about a mile to where I could turn around and I came back here, to my office. It took all of twenty minutes, including the roundtrip."

"Would you recognize the man if you saw him again?"

WW jumped in. "He wouldn't recognize him, Detective. No need to take him in for a lineup. Or a photograph spread. Anything else?"

"Yes, I'd like to ask just that, if Mr. Loden would come down for a lineup when I've rounded up some people who might be of interest. His help might very well take a very dangerous man off the street."

Steerman spoke up, sounding to Harley exactly like a good business lawyer should. "Mr. Loden realizes that there might very well be a conspiracy behind Dinah's disappearance. Knowing this, he doesn't want to anger these same people and see the same or worse thing happen again. It's very obvious that the LAPD and the FBI cannot protect his family, so he declines being involved further. Is that all now?"

"I'd like to interview Dinah. Then that will be all. She can come in voluntarily or I'll issue a subpoena."

"What kind of subpoena?" asked WW, suspicious and scowling.

"A grand jury subpoena," Harley lied. There was no grand jury meeting on the case because there was no state-level kidnapping case. But she used the GJ ruse nonetheless, having worked magic with it before.

"It could be arranged, Detective," WW said. "I'd much prefer an informal interview than testimony given. She's been through enough already. With a couple of stipulations. First, it would have to take place at Mr. Loden's home, where Dinah still resides."

"Done."

"Second, we would want a court reporter present in order to take down facial expressions, body language, all those things that get missed on a simple tape recording. Agreed?"

"Agreed. I just need about a fifteen-minute statement from her and I'll be on my way."

"The third thing—yes, I just thought of a third. Why is the LAPD involved in a kidnapping? The FBI is already working the case and has already taken her statement the day after she was returned to her family."

Harley was caught flat-footed on that one. Time for a quick two-step and a feint to the side. "Because the LAPD is running a parallel investigation. We believe state crimes were violated. We have every right."

"Of course, you do," WW had to agree. "It's just odd, that's all."

"Dinah's been through a lot," Loden said with an angry, glaring look. "I expect you to be very gentle with her."

"Very, I promise."

"And limit your questioning to the kidnapping," said Steerman. "Don't try to use this opportunity to collect her statement to discover more facts about her father. Of course, you'd never do something like that, would you, Detective?"

Busted. But side-stepping, again. "No need to do that. I'm sure Mr. Loden will be willing to answer any other questions I might have about that on down the road. Am I right?"

"Yes," Loden said. "I have nothing to hide."

Right you don't, thought Harley. *Until I hold your feet to the fire about who killed Spielman. Then we'll see.*

"You know, since you have nothing to hide, I wonder if you're ready now to answer my earlier question. Did you personally know Ira J. Spielman?"

"No, we'd never met."

"You know nothing about the Screen Actors Guild, either?"

"Hardly even know what that is. Never dealt with any such."

She knew she was pushing the issue and now wasn't time for that yet. Time to leave on friendly terms so the meeting could be resumed on down the road. Maybe she'd even catch him without his two legal goons next time.

"One more thing. Two detectives left LA yesterday to visit with you. Names of Sullivan and Black. Did you meet with any LAPD personnel yesterday or overnight?"

"No."

"Did they call you to try to meet with you?"

Loden shook his head violently. "Nope."

"Would you ask your workers if they saw our officers?"

"I'll ask. Leave your card in case I need to call."

Harley two-fingered a card across the table.

"That's all I have. For now. I trust we can do this again if I need?" She directed this specifically to Loden.

"I'm game," Loden spoke right up. "Nothing to hide whatsoever. Just call."

She stood and closed her file. "Thank you. I will do that. Gentlemen, good day."

With that, she turned on her heel and left.

Outside in her unmarked, Harley was cursing the two lawyers under her breath. It was going to take time, a little cunning and a lot of artifice to do an end run around those two. But she'd do it, come what may. She was sure she'd do it.

She backed out of the gravel lot and headed back the way she'd come.

"Lawyers!" she spat when she was down the road. "Lawyers!"

Marcia said, "What about Sullivan and Blackie? Loden seemed pretty firm about that."

"I know. I had the feeling he was telling the truth. I don't believe he's seen them."

"Same here. Damn them anyway."

"Call it in. Advise no actionable information."

"Roger that."

Marcia called Dispatch.

26

The next day, Marcia took the train north to San Francisco. Her plan was to hit San Quentin and meet with Matin Ordañez, Reuben's brother, and see what he knew about his brother's involvement with Spielman. After all, much to the detectives' surprise, Matin had been out on bail during the time Spielman died months before. It was time to pin him down. She also planned to discuss his case, as Harley had told Reuben would be done.

The train headed north, a full day's trip. She spent that night in the Mark Hopkins Hotel—her per diem paid for this, adding another hundred bucks of her own, and she ate lobster at Fisherman's Wharf that night. It had been her intention to make a mini-vacation out of the trip, which she did.

The next morning, bright and early, she passed through prison security and down to a police interview room. The deeper into the heart of the prison she was led, the more Marcia felt the walls closing in. She hated jails; prisons, she'd found, were a hundred times worse. Many inmates left there by way of hearse, inside caskets. That's how unforgiving a penitentiary could be.

The room she found herself inside was state-facility-green with painted pipes and a single overhead lightbulb inside a steel welded-wire basket. The table was steel, and the chairs were steel. Everything was bolted to the floor. There was a thick door on the room with a large double-plated window through which the interview would be closely monitored for the officer's safety. Marcia sat down and crossed her legs. Then she uncrossed and sat ramrod straight, her hands folded on the table, all business.

They brought Matin Ordañez in and he frowned at her. "You're my new public defender?" he asked. His ankles were hobbled, and he was waist-chained. His cuffed hands were attached to the waist chain. The guards locked his chained feet to two loops extending up from the floor for that purpose.

She produced her shield and ID, laying them flat on the table between them. "I'm a police officer."

"Guard! Guard! I dint agree to meet no fucking cop! Guard!"

"Wait! Listen to what I have to say. We met with Reuben last week."

"Reuben? My brother, Reuben?"

"Yes, and he wants you out of here. He made us a deal."

"Why Reuben make you a deal? He doan owe you nothin'."

"Because, we need information and he wants you free. It's a good deal for both sides."

"Bullshit."

"No, for real."

Matin scowled and chewed his cheek. Then he spoke.

"Tell me what I gotta do."

"Simple. Tell me who killed Ira J. Spielman."

"I doan know no piece of chit Spielman. Do I get out now or fuck you?"

"You don't get out yet. Not unless you help me. I'm here to ask for help off the record. Nothing you tell me will be used against your brother. Even if you tell me Reuben killed Spielman I won't use it against him. Let me ask again, who killed Spielman?"

"I choot that piece of chit. How's that?"

"That's good except he wasn't shot. Are you going to waste my time, Matin, or are you going to tell me something that gets you out of here?"

"Hey, man, I doan know nothin. How many times I gotta say it? Besides, I ain't no snitch."

"Who kidnapped Dinah Loden?"

"Lady, you talkin outta your ass now. I doan know no Diana."

"Dinah, Dinah. Do you know her name? Loden?"

"I doan know nothin about no Dinah. Ax me somethin gets me out, why doan you?"

"That's a great idea. I would like to set you free out of here. You were found guilty of selling narcotics to an undercover officer. Six different times. Were you a dope dealer at that time?"

"No, I was a mule."

"You were a smuggler."

"I was a mule."

"Right. But were you also selling narcotics?"

"Hell no, they put you in prison for selling. Mules get probation. I was jus a mule, but look at me."

"Had you ever sold narcotics to anyone?"

"Only in Mexico. Never United States. Too fucked up."

"How did it happen you sold narcotics to a narc?"

"He tole my brother was his friend. He tole me he just talked to Reuben and Reuben said to drop the brown dope with him and take his money. I thought okay."

"Yes, but you did it six times. How could you possibly think six times was okay?"

"It was six kilos. They got me for each kilo I gave him. All at one time."

"It wasn't on different days?"

"Fuck no. It was all right then. One load, all to Bill Withers. Not his real name. He narc'd me out. I'm goan kill that motherfu—"

"Right, don't tell me you're going to kill someone, please. That ruins what I'm trying to do for you, Matin. Nothing about killing, okay?"

"Okay. You got cigarettes?"

"I have Salem's. You want a Salem."

"I do."

She lit a cigarette and passed it to his lips. He took a drag then moved his head back. They repeated this several times before she ground it out on the floor.

"Okay, then," he said, obviously grateful. She then took the pack and slipped it down inside the breast pocket of his striped shirt. He seemed not to notice but she knew it went a long way in there to have cigarettes, even half a pack. A pack only cost twenty-three cents, so it was a wise investment on Marcia's part.

"Now," she continued, "you had a jury trial, right?"

"Yes."

"Do you know, did your lawyer ever talk to you about entrapment?"

"No traps. Except the narc was a trap maybe. He got me to sell."

"Did you want to sell to him?"

"No. I was too fuckin scared to sell to anyone."

"How did he get you to sell?"

"I told my lawyer these things. He told me he talked to Reuben and Reuben said I should sell."

"Did you call Reuben and ask him?"

"Yes."

"What did Reuben say?"

"Reuben said I should sell him."

"So, your own brother wanted you to sell?"

"Yes, he dint know about no narc. We kill that mother-f—"

"Never mind. Don't mention killing again or I have to go. Understand? Comprende?"

"I do understand. Reuben told me we delivered tons of stuff to guy before. He said it safe. So, I sold all six kilos. Fucking narc!"

"I know you're upset. I don't blame you. But was it really Reuben who instructed you to sell?"

"Yes."

"It wasn't the narc who got you to sell?"

"Hell, yes. It was all his idea. He asked me first."

"And at first you didn't want to sell?"

"Hell, no. I say to myself, stupid. What if he a narc? Stupid."

"Did he pressure you to sell?"

"He said he wouldn't need no more if I don't sell."

"Let me back up. You were just there to deliver the kilos? You weren't there to take money for them?"

"That's right. No sell. Just take to this warehouse and leave beneath tire rack. That's my yob. But this time, he come out and said, 'I give you money for those.' He said Reuben said it okay."

"Okay, I'm pretty clear on that. Well, I don't know how much good I can do you, but I can try."

"I just want out. They fucking with me in here."

"Who's fucking with you, Matin?"

"Everybody. Guards, gangs, brotherhoods. All of them."

"All right. I'm going to do whatever I can. But I need you to help me, too. Tell me who killed Spielman?"

He spread his hands in his lap. "I dunno. Not me."

"All right. You tell Reuben I was here, okay?"

"Sure. Fucking A."

"One more thing. Tell me about Reuben's family. He got kids?"

"Fuck you, now."

"You want out? Tell me about his family. Start with the youngest kid."

Matin then launched into what Harley could only later describe to Marcia as a complete family tree. Harley made notes. She learned Reuben's kids' names, where they lived, mother's names, where the mothers lived, schools, everything Matin knew. At the end, she knew she had enough. So she broke it off.

She smiled at Matin.

"We friends?"

"Sure. You get me out now, I do anything."

"I know, Matin. I know. Guard!"

The prisoner was removed, and Marcia packed up her accordion file and notepad. She wouldn't breathe freely until she was outside those high walls again.

It was stifling in there. She almost wanted to bolt and run.

But she walked. She forced herself to keep it to a walk.

27

She had just loaded the washing machine with whites when she heard her.

"Mom," said the voice in the family room, "help me, mom."

Harley stood up from the washer and listened. There it was again, "Help me, mom!"

She reached and pulled out the dial on the washing machine. It shut off; the roar of the water immediately stopped. She listened again. Nothing else was said. So, she pushed in the dial and the water began rushing into the machine again.

"Mom, help me, please."

Harley spun on her heel and ran to the family room. She looked at the fireplace, the glass door was shut. She examined the RCA TV. It was off and black. She went to her telephone on the coffee table. She lifted the receiver and listened. Again, nothing. Just for sure, she examined the amber ashtray on the coffee table. Which was when she saw. Wendy's face had returned to the amber glass. She looked frightened, her forehead creased and her eyes wide with fear. "What is it?" Harley shouted into the object.

Then she listened. She looked. Wendy's mouth appeared to move.

Harley set the ashtray down and picked up her pack of Camels. She shook one out and flipped open the Zippo that Robert had left behind when he shipped out. The smell of lighter fluid lingered over the table. She spun the wheel and it flamed up and she lit her cigarette. "Talk to me, Wendy," she pleaded. "Tell me where you are, honey."

She looked again into the ashtray. Nothing. Just dull, amber glass. There was no glow, no face.

With her cigarette sweeping the air in her right hand as she walked, Harley went into the kitchen and pulled a mug out of the cabinet. She poured coffee from the silver percolator and dosed it with canned milk. Then she returned to the family room.

Sitting on the couch, tipping a cigarette into the amber ashtray, sat Wendy.

Wendy. Transparent—the couch's floral pattern showing through. Harley blinked repeatedly and swiped a hand across her eyes.

"Hi, Mom. Got coffee?"

"I do," said Harley. "Would you like a cup?"

"No, thanks. I really can't stay long. I came by to ask a favor."

"Sure, honey. What's that?"

"Stop looking for me, Mom. I'm gone now and I'm happy where I am."

"Okay. I can stop looking. As long as I know you're all right."

"I didn't kill him, Mom. You know me better than that."

"How do I show the others you're innocent? I need proof."

"Take my statement. I'll give a statement. I know, I'll take a polygraph exam. Would that be okay, Mom?"

"That would be fine. Are you hungry, Wendy?"

"No, Mom. I never eat anymore."

"Pardon?"

"We don't eat here. No need for food."

"Can I have a hug, Wendy? It's been so long."

Wendy stood and held out her arms. Harley stepped to her and wrapped her arms around the—around the air. Nothing.

She staggered backward and plopped down onto the couch.

"Jesus," she said. "I need to see someone."

Tears formed in her eyes and she began crying. She picked up her coffee cup and took a long swallow. It was very hot—and very real as it burned her throat.

"Oh, my God," she exclaimed. "What is happening to me?"

The stresses of the past weeks settled upon her shoulders and squeezed all at once. The tears flowed and her shoulders shook while she cried. She knew better—she had known better when she came into the room, hadn't she? Hadn't she known it was an apparition? Then why had she played along?

She was alone and lonely. Harley had called Angelina's mother and explained about Angelina. Her mother and father were shocked but forgiving. They wanted to see her, and the girl was spending three days there. But, Angelina was living with her now. She was accustomed to hearing her Elvis Presley records coming through the walls but now there was nothing. Even Mira the cat was off on the visit. She pulled the phone across the table and called CV, her old partner at Hollywood Division. The last time they spoke he was living in his ex-wife's duplex in order to save money. He now had huge child support to pay, which gobbled up half of every paycheck. He answered on the first ring.

"CV, Harley. *Como esta?*"

"*Bien. Bien.* So good to hear your voice. We haven't talked since they divorced us."

"I know. I hated losing you as my partner. You're working with Mounce now"

"Yes, Jerry Mounce is a good guy. Hey, I guess you haven't heard anything new about Sullivan and Black?"

"Not a word."

"What about Wendy?"

"Not a word. LT wants me to find her without further delay. Turns out she was in Spielman's office the day he was killed."

Long silence. "What for?"

"Screen test, near as I can tell. I took her once, then she returned a second time on her own. Like always, she didn't discuss it with me, CV."

"What the hell. You deserve better, Harley."

"Don't we all? Anyway, I'm calling to see if you want to go out later. It's Saturday night and I'm lonely."

"Can't. I have the little ones tonight. Ellie Mae is out with her girl-friends. They have a new singles club for amateur chefs. She's studying French cuisine. Too fucking bad she didn't think of that when I was gobbling down TV dinners."

"You need to get out, CV. Let's see if we can't get you laid."

"I know, I know. Truth is, I don't have the money to even take a lady to dinner. I'm thinking of going over to the dark side."

"You? Never. You're a straight arrow and always will be."

"Yes, but I know some people."

"Don't we all? But cops like us are too dull to be on the take. We have very limited imaginations. Or don't," she added, remembering her hallucination of twenty minutes ago. It was working; talking to CV always calmed her down, grounded her. It was like a friendly voice on a very foggy sea on a very dark night. A voice in the wilderness.

"CV, I'm wondering something. Can I talk to you off the record?"

"Sure, Harls. What's up?"

"I saw Wendy tonight. Or thought I did."

"What, you were hallucinating?"

"It would be funny if it weren't true. I think I was hallucinating. Right here in my living room."

"You saw what you thought was your lost daughter?"

"I did. Then I cried when she evaporated."

"Harley, you need to see someone. You've had way too much stress. Listen to me. Losing Bobby, then Wendy. Anyone would understand. Plus, you're working ten- and twelve-hour days. Something had to give. I want you to call Devonna Stacey first thing Monday morning. You need to talk to Devonna."

He was referring to the LAPD psychiatrist.

"What happens? Does that go on my record or something?"

"No, it's totally voluntarily and totally confidential. No one even knows you were there except Devonna. And her files are doctor-patient protected. No one sees them ever. She's distinct from the LAPD. They can never touch her records. So, do it. That's an order, Harley."

"Yessir. I think I need to talk to someone. I'll do it."

"And let's get lunch Monday. We can talk about how it went."

"I don't know if I can do Monday. Marcia and I—"

"Monday. Noon. You and me. Lunch."

"Yessir."

They disconnected. Harley timorously leaned forward and peered into the ashtray.

Nothing there.

Good. She'd call Devonna Stacey Monday. First order of business. She removed her shoes and put her feet on the coffee table. She closed her eyes.

Then she cried.

28

D evonna Stacey's office was located in a small building five-
blocks from the Police Administration Building. Her office
was unlisted on the building register. Other tenants in the small
building included lawyers, several dentists, architects and a smat-
tering of doctors. Harley walked into the lobby, made her way
around a water feature and pool of water plants, back to the eleva-
tors. She pressed the *up* arrow. Nervously, she looked several times
to her right and left, hoping against hope that she would be traveling upstairs alone in the car. Her luck held as the elevator settled
on Lobby and she hurried inside and immediately pressed the
close >< button.

She scampered off on six and made her way to the far right,
another right, and to the end of the hall. The office was small and
smelled like the potpourri in the wood bowl at check-in. The
young woman behind the counter didn't require her to sign-in, a
relief in itself. She said it would be about three minutes. Actually,
it turned out to be less, as Dr. Stacey didn't want to leave police
patients exposed for any time in the waiting room. Nothing would

ruin an officer's day faster than waiting and running into another officer—or worse, police official. So, appointments were managed with an absolute minimum of heel-cooling.

She was shown in and was relieved to find Devonna Stacey was a diminutive, smiling woman who shook her hand vigorously and told her how happy she was that they could meet and talk.

"How many times will this take," Harley asked.

"Maybe just one," said the doctor, settling back into a chair much too large for her. She was seated at her desk, spun around facing Harley on a loveseat. It was a small office, felt homey to the visitor, and the blinds were closed. On either end of the loveseat, a lamp burned, set to very low.

"Good. I'm actually quite nervous," Harley said. "I never thought I'd be seeing a psychiatrist. Never in my life."

"It happens with police officers. Your high-stress lives can be very hard on the nervous system. Adjustment disorders are very common in here. Help me get oriented, please. First, you're an LAPD detective?"

"Yes. I've been a detective just over two years."

"Rank?"

"Sergeant. Which is as high as I can go under current policy."

"That stinks."

"Tell me."

"Yes. Your age?"

"Thirty-three."

"Marital?"

"Widow. Husband killed in Korea June 11, 1952."

"Any serious relationships since then?"

"Only with my daughter."

"What's her name?"

"Wendell—Wendy. Age fifteen now."

"Where does she live?"

"I don't know. She's a runaway."

"I imagine that's quite a stressor right there?"

"That's why I'm here. I worry about her night and day. There's probably not ten minutes that goes by that I don't think about her. I drink over her, cry over her, spend weekends in bed over her. Search terrible neighborhoods at random thinking I might get a glimpse."

"I'm sure. Have you seen her at all since she left?"

"Yes, this weekend I hugged her and said hello right in my own living room. Except, guess what? She wasn't really there. I was hallucinating."

"Had you been drinking?"

"I was having coffee. I really don't much care for alcohol. Occasional vodka on paydays. Some wines—one reason I love weddings is the champagne. Anyway, yes, no, I hadn't been drinking. I heard her from the laundry room. So, I walked into the living room and saw her sitting on my couch. She had been asking me to please help her. I went to her and tried to hug her and got a face full of air. Scared the hell out of me, doctor."

"I'm sure you were very frightened. Do you have a history of any kind of psychiatric illness or problems?"

"Nope."

"What about your family?"

"My cousin Sue has been a real problem for her family. Very stuck up but a very hard drinker. I don't know what that's about."

"Has Sue ever seen someone like me?"

"I wouldn't know, but I highly doubt it. My family was never one to use doctors unless an arm was hanging by a thread. Pretty tough bunch of people."

"Where is your family?"

"San Diego. My dad works for the city. My mom's a welder. At the shipyard. She worked on the production line as a welder in World War II and just can't let it go. Because of the money. It's a great job for a woman nowadays."

"Well, let me ask you, Harley. Have you ever had moments like this before?"

"Seeing people that aren't there?"

"Yes."

"Well, I've seen her face in my ashtray a few times."

"Does she talk to you then?"

"No, her mouth moves like she's talking but I don't hear anything."

"How long do these moments last when you see Wendy?"

"Maybe a minute, probably much less. I just see her, and she tries to say something to me, then it's over."

"Medications you're currently taking?"

"Aspirin for my monthly."

"Anything else?"

"Not really. I still do mustard plasters when I have a chest cold about once a year. But that's about it."

"Any problems at work?"

"No—except I want to kill a victim who's already dead."

"Who's that?"

"A movie producer who raped my daughter. I could kill that bastard."

"Yes, I hear that in your voice. What are you doing with that anger, Harley?"

"I don't know. What does that even mean?"

"It means there's a huge amount of energy building up in you that's going to need to come out sooner or later. Anger at somebody or something like you've got is very destructive to your system, too. It wouldn't surprise me to see that anger you feel at the producer somehow being connected to your hallucination."

"We're going to call it a hallucination?"

"Do you have a better word for it?"

"It is what I had, isn't it? A plain old hallucination. So, do I need medicine or electroshock or what, Doc?"

"You need to come in a few times and talk to me about things. We need to work on your anger before you shoot someone."

"What if I shoot someone who needs shooting?"

"Well, that would be better than somebody who didn't need shooting. I'm not convinced you can tell the difference between the two right now. I'm going to recommend at least three sessions, or I'll recommend a leave of absence. Your choice. Harley?"

"Hell, I can't take a leave right now."

"Then we'll make your next appointment."

They talked another ten minutes then time was up, and Harley left.

Her next appointment was a week away.

29

Los Angeles Times

The LAPD scores another big win in the shooting gallery.

Wednesday night came a call to all-units in the vicinity of Hollywood and Vine. A 211 was underway. Every cop and detective in the vicinity hit the reds, running to the robbery.

The two robbers were a couple of young toughs, two years out of New York's Elmira Reformatory. One of them did the juvie jolt for shooting his father to death. Now they'd been out thirty hours and had landed in LA, intending to start over. They happened upon a gin mill called the Melody Lane, complete with a front door in the shape of a heart. Their names were Stuart E. Cordovan and Vernon Z. Dillard, both from Lockport, New York. They walked inside, bought a bottle of Old Grandad, and took two civilians as hostages, threatening to shoot them unless the manager turned over the safe's contents. Stan Morris, a Marine, noticed that they were armed and called LAPD. Officers R. L. Newslyter and David Tutor arrived. And, unknown to the toughs, two detectives were lurking out on the sidewalk. Their names were Harley Ellis and Marcia

Meriwether, who were just passing through the intersection when the call went out. They'd just observed the two uniformed officers duck inside and they were waiting outside to assist with transport of the armed robbers if necessary. Back inside the Melody Lane, the young toughs were waiting as the uniformed cops came in. They disarmed the cops and marched them outside at gunpoint. They were heard saying between themselves that they were going to take the cops and their cruiser and drive them off a cliff into the ocean and see if they could float. In other words, a long night ahead for LA's finest.

Detective Ellis said afterwards she knew the cops were either coming out in the lead, which would be some kind of bad news, or following behind, which would mean she and her partner could go on with their shift and leave. Not ten seconds later, here came the two cops, minus their hats, hands held in the air, walking in front. They'd been had. They went walking past, followed immediately by Cordovan and Dillard, guns pointed at the spine of both cops. Detective Ellis stepped in behind, fired one shot into Cordovan's spine and one shot into Dillard's left underarm, just at his heart. Dillard fired off a shot that went harmlessly into the air. Detective Meriwether's pistol chattered, combat mode, and Dillard was struck in the face and he fell back, and Cordovan, still going for his gun, was then shot one time in the head. Passersby on crowded Hollywood Boulevard shrieked and scattered.

Story will be updated as more details become known.

30

"So, Harley, how are you feeling about the killing?"

Dr. Stacey was referring to the shooting from two days ago at the Melody Lane tavern. Psychiatrist visits were mandatory after officer-involved killings.

"I feel it was justified," said Harley. "They were marching our officers out to their squad car to take them someplace and murder them. I had no choice but to shoot."

"I know, but how are you feeling?"

Harley thought long and hard. "I feel—I feel—like you predicted I'd be in here after shooting someone. I feel like you saw this coming. And that now I'm somehow at fault for what happened. But I'm not. Any officer would've done what I did."

Dr. Stacey seemed to choose her words carefully. "Please don't feel like I'm judging you, I'm not. These shooting meetings are held just to help you process what happened."

Harley sat back and crossed one booted leg over the other. She drummed her fingers on the arm of the loveseat, thinking. "To be honest, I don't need to process, Doc. I took out two bad guys, end of story. I don't really need to think much more about it."

"All right, Harley, if you're okay with it, so am I. Shall we call that part a day?"

"Yes, let's call it a day."

"What about the other things we've spoken about? Anymore new stresses taking you down?"

"Do you mean have I hallucinated since last time? Luckily, no. I've actually been feeling better since we talked. But I am searching for Wendy now, officially. She's a person of interest."

"How does that feel?"

"Like shit. It's hard to search for your own flesh and blood on the idea she might be a criminal. Criminals are what I do. Daughters are not. You know what I mean?"

"I think I do. We need to help you separate out your work from your family. I've been thinking it might be a case you want to turn over to someone else. Would you like me to speak to your lieutenant about doing that?"

"God, no! Please! I need to keep this case so I can keep looking for her on the city's dime. Someone needs to make sure she's not hurt or killed if it comes down to making an arrest. I've got to be there for that, Doctor Stacey. No, please don't say something to my LT."

"It's okay, I won't say a word. I just meant it as an offer of help to you if you needed help. Obviously, you don't. You're a remarkable woman, Harley."

"Not remarkable. Just a mother with a badge."

"Okay, well, we're about out of time here unless there's anything else."

"We've misplaced two detectives. They were interfering in a case of mine. No sign of them."

"I heard about that. Two guys out of Hollywood Station."

"Yes. Oh, I also got a new roommate. A girl who's pregnant and needed a place to save some money for doctors and hospitals. She's a great kid and it helps with the loneliness to have her around."

"Good for you. It seems very healthy that you can reach out and help someone. Very healthy, indeed."

Harley smiled. "Did I pass, Doc?"

"Pass?"

"Did I pass the shooting review? Will you tell the department I'm good to go?"

"I will. I see no problems, Harley."

"Good, then. Thank you."

Harley stood and left the office. Just outside in the waiting room sat Marcia.

"My turn?" her partner said.

"Yes," said Harley. "I think she's coming for you."

"Anything to watch out for?"

"Don't say you enjoyed the shooting. I wanted to say I always love kicking bad guy ass, but I held back. They don't need to hear that."

"I loved shooting those assholes. But I'll keep mum. You're right."

"Right."

The doctor came and walked Marcia into her office. Marcia winked at Harley as she followed Dr. Stacey. Harley took a chair and selected a *Life* magazine off the waiting room table. She began flipping pages, studying the cover story about the Air Age. She knew there was no faster way to get suspended than to let it into the official dialogue you had enjoyed killing a bad guy. That could get you grounded indefinitely.

So, she flipped pages and soon was humming softly, just to herself.

31

F ollowing their interviews with Dr. Stacey, Harley and Marcia
piled into Harley's unmarked cruiser and set out for 1667 N.
Latham, unit eleven, Long Beach. They talked on the way there
about Danny Sullivan's visit to Annalee after Sullivan had been
removed from the case. Annalee was out on bail now. The DA
thought the case very weak and hadn't resisted releasing her. She
still had no lawyer and had no money to hire one.

Orange trees shaded the sidewalks on both sides of North Latham
Street. The detectives parked just inside the trailer park and began
scouting for unit eleven. It was a forty-footer, set back about ten
feet off the great circular drive that constituted the mobile home
park. A makeshift carport abutted the near end of the trailer, an
add-on that someone hadn't planned out all that carefully before
hammering the first nail. Harley climbed up to the top of the
wooden steps, trailing her hand on the splintering railing. She
rapped on the aluminum door.

Annalee Johnson appeared on the other side of the door. She
pushed it open and stood back for the detectives to enter. They

settled on the small turquoise couch, and Annalee plopped into the orange swivel rocker. In between them was a circular coffee table with a glass top covering a papier mâché rendering of a Paris sidewalk scene.

"I don't have any coffee, we're out," explained Annalee.

Harley raised her hand. "No need, we're coffee'd out. But thanks for letting us come here."

"I don't know why you need to. Didn't Detective Sullivan make notes about his visit? I told him and his partner I don't know jack shit about who killed Spielman. I'm getting a little annoyed by it, in fact.

"Annalee, we've discovered there was another girl there for a screen test the same day as you. In fact, she was there about the same time. Do you recall seeing another girl?"

"Yes, nobody asked me about her. Her name was Wendy."

Harley's neck hairs stood up. "You spoke to her?"

"She loaned me her lipstick, I'd bit mine off my lips and my tube was empty. We talked about the Gayle Howard role. Evidently, Spielman was promising the Gayle Howard role to everyone."

"Did this Wendy say she'd been raped?"

"She did. She said that she was in some school plays and everyone loved her. On the bus ride I told her that I was taking acting lessons in Hollywood. I told her my mom was trying to get me an agent. Do you know how hard it is to land an agent, detective? It's just about impossible if you don't already have a part in something."

"I've heard it's quite difficult," Marcia said. "A friend of mine's been trying for years. She's got to the point where she's too old for a beginner's role now. What do you do then?"

"My point, exactly," Annalee agreed. "I'm almost over the hill and I'm only nineteen. They're looking for the next Dorothy in Oz, you know, someone younger than me. It's very depressing."

"Annalee, do you work anyplace?"

"I did. I worked at Tiemann Motors in parts. But I got laid off because I went to so many casting calls. It was a good job, too, almost a buck an hour."

Harley looked at Marcia, who shuddered. Annalee missed this exchange. The minimum wage was one-dollar an hour; Tiemann Motors was paying scale. Still, the idea that someone could live on that—the detectives could only make a note and go on.

"Do you have any other sources of income?"

"My boyfriend works. He paints cars for Scheib. He paints six cars every day. Brings home almost a hundred bucks a week, too. We're talking about announcing our engagement."

Harley looked up from her notes. "You're engaged?"

"Not yet. It doesn't do for a young actress to be married. Not good for her fans, you know."

"Sure, sure."

"Let me get back to this Wendy, the girl at Spielman's. Did she seem angry to you when you spoke with her?"

"Not any more than anyone else who'd been messed over by Mr. Spielman."

"Did she say bad things about him? Cuss him out?"

"Not really. Two weeks later, I was there on a callback. She was there, well, just because. I don't know why she was there, but it wasn't a callback. Come to think of it, why was she there? Do you think she did it?"

"No," said Harley, "and we don't think you did it, either."

"Then why do you keep coming here and talking to me? Why did I get arrested? I read about my detective going missing. Has he been found? My dad says I shouldn't even be talking to you now. But I figure I'm home anyway, so why not? Besides, I actually don't mind having company. Otherwise, I'm very isolated in this place."

"Who owns this trailer?"

"The park owns it."

"So, you're just renting?"

"Randy is renting. He's my boyfriend. He hasn't signed anything."

Harley climbed to her feet. "You know what? This is the last time we'll be bothering you, Annalee. Thanks so much for allowing us to come here."

"Sure, and do you mind if I tell you something?"

"Sure, what?"

"You look an awful lot like that Wendy. I'd swear you two are related."

"I'll make a note, Annalee. Thanks, again."

"Okay, I hope I don't see you again. Oops, that came out wrong."

"We know what you mean. Goodbye."

"Goodbye."

32

W hen they returned to the squad room at Hollywood Station, Harley found a pink phone message from CV: "Go to the private phone in the hall and call me. Thanks, CV."

She poured a cup of brackish coffee and carried it out to the pay phone most detectives used for very private calls the others didn't need to hear. A detective's trip to the pay phones was always the subject of conjecture among the other dicks sitting around the bull session that was always underway. "My turn in the barrel," she said to no one and everyone as she carried her coffee away. No one appeared to pay attention, but she knew the comments would begin the second the door closed behind her separating the hallway from the detectives. She shot a look behind her. Even Marcia could be seen deflecting questions.

She caught CV at home, his day off. He answered on the third ring, "Hello?"

"Hey, big guy, it's Harley. What's cookin'?"

"Oh, hi, thanks for returning my call."

"Sure, everything all right with you?"

"Yeah, you know, the ex is giving me a ration of shit about more child support, but what's new, right?"

"Right."

"So why I called—this is awkward. How long we known each other now, Harls?"

"I don't know. Let's see, we partnered two years, and I was on patrol before that and you were working—did we know each other then?"

"No, yes, I think in detectives until we got our first call-out just about. Maybe—I don't know. Anyway, it's been awhile, right?"

"Right."

"So, I was wondering if you'd—I mean I'm wondering if we could maybe take it to the next stage."

She paused and chewed her cheek. "Meaning?"

"You know, I wonder if you—if you ever have any feelings."

"I have feelings, sure, everyone has feelings. Do I have feelings for you? Yes and no. I mean I love you like a brother, CV. You've gotta know that."

"Could it ever be more than that?"

"Could it ever be more? Holy shit, since Bobby died, I haven't even thought like that about anyone. Not even once. To answer your question, I don't know. I'm kind of dead inside, CV, you know what I mean? You know, you've got me seeing the shrink because I'm seeing things and now you wanna know if there's something else? Holy shit, I don't know what to say. Yes, I do. A smart guy won't have anything to do with me right now. I'm probably a heart-breaker. Me, I wouldn't touch me with a ten-foot pole. Too dicey."

"Uh, I thought maybe we could have dinner, like get dressed up and have a romantic meal."

"Holy shit, CV, what brought all this on? We already have dinner together. How would it be any different?"

"You know, romantic. Like I could bring flowers or something. Oh, shit, Harls, I've got this all screwed up. I'm not saying what I gotta say. The best day of my life was the day they separated us as part-ners because now I can say what I've gotta say. See, I've got feelings for you. Strong feelings. I think about you lots during the day. You're just the first thing I think about when I wake up, too. I don't know what to say to make you see me like that. I don't want to be just a brother. I want to be your boyfriend."

Harley thought long and hard. The whole thing had caught her flat-footed. This conversation was the farthest thing from her mind when she called CV. Ordinarily, he wanted to talk about how rough it was with his ex or how his kids were screwing up at school or how the fish weren't biting—they fished a lot off the pier at Santa Monica—those kind of things. But romance? Well, she couldn't even. Then it occurred to her, what her real feelings were.

"You know, CV, I've always thought of you as my best friend. Ever since we started palling around together. But, like Marcia always says, our goal is to marry our best friend. So sure, why don't we give it a shot and see where it goes. With the understanding that right now my feelings are a mess and it may turn out I don't feel shit. Or it may turn out like you're feeling things. I'm willing to try if you can take me like I am, fucked up in heart and head."

"Of course, of course, jeez, Harley, I'm sorry you're feeling like that.

I just want to take it slow, but I don't want to hide my true intentions."

"Which is to get me in bed and make me see I love you?"

"Something like that. Oh, shit."

"It's all right. Isn't that the whole point of how it always goes? Dating, then bedding, then figuring out how to pay the bills, get a house, send the little darlings to college, make lieutenant, make captain, don't get IA up your ass. Isn't that all there is? We don't need to make it into something it will never be. My father was a contractor and had a great subdivision in the Valley until he lost it. I had a great marriage with Bobby until I lost him. I have a great daughter named Wendy but then I lost her. My point is, if I stick my neck out, I don't want to lose you. It would just fucking kill me. So be very sure about what you're getting into here. That much you owe me, as the healthy one."

"I know my feelings. That's all I know. In fact, I could say more, but not on the phone."

"No, CV, don't say more. Not now, not tonight, not next week. Let's just have dinner and have a look at those flowers you're talking about. Can we just start with that?"

"My idea exactly. What time should I pick you up tonight?"

"Tonight? Jeez, you don't waste any time."

"I've already wasted too much time already. What time?"

"I don't know. Five, then we can let me get back to work after?"

"Sure, if that's what you've gotta do."

"It is. Marcia got the name of another Spielman secretary today who saw something. We can't wait to buttonhole this one. So, let's say five, then you're out of there by eight, does that work?"

"That works perfectly. It's a start and that's more than I hoped for."

"All right. You've said enough. Now let me off here before I start kicking myself for saying yes. You know how I second-guess every friggin' thing I ever do."

"I do know that. See you at five."

She hung up the pay phone and looked around. She looked through the glass wall back into the squad room. No one at the detective desk appeared to be watching her. Was it possible they'd all forgotten about her and actually turned around to get some work done?

But then Marcia made a beeline for her. She came into the hallway, brushing a strand of hair out of her eyes. "Hey, I got Mia Knowland on the phone. She can meet us this afternoon."

"Where is she?"

"She works at Capitol Films still. Next office from Spielman's. She's in production."

"Let's go. We can leave now so I don't have to go back in and face the wolves."

"They saw the phone message was from CV. I think they know something's up."

"Wait. How did you know my phone message was from CV?"

"Darling girl, we're all detectives, remember?"

Harley laughed long and hard. "God, that feels good, just to laugh."

"So, did he ask you out? No, don't tell me. None of my business."

"No, it isn't any of your business, partner. And yes, he did ask me out."

"Good! I can see you two together! He's handsome, tall, and bedroomy eyes. I'm surprised you haven't jumped his bones before."

"Who says I haven't, detective?"

Marcia rolled her eyes. "Sister, I know better."

"You sure of that?" Harley laughed a Lon Chaney horror laugh.

"I've got my car closest to the door. I'm driving."

"Whoopee, then. Let's go bust this fucking case wide open before it makes a babbling lunatic out of me."

"Makes? Did you say makes?"

"Don't push me, Marcia."

"Don't worry. Detective."

33

The detectives left Hollywood Station on Wilcox, heading south to Santa Monica Boulevard then west to Sunset, southwest to West LA, down to Santa Monica, back east on 5th Street to the Pacific Arms apartments. Mia Knowland had confirmed an appointment.

The apartment was on the ground level, next door to the manager's office.

A fiftyish woman wearing a purple caftan and smoking a filtered cigarette answered the door. Harley and Marcia produced their ID and shields and were allowed inside when the screen door was unlatched. "I'm Mia," said the woman. "Welcome to our humble abode. I live here with Cathay Cautier, another secretary from Mr. Spielman's office. You could talk to her too, except she's home in Merced for a few days. Anyway, make yourselves comfortable."

"Thank you."

"Thanks."

"Now, would anyone like coffee or sun tea? I have both ready to pour."

"Not for us, thanks," Harley said. "We'd just like to ask a few questions and then scoot on out. In particular, I'm wondering about the episode involving Mr. Spielman and Annalee Johnson. You saw something there?"

"I did. It was the damnedest thing, too. See, staff keeps his appointments to fifteen minutes. He wants us to knock and come in after that and pretend there's another appointment waiting. This is so he doesn't get held up with nonstop talkers."

"Okay. How did that happen to involve Annalee?"

"Well, on her first visit, the fifteen-minute hourglass I keep on my desk ran out. So, I got up and knocked on his door. Guess what, no answer. I knocked again and again. Still no answer. But I knew they were both in there together cause no one had come out. I turned to Cathay."

"She was in the outer office with you?"

"That's right. I turned and sort of shrugged to her. She smiled and said, 'Go on in. That's what he wants, Mia.' She was right, so I knocked once more and entered. Well there, on his casting couch, Mr. Spielman had straddled poor Annalee and I couldn't tell if he was doing it to her or not because I was behind, but she was beating on his shoulders with her fists. That's when I saw he had a hand over her mouth. She was crying, 'No! No! No!' but it was muffled because he had his hand in there. Also, his hand was bloody. I guess she'd bit him and hard. Just as I got over to them, he—he—he climbed off. I used to be married so I know about these things. She bit him so hard he lost it."

"He lost his erection?" Marcia said abruptly.

"Exactly. Then he slumped to the side and sort of rolled onto the floor. Now he's sitting on the floor trying to tuck his business back into his pants. Annalee has rolled onto her side and pulled her knees up to her chest and she's crying loudly now. He goes half cross-eyed and his head falls back against her shoulder. She screamed, 'Goddamn you, bastard! I'll come back and kill you!'"

"You're certain she said she'd kill him?" Harley asked.

"Very certain. You don't forget something like that, detective. Well, at this juncture I didn't know what to do. I didn't know if I should call the police or what. Then she sat up and pulled her dress down. Her dress was very tight, and she wasn't wearing any stockings, just panties with a garter belt. Her lipstick was smeared half onto the side of her face and her bouffant hairdo was mashed flat all the way around. She started trying to throw up then. I think it was because she had some of the blood from his hand in her mouth. But it wouldn't come up. So, I went over to his water cooler and poured her a paper cup. He held up his hand for me to help him up."

"Did you help him up?"

"I did not. Any man capable of trying to rape someone can get on his own darn feet. I turned right around and stomped out. I didn't close his door, either. I wasn't going to leave that poor thing in there alone with that brute."

"What happened next?"

"A couple minutes later, she comes storming out and slams his door. She stopped at Cathay's desk and tried to say something. No words would come out. So, she stomped on out the sidewalk door and off she went."

"What did he do next?"

"We heard the pipes in his bathroom rumbling like they always do. Pete—Maintenance Pete—says they've got air in the lines. Something like that. Then he goes on with his day like nothing's happened. I mean there's letters to transcribe, calls to place, contracts to type—the whole nine yards. Just like nothing horrible happened in there."

"Did Mr. Spielman ever mention it to you? Say anything? Apologize?"

"Not to me. I guess not to Cathay either, or she woulda told me. You sure you don't want some nice dark sun tea, you two?"

"We're about done," Harley said. "He never said a word about it?"

"I did get a double paycheck on Friday. Just outta the blue. Nobody said why or wherefore, I just got paid double. Never happened before, hasn't happened since. Cathay says he's buying my silence."

"How did you feel about him after?" Marcia asked.

"How did I feel? I hated him. Cathay and I wanted to call that poor girl and check on her, but we decided that would be foolish."

"Let me show you her picture and ask if this is who it was."

Harley pulled an 8x10 from her file. She turned it top to bottom and handed it to Mia.

She studied it for a second then said, "That's her. Look at that nice, serene smile. If he'd finished the job, I'd have killed him."

"She was lucky, given how young she is. But what a fighter!"

"Poor girl. I know he did it to other girls, too. One girl had her brother calling him up and asking where he lived. He'd call us three or four times a day like he was a delivery man and needed Mr. Spielman's address. One time he called and said he was a cop and he needed to go to his house to deliver his wife some bad news. Stuff like that. And he wasn't the only one. There were boyfriends, fathers—I'm surprised someone didn't...wait, someone did, didn't they?"

"That's what we intend to find out, Mia. Look, you've been a great help so far. But there's also one other picture I want to show you and just ask for your comment."

Harley pulled out Wendy's picture, turned it and passed it to Mia. The woman took the picture and held it closer, then moved it away, then clucked and shook her head.

"Shame about this one," said Mia.

"What do you mean?"

"She was so young. He raped her. I was there that morning. When she first came out of his office she was crying. Now, we had our orders from Mr. Spielman. So, I told her, don't call us, we'll call you. You'll need an agent before anything can happen. It'll be at least six months before you hear anything—all the roadblocks he told us to use with the girls on the screen tests. When I first started working there, I believed him. But after a few months I knew he was just using it to ruin any hope they had. They couldn't get agents. They couldn't wait six months, they'd have to move back to Iowa or New Jersey first. We never called them, never called even one of them. But this girl in this picture, she sticks with me because she was so young. I'm sure it was statutory rape even if she agreed to it. Did she agree to it?"

Harley shook her head. "No, she didn't consent to it."

"What's her name again?"

"Wendy Ellis."

"But—wait, didn't you say you're Detective Ellis?"

"I am. She's my daughter."

"He raped your daughter? Jesus, Mary and Joseph. And now she's run away, I'm guessing, is that it?"

"Yes, that's it."

"And there's the chance she killed Mr. Spielman? That's why you're looking? Your poor, poor girl. Let me give you a gallon of new sun tea to take. It'll help you later when you're hot and need a break. Please wait right here."

Harley stood and began placing her file back in order while Mia Knowland left the room. Then she reappeared, carrying a gallon jug in two hands. It was ringed around the lid with tea bag strings and teabags at the other end. "Now, you must take this."

Harley had nothing to say in response, so she accepted the tea and shifted it up under one arm. "Thanks for talking to us," she said. "And thanks for the tea."

"If you can ask Cathay to call me, here's my card," Marcia added.

"She'll call. I promise. Please take care of Wendy. She didn't deserve anything bad to happen at her age. If she killed him, get me on the jury. I'll tell them all good riddance. Hope the bastard rots in his grave."

"Thank you, Mia," Harley said. Off she went, then, carrying her file and the jug of tea. Marcia, bringing up the rear, muttered under her breath, using every curse word she could muster against

Ira J. Spielman. "And her? How the hell could she keep working for the slug?"

"Another unhappy customer, are we?" Harley said over her shoulder.

Then they climbed into their unmarked car and headed back to the Hollywood station.

34

She wore her sleek black evening dress with her grandmother's pearls and a fine gold watch from her police academy graduation. A gift from her mother and father. CV wore evening clothes and brought her a single red rose bud, which he pinned on her.

"We're taking a cab," he told her.

The taxi was waiting out front and he, every millimeter the gentleman, pulled open the rear door and stood aside while she entered, pulled her wrap around her shoulders, and settled back. He came around to the other side and climbed in.

He two-fingered a twenty up to the driver and softly directed, "Take us to Ciro's."

Thirty minutes later they arrived at the world-famous restaurant on Sunset Strip. The cab pulled into a long line of waiting cabs, slowly making its way to the front. While they waited, CV gave Harley a brief history of the restaurant's name.

"Louis Adlon, son of the proprietor of Berlin's Hotel Adlon, opened Hollywood's first Ciro's in 1934. That club was located on Hollywood Boulevard and was informally part of a chain with locations in London, Paris and Berlin. The Hollywood Ciro's was not a success, apparently, because it soon folded.

"In 1935, the building at 8433 Sunset was rebuilt. The first tenant was Al De Freitas' Club Seville, where the gimmick was a dance floor made from sheets of glass over a giant aquarium. But dancing on fish proved not to be popular, and the club closed within a year."

"How do you know all this?" she asked. "But you were born in LA, I know that. I just didn't know you were such a local history buff."

"I've made nearly a dozen arrests out of the joint," CV said with a laugh. "Sooner or later it rubs off on you."

When the cab arrived at the door, he helped her from the car, then took her lightly by the elbow and they made their way inside to the maître d. Their table was waiting.

Harley glided through the maze of tables as they followed the gentleman in tails, down to the small dance floor, and to a small, intimate table. A string quartet was making dinner music. They were seated less than three minutes before their waiter, George, arrived with menus and a request for drinks. CV ordered a bottle of 1945 Chateau Paulet champagne. They talked quietly, while three couples danced, and different tables erupted here and there with laughter and joviality. The wine arrived, and she sipped once, twice. She felt the fine spirit go straight to the center of her brain after one glass and, in one impossibly sped-up moment, she lay her hand on top of CV's hand while he told about serving at the end of World War II. His assignment had been Paris, where he and his sergeant and two other corporals were charged with escorting war correspondents to various pockets of resistance while the writers and photojournalists captured their stories to help keep up the struggling spirits of the French. Without realizing she had so placed her hand, she listened to the end of the tale and then, in alarm, jerked her hand away, only to replace it there at the beginning of the next story. CV had a way about loving life and loving to tell his stories that had always enthralled Harley. More than once she had told him he should be writing books but, in his own subdued way, he pooh-poohed the notion for the headier romance of writing reports of homicides and suicides, the most time-consuming reportage in the entire LAPD. "Lucky for me I do like to tell stories," he finished. "There's a new dead body just about every day to keep me going."

Then they danced, not close at first, until they played *Some Enchanted Evening* and she lay her head upon his chest. He touched the small of her back and she felt herself relax against him.

Halfway through dinner, Harley noticed their conversation was covering items they'd never shared before, not even during the two years they rode side-by-side in a Vice vehicle, moving from one setup/arrest to the next. During all that time, she'd never told him, as she did that night, about her own dad's drinking problem and how he'd finally found respite in the new thing called AA. For his part, CV told her about his trip to the White River in Arkansas after the war when he'd taken a tour guide and spent a solid week fishing for trophy trout, camping on the riverbank at night, and staring up at the stars and crying about all the dead faces from the war that plagued his sleep. "Even the smell of fish frying in crystal clear air couldn't scrub me clean," he said. "It's the first time fishing ever let me down."

～

WHEN THEY GOT HOME to Harley's, CV led Harley by the hand to her room. Harley knew Angelina was in bed asleep, but she kept her voice low and CV got the hint.

He'd been in the room before exactly once: when he brought a carafe of chicken noodle soup the day she was shaking and shivering with the flu and he was her Vice partner.

He shut the door quietly and then wrapped her up in his arms. She locked gazes with him, a slight smile on her face.

CV gave her a soft kiss, just a peck, before he removed the pins that kept Harley's hair away from her face, just enough messy to show her she could unwind. He ran his hands through her hair, massaging her scalp as he did, until her hair lay against her jawline.

Then he unhooked her dangling earrings, the ones she had bought at the Hotel Del in Coronado the weekend before Bobby left for Korea. They reflected with a bit of red coral in them. He placed them on top of the dresser. He had loosened his tie at dinner so that she just needed to pull the tail through to remove it. She dropped it to the floor and began to unbutton his shirt. He stepped closer and sucked on her ear, now free of any ornamentation.

She moaned and lifted his tucked shirt from his trousers. At her insistence, her pushing the shirt off his shoulders, he removed it entirely and it, too, fell to the pile on the floor. Harley ran her hands up his bare chest, gently grazing his nipples.

He captured her mouth with his, greedy for what she gave him, chasing her tongue with his own. He unbuttoned her dress and slid it off her shoulders, then unclasped her bra. Her breasts finally free, he massaged them both, running his thumb over nipples that swelled at his touch. He pinched one then soothed the sting with his palm, then did the same to the other.

At her groan, his kisses turned aggressive and he pulled in her lower lip and sucked hard. He slid her stockings and panties down her shapely legs. On his way back up her body, he took a nipple into his mouth. She arched back and dug her fingers into his hair.

Her best friend, and now her lover, stood before her naked from the waist up. Her hair mussed from their passion, her lips swollen from his kisses, she looked at his trim, athletic body and she had never known a more beautiful, heart-wrenching sight. CV scooped her up in his arms and laid her on the bed. She scooted back and settled on the pillows while he removed his shoes, socks, belt, and trousers. She was glorious with her flushed skin, her breasts perky, her legs open and inviting.

CV crawled onto the bed, kissing up her belly, and nestled between her thighs. She arched up to him. "Please, CV," she begged, "I want you now."

So, he slid into her, his gaze on hers, the love there surely reflected in her own. He stayed still, but she urged him by grabbing his buttocks and pressing her mound against his pelvis. He started sliding in and out, slow but then faster, her hips arching to match his rhythm. As her breathing turned to pants, he must have sensed she was close, so he bucked into her, murmuring her name out loud over and over again until they both came, his eyes watching her face and exciting him to climax.

He lay on top of her while the orgasm subsided, holding her close. When he shifted off her onto his side, she rolled to face him. She smiled and then gave him a slow lingering kiss. "That was lovely."

He tucked a strand of hair behind her ear. "You're lovely."

She sighed deep and closed her eyes, but he didn't let go, and they both drifted off before midnight. However, Harley didn't sleep all that well. It had been her first time since Bobby and her feelings were cross-wired.

At four a.m. she was still awake, tossing and turning, so she gave up, climbed out of bed and headed downstairs for the coffee pot.

CV continued sleeping the sleep of the righteous who finally has pulled into a safe harbor.

She smiled at him in her mind.

He had come to the right place at exactly the right time.

She said goodbye to Bobby then, and took CV a steaming cup of coffee.

It was time to talk.

And maybe repeat.

35

The next day, after saying goodbye to her lover, Harley drove to the Property Division. It was time for her to review the Spielman evidence box just to compare notes with Marcia and be sure no hint, however small, had been passed over. She was considering dismissing the charges against Annalee. Now she wanted to double-check first.

Like Marcia before her, she gingerly sorted through all items marked as evidence, she came to the letter opener, the actual thin-bladed device that had been plunged deep into Spielman's brain, triggering the massive hemorrhage that killed him.

She studied the long, flat, silver blade, with an offset handle. Along the blade, partially covered in blood, she could make out *Wang's Hardware, Las Vegas.*

She kept going until she found the white scarf with the monogram "WE." Wendy Ellis. She read the identifier clipped to the scarf: "Found on the victim's sofa, hanging across the left arm of the sofa, half on and half off." The tag was initialed "LF"—the initials of the CSI tech who had chosen to seize and tag and box the item. Harley recognized the scarf: she'd had it monogrammed and given it to Wendy as a gift for a dance recital.

She took the letter opener up to the front of Property, to the desk officer, and asked for a photo. A snap was taken. They'd have a print on her desk that afternoon.

She returned to the squad room, where she found Marcia doing paperwork at her desk. Harley sat at her desk, abutting Marcia's. She said, "What do we know about Wang's Hardware in Las Vegas?"

Marcia looked up. "The letter opener? I know. I've called them and they've confirmed they're the only Wang's hardware store in Vegas. I didn't send them a picture of the instrument. I suppose one of us should run over there with a picture and get a confirmation it came from their store. The DA will ask."

"And show them a picture of Wendy and see if there's a connection. I guess I'm up for that. I'll leave in the morning."

"Want some company?"

"I think I'd rather have you run down Loden's daughter and see what you can find out. I doubt she knows anything about the murder but maybe she remembers something about her kidnappers that's a clue. We're looking for anything that might link them to Ordañez."

Marcia nodded. "Right, agree. All right, I'll hang back here and see what she's up to now. Are we still looking at her as a person of interest?"

Harley shook her head. "Two things. First, Ordañez says he did Spielman. I don't believe that. Did Loden's daughter? She might have been another angry one, I don't know. I think I want to reserve judgment until I go to Vegas and see what Wang's knows."

"No fingerprints on the damn thing. That makes it that much harder."

"No, but I saw the note the lab attached. Somebody had wiped the handle clean."

"I know."

"I think Dinah Loden is a dead end. Daddy might not be. He's put two and two together and knows Spielman was in on the kidnapping to force him to pay up. He's a much more likely candidate than his daughter. But you know what? Wendy's scarf really scares the shit out of me. My daughter's scarf found at a murder scene, plus a letter opener from the town she's living in. Plus her letter to Spielman? I don't like it, Marcia."

"You've been reading my mail."

"I know. Don't be afraid to speak up about this stuff, you know? She might be my kid, but we've still got a job to do. If it turns out to be her, so be it. There might be mitigating circumstances and I'll be the first to stand up and help her assemble that kind of evidence for sentencing. It works both ways. I might help convict her, but I'll work just as hard to mitigate her sentence."

"I disagree. I think we need the case reassigned. It's not right, you having to chase your own daughter."

"LT gave me thirty days. I'm hanging on that long."

"He gave you thirty days to find her. I doubt he knows about the name on the letter opener and the scarf. And what about the letter? That's a smoking gun, isn't it?"

"Let's just drop it for now. I've got to be the first one to her."

Marcia sighed and turned her attention back to her desk. It looked chaotic with files, pink notes, old newspapers, soft drink bottles, and two coffee mugs. She looked back at Harley.

"By the way, CV was looking for you. Maybe he wants you back."

Harley's heart jumped. "Wants me back?"

"You know, as his partner. I'm just kidding."

"Oh, sure. Tell him I'll catch up with him tonight, if you see him again. Right now, I'm going to go through the murder book one last time before I head out for Vegas. Just making sure I don't miss something before I cut Annalee loose."

"Sure."

THAT NIGHT, after making herself and Angelina tuna fish sandwiches and downing them with chips and milk, Harley went into the family room with her file and began making calls. One of those was to CV, who'd dropped by her office earlier that day, wanting to talk.

"Hey," she said when he picked up. "What's going on besides time and taxes?"

"Thanks for calling," CV replied in a low voice. "I'm just missing you today and wanted to hear your voice."

"Well, we had a great dinner and I thank you again."

"What else? Do you remember what happened after our dinner?"

Her lower abdomen warmed. "I do. You probably don't know, but that was my first time with a man since Bobby was killed. It was a huge moment for me."

"Me, too. I've been out and around with this gal or that. I won't lie to you about that. Nancy in our divorce made me feel like a bottom feeder. Her lawyers called me a deadbeat dad—after I always paid child support. She slimed my name with the department. I've been feeling like a bum ever since. But now, when someone of your caliber is willing to spend a night with me, I feel like I've climbed up out of that dark place and I'm catching a glimmer of light. That's why I want to see you again. You make me a better man, Harley. I sincerely want to see where this goes."

Harley took a drag on her Camel cigarette and blew two smoke rings. Then she responded. "I don't have anything to offer anyone at this point, CV, much as I'd like to. I'm so wrapped up in my daughter and is she or isn't she involved in Spielman's murder. Plus worrying about her welfare and whether I'm a grandmother and have a grandchild I want to know. There's so little of me left over. But I'll tell you what. The part of me that is left over, I'd like nothing better than to spend it with you. You're my friend, probably my best friend. I value that more than anything else between us."

"Tell you what, Harls. I'm going to help you find Wendy. And I'm going to hold your hand while you go through some stuff with her if she is involved. Same with the grandchild. Maybe we can help there. And when you come out the other end, I'm going to be there waiting for you, asking you for anything you have to give then. You're my best friend, too. It doesn't get any more real than that."

"So," she said. "Tomorrow I'm going over to Vegas. We have a letter opener from there that was used to kill Spielman. I'm going to track down the merchant who gives them away."

"Want some company? I can take a couple of days of leave and go with you."

"No, give me a day alone with it first. Let me just follow up on some hunches. Then come over the second day and we'll paint the town red. Maybe even spend twenty bucks on the nickel slots. That's about my speed."

"Sounds great. Just call and let me know where you're staying."

"I already know. I'll be at the Flamingo."

"Oh, that sounds dangerous. Lots of good-looking movie stars hanging around there."

"I've got my eye on a certain detective from Hollywood. That's as Hollywood as I care to get, thank you very much."

"Ah, you just made a forty-year-old detective feel like eighteen again. You make my heart melt, lady."

"See you in Vegas. Don't check in. I've got the room."

"Done and done. So long, Harls."

"So long."

She went into the bathroom and felt the hosiery she'd hung over the shower bar to dry. It was dry and ready. She called goodnight into Angelina, who called back goodnight herself.

Harley began packing.

It was time to find her daughter.

36

The drive took six hours. Every inch of the way, Harley was scanning other cars, crowds at eateries, faces at service stations, for a glimpse of Wendy. Halfway there, she stopped for lunch at a roadside barbecue, Tex's Mesquite BBQ. She surreptitiously studied the face of each and every diner. Then, after eating, she smoked a cigarette and played the slot machine at her booth. She lost $1.25. Harley arrived at the Flamingo hotel at two p.m. and went inside to check-in.

The room was typical: double bed with upholstered headboard, trestle table beside a sliding door opening onto a tiny patio, window AC, well-lit bathroom with plastic cups and a wrapper across the toilet, telephone with all the right buttons (room service and wake-up calls).

The bellhop plunked her suitcase down on the dresser and stuck out his hand. Harley laid a fiver on him—a king's ransom. But she was feeling extravagant because she'd neither gone anywhere nor spent any money on herself since Wendy disappeared. It was time to loosen her grip on life for a day or two and spend some of her per diem, besides.

She changed shoes and removed her sweater as the desert air was very warm. She pushed a button and turned the AC on high. Holding her head in front of the vent, she dried her sweaty hair. She then exited her room and went back through the lobby, out to her unmarked vehicle. It was time for a trip to Wang's Hardware.

She drove slowly, enjoying the strange sights and sounds of the tiny town that gambling addiction had built. Down Las Vegas Boulevard to its intersection with Warm Springs Road and then three blocks to Bermuda Road. Ahead another street, and then, Wang's Hardware was on the northwest corner. She was able to park almost right in front and went inside. The main counter was staffed by a boy of maybe twelve. Harley approached and asked him to go get the manager. An Asian man wearing a short-sleeved white shirt with a black necktie, black pants and black dress shoes, appeared behind the counter. "Yes?" he smiled.

Harley held out her ID and shield. He nodded. She withdrew one of Wendy's pictures from her folder. She turned it around for viewing and lay it on the linoleum countertop. "She came in here and left with a Wang's letter opener. Do you remember?"

The manager smiled engagingly. "Oh, yes, a very young woman with a leaking toilet."

"Leaking?"

"She needed to reseal her toilet. But telling her how to do it was impossible, so I sent our crew with her. They said they got it done in about an hour. I only charged her twenty dollars, which she's never paid. But that's neither here nor there. She also had a baby with her. A nice baby without crying."

"Wait, she owes twenty dollars?"

"That's right. I still remember because I knew she was going to stiff me. But I wanted to do her a favor. Someone so young."

Harley pulled a twenty from her wallet and laid it on the counter. "I'm her mom. Let's just say she's even now. Did you by any chance get her address?"

"I did. Let me look it up."

He opened a large accounts book and traced down line-by-line with a clear ruler. Finding what he wanted, he said the address was on East St. Louis Avenue just south of Bonita Avenue, unit 290. Harley wrote down the number and his directions.

"Do you still give away those letter openers?" she asked.

"We do. Jamie!"

The twelve-year-old rounded the door into the office and returned in seconds with a letter opener. Sure enough, exact same model and lettering as the one in the property box. Harley slipped it into her jacket and thanked the man. She felt closer to Wendy at that moment than she had since her daughter had run away.

Harley drove back into traffic and retraced her path, heading north, passing the Flamingo and continuing north to East St. Louis Boulevard, where she stopped then proceeded right on a red. She drove 15 mph past the Desert Aire apartments first, west to east, taking in points of ingress and egress and praying she was very close to Wendy. Then she parked at the far north end of the units and began walking back south.

Harley walked through the iron gates—they were permanently fixed open—into the second building where the numbers included 290. She climbed the concrete stairs to the second floor.

At the landing she entered the hallway and walked down to number 290. Then she knocked and stood back. The door slowly opened.

There stood Wendy.

Harley's first thought was that her daughter had aged five years though she had barely been gone fourteen months by now. Her look was one of bewilderment. Her long, blond hair was scraggly, and she wore no makeup. A word formed on her lips: "What?"

"Hello, sweetheart," Harley said in a very soft voice. "I've come to say hello."

Wendy's expression didn't change. She appeared shocked to find her mother at her door, almost at a loss for words. Then she responded to Harley's words with a toss of her head and a move to shut the door. But Harley pushed the toe of her boot into the opening and it wouldn't close for Wendy.

"Please," Wendy said, "you're blocking my door."

"Please talk to me just for a minute," Harley pleaded. "I miss you and just need to know you're okay."

"I'm okay. Now move your foot."

Then, from behind, came a man's voice. "Who's that, Wendy?" he yelled. "Someone bothering you?"

A man Harley didn't recognize appeared. He looked at Harley's foot, blocking the door from closing and he swept Wendy aside. "Listen, lady, you really want to move that foot before I break it off for you."

"I'm Wendy's mother."

"Lady, I don't give a good goddam if you're her mother or not. Move your fucking foot. Now!"

With that, he kicked at Harley's foot, driving it back out of the opening. He slammed the door and she could hear the deadbolt lock. She knocked several times but the man hollered he was calling the cops, and it dawned on her she had no authority there, in Las Vegas. Shoulders slumped she retraced her steps to her unmarked unit.

It was frustrating. And humiliating. But, by all that's holy, she was alive! She'd found Wendy alive, though looking stressed and aged. Still, she was alive!

Harley climbed into her car and numbly drove back to the Flamingo. All the way, her mind was whirring with thoughts of how she could get a chance to talk to her daughter. Then, she realized her daughter wasn't going to talk and Harley had no authority to grab her and take her in for questioning. This was Las Vegas, a foreign jurisdiction to LA. Any conversation was going to have to be voluntary on Wendy's part. But with the man there running interference, Harley couldn't even let Wendy know she wasn't there to interfere, she was only there to determine that Wendy was okay and that she knew nothing about Spielman's death. Harley was certain that's what Wendy would say if only she could spend five minutes with her. She also wanted to find out, of course, whether she was a grandmother. *Who wouldn't want to know that?* she thought as she made her way through the downtown Las Vegas traffic. *And didn't she have some God-given right to know that?* Of course, there wasn't, at least not a legal right, but, hey, wouldn't Wendy take pity and let Harley know?

Harley wasn't the kind of mother who doted on their child's every word and comment. She never had been that way. She'd always given Wendy her own free rein to make her decisions and decide what was best for herself—within normal limits, of course. But now, with some strange man in-between them, there wasn't even a history she could rely on between them to try to take Wendy back to a more forgiving, loving time. Harley wanted to access that time when Wendy did have good feelings for the mother who had helped her grow up to be a woman with the ability to make good decisions for herself. She wanted to connect emotionally and try to rebuild from there.

Harley also realized she bore a great burden of guilt over losing Bobby in the war. It almost felt like Wendy believed, and had made Harley believe, that Harley had lost him intentionally. Of course, it had been Bobby's decision every step of the way to go to the war, to enlist and fight and get himself killed. In fact, he had done those things almost without regard to his family. Men with children weren't being drafted then and what he'd done, in enlisting during wartime, he had done freely and voluntarily. If there was any fault to be assigned, Harley had decided on her worst nights, it was Bobby's fault. Harley had loved her husband totally and he had returned that love. There was just something, though, that drew him to war. Something very male and preternatural.

She returned to her hotel room and kicked off her boots. She hung up her cotton jacket and shed her holster and gun. These she hung up alongside her jacket. Then she removed her shirt and pants and shrugged into the hotel's bathrobe she'd found hanging on the back of the bathroom door. It featured a small flamingo on the breast pocket with the letter "F." Nicely done.

Room service answered Harley's call and she ordered a club sandwich with iced tea. While she waited for her food, she stretched out on the bed, hands clasped behind her head, and let the cool

AC air blow over her. It felt wonderful and she dozed within minutes.

Her sandwich arrived twenty minutes later. It came with chips, a pickle, and a mint wrapped in tinfoil. Harley had it placed on the trestle table, tipped the server, and closed the door behind her. While she ate her sandwich, her thoughts roamed back over the moments she'd been at Wendy's door, seeking out every last detail of information. Had she heard a baby in the background? No. Had she caught a glimpse of a playpen back beyond Wendy framed in the doorway? No, she couldn't say she had.

Eventually, she decided she would wait for CV to arrive and then, perhaps, try again to get through to Wendy. Maybe having CV along would be enough to quell Wendy's husband or boyfriend and get him to act reasonably toward Harley. She didn't mean to intimidate the guy, but, in comparison, CV was probably six inches taller and fifty pounds heavier, so maybe the fellow would be sweetly reasonable. It wasn't that Harley couldn't have handled the guy; it was just that she didn't want it to come to a police-citizen moment. Didn't want there to be a confrontation.

Harley also considered going to the LVPD to make arrangements, if the need arose, for an officer to accompany her to Wendy's. This would be done if CV had no impact there. After all, the bottom line was Wendy was a witness to some of what Spielman was doing to young women. Not to mention that she was also a person of interest. Harley needed to ask about the letter opener from Wang's and the monogrammed scarf. The case demanded that information and Harley wouldn't leave town without it.

She finished eating, then washed her hands.

CV couldn't get there fast enough.

37

She picked up CV from the airport. He was wearing khaki shorts, blue tennies, and a T-shirt that said *USC Football*. The T-shirt was extra-large and bloused over his waist. There, beneath the fabric, she knew he would have strapped his gun. They kissed and hugged, and Harley led them to short-term parking and her unmarked vehicle.

"So, what's my Harley been up to?" he asked when they were underway from the airport back into town.

"I can hardly wait to tell you. I found Wendy! She's living in an apartment. With some guy who got between us and slammed the door in my face. I'm hoping you'll go back there—"

"Say no more. Let me knock next time. I'll badge the guy and we'll get some time with Wendy. You have some things you need to clear up. We'll get that done, sweetheart."

"I'm so glad you're here. As her mother, I can't, absolutely cannot, imagine myself getting pushy with her guy. That goes nowhere fast and I lose her forever again. If you can at least draw him outside and let me have three minutes with her, I can at least ask my questions and gauge her response. I know when my own daughter's telling the truth or not. That much I can guarantee the lieutenant and the case."

"Sure, you can. You're her mother and, besides, you're the detective on the Spielman case who needs some answers."

"I also thought of going by LVPD and getting a uniformed officer to go with us."

"No need for that. At least not yet. I think my badge will work every bit as well."

"All right, then. How about we retreat back to our room, hit the pool, and head over there this evening?"

"Sounds wonderful. I can hardly wait to get you alone."

"I figured. Me, too, CV."

"You just made my day. I've really been missing my buddy."

"Same here. You grow on a girl. Not to mention you're my buddy, too."

They drove on in silence. CV carried his bag to the room, and they went inside and shut the door.

ONE HOUR LATER, they swam and had a drink poolside, then ordered two coffees to go. It was time to see Wendy.

Thirty minutes later, they'd changed from bathing suits into street clothes and were driving to Wendy's apartment complex. They parked directly in front of the manager's office this time and went straight upstairs. CV stood closest to the door and rapped his knuckles against the green door three times.

No answer.

He knocked a second time, and again no answer. Harley stepped up and rapped the door with her fist and called out Wendy's name. Again, there was no response from within. She turned to CV and shrugged as if asking what happens next.

He shook his head. "Let me get the manager."

"Then, I'll go with you," she said, not wishing to be there alone should the man suddenly answer the door. She had zero fear, she just didn't want a confrontation to escalate. Had it, she would have won in any case, but it would probably ruin her chances of connecting with Wendy.

Downstairs they went to the manager's office and went inside. An older man was sitting behind a desk sign that said "manager." He looked up when the two detectives entered and smiled. "Renting today?" he asked.

CV showed him his shield and ID. Without bothering to examine closely, the manager groaned. "We have another bad actor here, do we?"

"Not really," Harley said. "We just need to speak with the young lady in 290. Her name is Wendy Ellis."

"You mean Miller? Her name is Wendy Miller. Her husband is Robert Ray Miller."

"Oh, she's my daughter. I didn't realize she was married."

"Well, I saw them loading their few things in his truck and driving away in the last hour."

"They loaded their furniture in that time?"

"No furniture, detective. Their apartment comes furnished. They loaded up the little boy's playpen and a few suitcases and small appliances and cookware. That sort of stuff."

"How long since they left?"

"Oh, I'm going to guess two hours."

Harley turned to CV. He shook his head.

"Look," said Harley, now showing her badge. "Can you let us in and allow us to have a look around?"

"I could if I knew for sure they was gone. But right now, I don't know that for certain. I can't let anyone in a rented apartment until I know it's either been let go or until they don't pay. If they're ten days late, we evict and go in and clean up."

"So, there's no way you can let us in for a quick peek?"

"I cannot do that, ma'am. I know you're the girl's mother, but if they came back and found police in there, they could sue me. Or worse, there could be a fight. I don't care for that to happen. Please understand. I'm hamstrung."

"We understand," Harley said with a sigh. "Thanks, anyway."

"Let's go, Harley," CV said. "We've got some other steps we can take."

Reluctantly, Harley turned away from the manager and put her hand on CV's shoulder as he led them back outside. They stood beside Harley's unmarked car. She looked into his eyes. "She's not going to let me back in her life, is she?"

"I don't know. She's very young and impressionable."

"I've lost her, CV. I give up. We're going to have to have the local police run her to the ground and then extradite to California. What a mess that's going to be. She'll hate me forever."

"Can't be helped, Harley. Don't forget about the letter opener and the scarf. You've got compelling reasons to want to see her in LA. My guess is, you present your case to the DA even as it is right now, he's going to indict her. He's going to charge her with first degree murder just based on what you have. Maybe it's time to turn the case back over to Lieutenant Chall and let him assign it someplace else."

"Not yet. He gave me thirty days. I've only used half of that. I'm going to see about having her picked up here and try talking to her alone, first."

"Then let's go to the LVPD and put that in motion."

"Agree. Let's go there now."

38

They made their way back downtown to casino world. Parking in the police officers' lot, Harley found her PD sign in her glove compartment and placed it on her dash to avoid being towed while they were inside.

Ten minutes later, they were meeting with Lieutenant Joseph S. Carroll, a bespectacled man of fifty with long white sideburns and close-cropped white hair. He was quick to smile and gave his full attention to the two LAPD detectives once they had a seat in his office.

"How can I help?"

Harley recited the particulars of the case, her relationship to Wendy Miller, and her need for LVPD intervention in locating Wendy and placing her on hold for extradition.

"We can do that. Just let me get some particulars."

He then took Wendy's name, age, occupation, marital status,

priors, and all the rest that makes a police agency able to locate and confirm someone. While the information was exchanged, she had to remind him that her info was old and for all she knew her daughter's particulars might've changed dramatically. But she did the best she could anyway.

"What's the underlying charge out of LA?"

"Homicide." Harley then explained the case. Lieutenant Carroll was patient and sympathetic.

Paperwork followed, and signatures. Robert Ray's name was run for warrants and came back empty. There was no license plate or registration of any vehicle in his name, either. It was speculated that he'd probably borrowed the truck the apartment manager saw him loading up. Or maybe purchased without a title transfer —typical on $500 vehicle transfers, said Lieutenant Carroll, and paperwork isn't bothered with.

The warrant was issued that afternoon with the particulars including description and vitals.

Before they left, CV had one last bit of business.

"Lieutenant," said CV, "We're dealing with Reuben Ordañez out of Juarez."

"Sure, good old Reuben. He has people here. They're moving high value narcotics in my town. Heroin and cocaine. And the marijuana is something else again. Every call girl shows up at the hotel with pot in her garter belt or bra. It's easily the most consumed drug in Las Vegas. Which is fine—I have a look-the-other-way policy on pot for personal use. Large quantities for sale, no, we'll bust your ass for that. But casual users, not interested. The man you're looking for in Las Vegas is Raul Castro. He's directly connected to Reuben Ordañez. The drugs come into my town by mule and get delivered to Castro. All local distribution is then made by him. If narcotics come to town, they invariably pass through Castro's hands. He's everywhere. If you're looking to talk to him, try Shady Noriega's Cantina off Washington. It's got a sign of a Mexican in a sombrero pulling a donkey with a rope. Neon sign. Pretty damn cute."

"Raul Castro. Thanks," said CV. "He's my next stop."

"Can I ask what you're going to tell Raul?" Carroll asked.

"I want him to get a message to Reuben Ordañez."

"I'm sure he can do that. They talk every day."

"You've got a tap on him?"

Carroll tossed a look left and right as an actor would. "On the hush-hush. The feds want his ass. If you've got a message for him to carry, I strongly suggest you don't dilly-dally. He's coming close to the end of his days in Nevada. Maybe in the United States."

"Thanks for the tip," CV said. "That helps a lot."

"Good luck with the punk. Watch out for a razor. He doesn't mind cutting."

CV lifted the hem of his shirt. The .357 magnum was displayed. "I win."

Everyone laughed. It was a good moment for Harley. She felt a weight lifted from her shoulders as her burden became shared. Especially she was grateful for CV in her life and in Las Vegas just then. He was forever the best friend she'd always needed.

Harley made a mental note to call Marcia that night. Marcia was tasked with interviewing Mickey Loden's daughter on the off chance she knew something or had recognized something about her kidnappers that maybe the FBI had missed. Not likely, but it never hurt to ask.

39

Marcia returned to the murder book to see what they had on Mickey Loden's daughter, Dinah Loden. She learned Dinah had been divorced just six months after a two-year ride in a driverless locomotive with a crazy man named Merlin O'Meara. Evidently, the guy was a made man in the New York Irish Mafia who'd come west to run his real estate scams in Southern California. His most recent effort was the purchase and sale of twenty-five homes in a small subdivision in the Valley. Except...O'Meara didn't own the homes he was taking earnest money on. No one who paid him got anything except a worthless contract and a disconnected phone number after the one weekend open house with half-price homes for sale. O'Meara was gone. Dinah Loden wasn't so lucky, because it was her bank account O'Meara used to wash the earnest money checks. One week after the weekend blowout and the checks had cleared, O'Meara had cleared, too, with all the money in a night depository bag beneath the seat of his Chevy pickup. Gone, long gone, O'Meara was never heard from again. But Dinah's bank account, where all the checks were cleared, was easily traceable by the police when complaints got filed by the defrauded home buyers. Dinah was going down as an accomplice. But Mickey, her father, stepped in and refunded all earnest money payments. He then, it was whispered, put out a contract on O'Meara.

Marcia also learned that Mickey Loden didn't scare easily. When his own capo remarked to him that O'Meara was a made man and a contract on his life was saber-rattling maybe he'd best avoid, Mickey told his capo no, he didn't care if every drunk mick in Tinsel town came after him, he was the real Mickey and he was ready to fight back. As it turned out, O'Meara had missed a switch-back down by Ocean Beach, went off the cliff, and died in a fiery crash. "See what I mean?" Mickey told his capo. "No good comes from fucking the real Mick."

Marcia considered these things as she prepared to pay a visit on Mickey's daughter, Dinah. She wanted to learn about the father through the daughter.

She called and made an appointment with Dinah. She was surprised at how easily that was done.

They met in Francisco's Grill, south of Calabasas. It was Dinah's choice to meet there. She wanted to be away from Mickey; he couldn't find out she was talking to the police. These are the things she told Marcia when they sat down and ordered drinks.

At Francisco's, Dinah was wearing light gray slacks and a yellow shirt with a scarf. The scarf normally hung around her neck. When she arrived at the meeting, the scarf was around her head to keep her hair from blowing. She was driving her Corvette with the top down and the Valley winds were wicked.

Marcia watched as Dinah took two large swallows of her martini. Definitely not a sipper, Marcia noted. She reached inside her purse and took out her notepad and pen. "I'm just going to write

---

down a few things," she explained. She wrote on the top of the page: *Dinah Loden, 1430.* She always wrote down the time an interview began.

"So, Dinah, thank you so much for agreeing to speak to me."

"Of course. I support the police. Especially since I was kidnapped."

"Yes, how did that happen?"

"I was at Daddy's Mobil station, getting a fill. A man came over to the driver's door and told me I was pretty enough to be in pictures. He told me he was a producer and he noticed me as soon as I pulled in. He asked me to get out and stand up so he could see how tall I was. So, I did. When I was out, he grabbed me and threw me in a car being driven by a Mexican. The man pushed me down in the back seat and sat on me. The car squealed its tires and off we went. They pulled off just up the road and put a bank bag over my head. Then we drove for what seemed like two hours. We stopped and they took me inside someplace with three steps down. I still don't know where that was. They kept me there for a week. Then they took me back to Hollywood Boulevard and let me go at the first stoplight."

"Did they hurt you in any way?"

"Well, I was hungry the whole time. Bastards only gave me Fritos and pop. I never want to see another Frito."

"How come they let you go?"

"My daddy says he paid them two million dollars. That's why. Otherwise, he says they would've killed me."

"Has anyone figured out who they were?" Marcia asked.

"The FBI will find that out. They haven't yet."

"So, it sounds like your father loves you very much."

"It's mutual. I love him very much."

"Your father is a very successful real estate man."

"He builds plenty of houses. We're so proud of him."

"How did he get his start? I mean, doesn't it take a lot of money to build houses?"

Dinah gave it some thought. "He worked and saved for years. My daddy is very smart about saving money."

"Do you know the names of any of the men he doesn't do business with?"

"He never has them over. I might hear a name or two, but no last names."

"It's remarkable your father is so lucky with selling houses. Does he have partners?" asked Marcia.

"He wouldn't ever tell someone like me. You're need-to-know with daddy and I don't need to know."

"What can you tell me about his banking habits? Where does he keep his money?"

"I know it's downtown somewhere. He goes there about every day."

"Do you know the name of his bank?"

"No, I wouldn't need to know that."

"Does he have an accountant?"

"You know, he must. Daddy is very busy."

"Do you know her name?" asked Marcia.

"I don't even know it's a her. It might be a he." This was said with a lingering giggle as she'd just eaten the onion in the bottom of her glass. Marcia still hadn't touched her beer.

"Can you tell me what you know about the FBI and your daddy?"

"I'm sure I cannot."

"The FBI saved you?"

"Not at all. Daddy's money saved me."

THE VISIT ENDED POORLY. Dinah was caustic and sarcastic and said the FBI was a bunch of dolts. They hadn't caught her kidnappers and she was thinking of suing them.

She said Marcia should talk to her father and said to follow her to a new subdivision her father was building. Marcia saw it as a great opportunity. Maybe the old man would slip-up—*wouldn't that please Harley if Marcia scored some major points?*

Dinah drove her Corvette while Marcia followed in her Ford. It was just starting to get dark, but Marcia thought nothing of it because the new subdivision already had its streetlights burning and many homes were already occupied and lit up. They came to the end of a long street of half-finished houses when Dinah suddenly whipped to the shoulder and parked. The women got out, Marcia expecting to meet with Mickey. Instead, two men came out of the last house. One was tall and wore khaki pants and a khaki shirt and a brown cap that said "CAT" on it. The other was a stout man with a heavy five o'clock shadow. He was wearing a natty black suit and Marcia could've sworn she saw the outline of a gun inside the breast of the jacket.

Alarmed and finding herself suddenly outnumbered, Marcia tried to sound streetwise and tough. "Where's papa bear? You said I should chat with papa bear."

Without a word, Dinah climbed back into her Corvette and sped away. Marcia made a move toward her own vehicle which was when the stout man came up and in one motion placed the muzzle of a gun against the side of her head. "You still need to meet papa. Now I'm going to reach inside your jacket and remove your gun. No sudden moves or you will startle me, and I will shoot you."

With that, she was disarmed. They marched her to her unmarked car. Her cuffs were removed from her belt and placed around her wrists in back. Then she was pushed down onto the backseat and told to lie very still. She wasn't going quietly. She struggled, turned over and kicked at the man in the suit. He raised her gun and struck her across the face with it. "Don't make me mad," he said. Her mouth bled and her nose, gushing blood, felt broken. He flipped her back over, face-down.

By now, the sun was setting. Marcia's heart was pounding as she realized she'd been had. There had been an appointment to talk to Dinah, yes, but Dinah had never meant to give a real statement. Innocent or guilty Dinah was not going to spend a helpful minute with a law enforcement officer. Now she was long gone, and Marcia was caught by her own handcuffs.

The man wearing khaki went over to a long flatbed truck on which was chained down a Wain-Roy backhoe. He fired up the flatbed rig and gave a thumbs up to the thug, who climbed inside Marcia's unmarked car and started it up.

Then they were moving. Bouncing along a rough road, she began to panic.

Her hands were bound behind her with her own handcuffs. She was face-down and struggling to breathe. Fear clawed at her lungs, threatening to drop her into an unconscious and defenseless state. She turned her face to the side and gulped in a lungful of air. Her mouth was bleeding where she'd been struck in the face with her own pistol. Blood, she tasted blood and every few breaths blew a giant blood bubble from her swollen lips. As they bounced along the dirt road, the gunman, reached over the backseat from the driver's seat. He would rest his hand on her buttocks and give a little squeeze every few seconds. It sickened her, the violation, and she knew what it meant to be overwhelmed with abject hatred for another human being. Had she been in a reverse position she wouldn't have hesitated to use her gun on him. Slowly, she realized he was doing it to just to frighten her and make her miserable and it was working. Was that it, then? Was all this being done just to instill a terrible fear inside of her? She prayed that was the case. She sent a mental message to Harley, telling her she was sorry she'd come without her.

Then her vehicle rocked to a stop. It was pitch black in the Ford's interior save for a faint glow from the dash. Her eyes had adjusted to the dark and she was aware of a dark form moving outside. Then she felt the summer heat when her driver climbed out. He stepped back to the rear door, swung it open and grabbed her by the upper body and ripped her up off the seat and into the night. He stood her up—such as it was, because she was swaying and fighting to keep her balance in the silt around her ankles. Her blouse was torn from the tussle and two fingernails on her right hand ripped away. She felt the pain, but it was almost a welcome relief from the horror she felt in her gut. Something, some little voice, said quietly in her mind, *there's no coming back from this.*

A flashlight was flipped on. They were standing next to a corn-field. She was pushed from behind and made to follow the heavy machine operator she recognized from the worksite. He had been the one driving the flatbed. She wondered where the others were, the laborers who'd been pouring concrete and sodding yards at the subdivision. Had they followed in their own vehicles? Would any of them decide the night was not for them and go for help?

Was there any chance of that? She clung to it, hoping against hope that just one of them had an attack of conscience and went for the sheriff. It would only take one.

On and on into the cornfield they marched. The flatbed driver would raise his arms in front to cut a path through the corn stalks then let them snap back against her as they went. With her hands caught behind, there was a constant whipping across her face and chest as she tried to keep up. Several times she stumbled and fell, only to have the stout one seize her by the back of her belt and pull her to her feet. Then he'd give a swat across her buttocks, telling her again and again that she belonged to him now, that she was his to do with as he pleased.

Maybe five minutes had passed when they came to a stop. At last. The lead man produced a cigarette out of nowhere and lit up. He tried to hold it up to Marcia's lips for a puff. "Last chance?" he asked. "One puff?" She jerked her head away and spat at him. Her spittle sprayed his chest. He looked down and smiled. "You think of that in a few minutes. You remember that."

"All right," said the second man. "You're a cop and I hate cops, but I have a streak of fairness. So, here's what's gonna happen. Instead of shooting you right here and raping your dead body, I'm going to turn you loose and count to ten. That's right. I'm a fair man and I'm giving you a full ten second head start. If you make it to the edge of the field and out the other side, we take you back to your car and you drive yourself back to LA. You win fair and square and we face the music for roughing up a cop. But if you lose, if I catch you before you get to a service road, then you'd best start praying because you're one minute away from meeting the Lord. You like to meet the Lord, lady? Are you ready for that?"

"I'm—no. I don't," was all she managed to mumble. "But I'm a fast runner. Just be fair is all."

"Listen to her, Damien! A cop wants fair!"

"Fair? The lady cop wants fair, Mr. Barkley?" Damien's eyes were dancing with fire. He was elated to be playing the chase game. He knew how it ended. Only Marcia didn't know how it ended; or maybe she did but she was pretending. Maybe she was just pretending.

"All right," Barkley said quietly, "Ima count to ten then I'm coming. So, you run, starting now!"

Marcia realized the best path was the one they had just made through the corn. She turned completely around and charged off through the broken stalks, jumping and dodging, jumping and jittering side to side and off at an angle then crossing again and always running as far as her legs would move. She'd been a great runner in the eighth grade. Beat everyone, including the boys. So, she had help now. The main difficulty that night, though, was the handcuffs. They made breaking a new path all but impossible except by plunging headfirst into the stalks and clearing the way with her head and her shoulders.

As she ran, she listened. She heard a heavy machine cough and start up from the direction of the flatbed truck. She imagined the thug would come up behind her with a flashlight, so light would be her first warning. Or would it? Maybe he'd just be following her sound. Maybe her first warning would be when he caught her, flung her to the ground, and raped her. She knew that's where it was headed, ultimately. She knew he was going to sexually assault her before it was all done. Dead or alive, it didn't matter to that man. She knew the type. *God help me,* she prayed.

In a sudden burst of hope, she broke out of the cornfield and stumbled upon the bank of an irrigation canal. Long aluminum pipes, with bends like crookneck squash, lay half in the water and half in the cornfield. She knew they were irrigation pipes that sucked water from the canal and set it loose on the cornfield. She lay down across one of the pipes, breathless and fighting to remain conscious from fatigue and the fear shutting down her body. She was lying there, on her side, thanking God she had won, when Barkley walked out of the field.

"Good for you," he said, and he began clapping. "You won, Marcia. You won!"

"I won," she smiled. "Please take me to my car."

"Not just yet. First, we have to go back and see Damien's prize. Do you want to see what Damien has?"

"No, I don't. I want to go home and take a bath."

"Hey, I'm right there with you. Imagine, you and me, bathtub, washing my back and touching my cock. Do you like that?"

"No. I want to go home alone. Please, I won."

He approached and grabbed her by the handcuffs and bodily lifted her to her feet. "Naw, let's go see what the prize is from Damien."

He began pushing her ahead in the corn, back in the exact direction as before. She stumbled, she fell several times as she was now exhausted. It took a good ten minutes of falling, resting, then staggering forward again. In the meantime, she could hear the sound of heavy equipment in the cornfield. But why heavy equipment?

The backhoe in corn? Her brain wouldn't follow the thought. Couldn't follow the thought.

Damien was sitting atop the backhoe when they made it back to the center of the field. He was working the huge bucket, digging a long, deep hole right there in the middle of the cornfield, doing his digging like it was only natural and holes like this were common.

Then he climbed down.

"Now look in," said Damien.

Barkley pushed her from behind. She staggered and slipped up to the hole.

"Know what we do to cops out here?"

She tried to form the words, tried to beg, but words wouldn't form. Then she realized. She was too frightened even to speak. Even begging was out of reach.

"Now, do we push you in the hole or do you climb in?"

"No—no—no—"

She felt a powerful shove from behind and she plunged headfirst into the hole. Now the ground was two feet above her head. She struggled to her feet. She leaned back against one wall, placed her feet against the other wall, and tried to walk her way up the side. She struggled at this for a minute or more, while the two men, lost in the dark night above, talked and smoked.

Finally, Barkley said, "I'm hungry. Let's go get a steak."

She heard the backhoe's chugging accelerate and saw the huge shovel overhead almost at the same instant she felt the first ton of damp earth hammer down on her from above. The first load knocked her off her feet and she was lying on her side, crying. She imagined the earthworms against her skin, the grubworms with their claw feet, and she vomited. Gasping for air, she begged at last. "Please. I'll do anything."

But the answer was another load of thundering dirt, which covered her body. Only her face was free. Then her shoulders broke through as she struggled for air. The next load covered even that.

Her last thought was of her mother, whom she desperately prayed to see again.

"Mama," she said to the dirt. "Mama come get me. It hurts."

40

They arrived at Clark County General Hospital just before eight o'clock the next morning. It had been a long night for CV and Harley. They had slept together, tried to make love but failed because Harley was still with Wendy in her mind, then tossed and turned until four a.m. when they made coffee and watched the sunrise over Frenchman Mountain east of Las Vegas.

"People call it Sunrise Mountain but it's really Frenchman Mountain," Harley said. The knowledge had been acquired on a prior visit with Bobby just after the war in 1947. They were celebrating their wedding anniversary with a free weekend hotel room at the Grand Hotel and Casino.

"We'll stick to Frenchman. It's more romantic," said CV, who knew Harley hardly gave a whit for romantic. She was a down-to-earth pragmatist, in his view, and he celebrated that, for he'd found someone who understood why he took a job earning half of what a good Allstate Insurance agent could make. Not only understood, she was right there with him doing the exact same job.

After showering—separately—they dressed and went downstairs for the breakfast buffet. Harley said she was too anxious to eat but that didn't stop CV from downing a plate of scrambled eggs and Canadian bacon. After their second cup of coffee, Harley signed the ticket and they were off to the hospital.

First, they went to records. The sleepy-eyed clerk, a beautiful young Mexican woman whose nameplate read *Sonia*, was very capable.

"Of course," she said after they'd badged her. "Let me pull that chart. Please remain here."

She returned a minute later with a chart labeled Wendy Miller. She opened to the first page and checked down the account ledger. "Says here she owes $155.67 for the birth of her child. Charges include labor and delivery room, Pitocin and pain killer, and nursing and hospital charges. Doctor would've charged separately."

"Who was the doctor?"

"Russell Hamm. He practiced OB-GYN in Las Vegas until recently, when he died. I see his charts all the time for this and that. Medical records never go away, you know. Someone, somewhere's always wanting something or other."

"I can imagine," Harley agreed. "Can you tell from the file what Wendy's address was?"

"Sure, 518 N. Apache. That's way out. Probably a trailer, unless I miss my guess. Now it's grown up more. Might not even still be there."

"Is there a unit number?"

"Nope, just the address."

"All right. Well, let me write you a check for her bill."

"Please, you'll need to take it to the cashier for that."

"All right, then, thank you, Sonia."

"Yes, ma'am. Always ready to help in these cases. We get detectives from all over. Las Vegas is very popular with killers and card sharks."

"Yes, thank you for your time."

"Goodbye."

Ten minutes later, they were on Apache Boulevard, headed north. The numbers kept climbing, one small wood frame home after another until, finally, they reached what should have been 518 N. Apache. But it wasn't there. Only a hole in the ground and a concrete foundation running partway around. The home itself— gone. Harley went up to the end of the block and drove back at low speed. She was searching addresses on the opposite side, but, of course, they were all odd numbers. It was true, then, the home where Wendy had once lived was gone.

"Son of a bitch," growled Harley.

"Afraid so."

"Now what?"

"Now we go find Raul Castro, then hightail it for LA in case Wendy heads back."

"You think?"

"Stands to reason. It's her home. We always go home when we're scared. Criminals on the lam are usually found within three miles of the house where they grew up. Did I teach you nothing, Harley?"

She laughed. "You probably covered it. I was OTL that day, apparently."

THEY FOUND Shady Noriega's Cantina off Washington just before noon. When they walked inside, they waited at the door for their eyes to adjust. Ray-Bans came off and were pocketed. Then they moved up to the bar, where CV ordered a tap beer and Harley a cup of coffee. At the far end of the bar, between the Schlitz and the Old Milwaukee signs, hung a black and white TV. At the strike of twelve, the TV flipped over to the news. The detectives, waiting to catch the bartender alone so they could ask about Raul Castro, watched the news.

The lead story on Channel 3 was the story of a tri-state manhunt. A manhunt in California, Arizona, and Nevada. A manhunt for an LAPD detective missing since about noon yesterday. Twenty-four hours they'd been looking for her. *Her.*

Harley's ears twitched as she focused totally on the TV screen. "Oh my God," she breathed the words, "give us a name."

"The detective is identified as Marcia Meriwether of Santa Monica, California."

Then came the official file photo and Harley dropped her cup of coffee onto its saucer. It rattled once, twice, then the story continued. The reporter had Marcia investigating a kidnapping in the San Fernando Valley, just outside Calabasas. The story had her meeting with a prominent Valley developer named Mickey Loden.

CV started, "Did yo—"

"Quiet!" she snapped. "We're leaving. Go out and get in the car, we're leaving now."

They stopped for suitcases and a five-minute checkout.

For the next four hours, while Harley drove, CV spun the radio dial for more news. At one point, just beyond the state line, they pulled into a gas station, filled up and Harley called Lieutenant Chall. He confirmed the TV story and immediately told Harley how sorry he was but not to worry, they had every cop on the force out on the streets and in the Valley, looking.

Harley attached the vehicle's red light to the rooftop and kicked it up to eighty-five. They maintained that speed, and greater, from that point all the way into the LA outskirts, where she had to slow. They stopped for no red lights all the way. She screeched to a stop in the police vehicles lot, and then broke into a run for the restricted entrance.

The detectives' bureau was up a flight of stairs, and she sprinted down the hall to Chall's office. His room was filled with suits and uniforms and he was manning two phones at once. He motioned Harley to come on inside. One of the detectives got up and let her sit right in front of Chall. The lieutenant finally hung up the phone and reached across the desk and grasped Harley's hands. "We're doing everything we can. I promise."

"FBI?"

"On it."

"Everyone on the street?"

"Done."

"What can I do?"

"Man your desk. Clear your messages. Then you and—you came in with CV. You're together?" He meant it in at least two ways.

"Yes, we're together."

"You can join the troops out at Loden's place. Be useful. Use your heads. Don't start trouble. Think. Now go on and go."

There was no stopping to clear messages.

Thirty minutes later they were entering the Valley and headed for Calabasas.

Loden's office at the model homes was five miles away.

41

Barkley pulled the plastic bag out of the trunk of his Buick and handed it to Damien.

"What do we have here? Hands and jaws? Upper and lower? Good enough."

Damien pulled the bloody body parts out of the plastic bag and began following behind the cement truck as it laid down a ribbon of concrete in the wooden forms. They had constructed a new home's foundation out of the forms and the concrete would be molded to fit inside the forms. He plunked the severed hands down below the surface of the concrete two yards apart until they disappeared, and then the upper and lower jaws containing the woman's teeth. "Tidy Friday, that's what today is."

"No fingerprints, no teeth."

"Just like that—" he snapped his fingers "no more detective. Just a body. How was she?"

Barkley smiled. "They always manage to work their head a couple inches through the dirt like they're flying off to heaven."

"You'd try to fly too, if you were dying under five tons of dirt, Barks."

"So, would you."

42

The next morning, after locating nothing useful the afternoon and evening before, Harley and CV were called into Lieutenant Chall's office. They sat in the two visitors' chairs, quiet and depressed. They'd been unable to locate Mickey Loden. Telephone messages went unreturned. No one at his job sites seemed to know who he was. His model home office was busy, but no one could say where he was. Chall looked them over and knew Hollywood Division had a skyrocketing morale problem. It was only natural.

"Look," he began with the two detectives, "we've suffered a huge loss. Harley, you've suffered the worst. CV, you're her partner from before. I'm throwing you two back together."

The detectives shifted in their chairs. "You're making us partners?" asked Harley.

"Smart move, LT," said CV. "Especially now, with the manhunt. We'll be good together."

"I know that. I want you two back in the Valley. I want you up Loden's ass and out the other end."

"No one knows where he is, yada yada yada," said Harley. "Green-light me and I'll start beating it out of people."

"Nobody knows, bullshit they don't. They don't because he knows what happened to Marcia and, by God, I need someone who's going to get it out of him. I've got Chief Parker and the mayor up my ass for an arrest. We can't lose Sullivan and Black and now lose Marcia, too."

"Wait," Harley said, coming up out of her chair. "I'm not ready to go there. I don't think she's dead. She can't be."

"Agree. Use all your wits to get Loden to tell us. It's open season, detectives. But I never told you that, get me?"

"Got you."

"Yes."

"I'd start with his kid. Dinah, is it? She's our kidnap victim, which places her on the front line of dad's payback. She's going to know what he did and maybe Marcia found out. She was paying a call on her, so I'm certain Dinah saw her last. Who knows, orders from the old man? I'm thinking Marcia had put together two-and-two and had a case. Now do me one better, find out what she found out and bring me back someone's head on a platter. Don't forget, I need this. So does Marcia, so does Hollywood Division."

JUST NORTH OF CALABASAS, a wrecking yard called Jim's Last Stop was running an LAPD unmarked vehicle through the crusher. It was black with black sidewalls and was a new model Ford. But it had seen its last pursuit, as the crusher made it into a heap of twisted metal the size of a mattress. Now it was ready for the meltdown.

The last vehicle Marcia Meriwether had driven.

43

Harley and CV spent an hour in the county clerk's office, poring over plat books and grantor-grantee indices. They were looking for a street address for Mickey Loden, as it was time to stakeout. Several housing development transfers were traced from farmer or rancher to Loden Enterprises, Inc., the name of the company that turned grazing lands into subdivisions. Those transfers were of no interest. But every now and then they found one from some individual to Mickey and Myra Loden, husband and wife, as joint tenants with right of survivorship—which meant that, where the conveyance contained improvements, they were looking at a residence. They found two such transfers, compared dates, and decided the one off 1109 Sorrel Lane, Calabasas must be his home. Then they were off.

One hour later they stopped at an EZ-In convenience store and loaded up on soda pop, and snacks—items required for a stakeout. They also bought a box of Kleenex—sometimes stakeouts required a urination break. All supplies set in, the detectives continued driving until they found Sorrel Lane. It was a simple matter, then, to find 1109.

It was an estate done in the French Provincial style, with all the right turrets and stonework, a rolling, manicured lawn, and two Cadillacs parked on the circular drive—lookouts, the detectives guessed. They breezed past the home and continued driving until they topped a hill a half mile away. Then they disappeared over the hill, turned around, and crept back to the crest of the hill and stopped. Binoculars were uncased and the watch began.

"Let me talk to her first," Harley said of Dinah. "I've got a very curious energy building up for that."

"Bullshit. You mean you're itching to slap the shit out of her."

"That's putting it...mildly."

Two Coca Cola bottles were uncapped with the opener kept in the glove compartment. They shared a bag of Fritos. A half hour into the stakeout, no vehicles had come or gone.

"How do we know which car would be Dinah?" CV asked. "She could be driving anything, and we wouldn't know. Or else we follow and turns out we're following the wrong person."

"Nope. These people have money. I'll know her car when I see it."

Another half hour. CV's head was tilted back, his eyes were closed, and he was snoring softly. It was okay; they had agreed he would catnap first. Harley kept the binoculars nearby, scanning the interiors of other cars traversing Sorrel Lane. But still, so far, no car had come or gone from the house.

At 3:30 in the afternoon, CV came awake with a startle. "What's that?" he gasped.

"Nothing. Go back to sleep."

"No, I heard something. I hear a big Chevy engine."

"You're dreaming."

"You don't know my hearing."

Sure enough, the garage door was open, and a shiny yellow Corvette pulled out onto the driveway. Harley quickly scanned the car with her glasses. She just could make out the form of the driver. Female.

Harley started her own unit. CV sat up and glassed the vehicle for himself. "Is she about twenty-five, give or take, blonde hair?"

"That's what the murder book shows. Sullivan got the picture from Spielman's head shots. Looks kind of like Lana Turner with blonde hair?"

"Too far to say which actress she resembles. But I think we've got our gal. I vote we follow."

"I vote we follow, too."

Soon, the Corvette rolled along the circular drive very slowly, came up to Sorrel, and nosed its way into a slow right turn. Harley released the clutch and began following, keeping a good half mile distance out on the empty country road. They followed her to the junction of 101, where she turned toward Los Angeles.

Staying two cars back proved easy enough. Going into the city was much faster than driving out had been. They were on Sunset Boulevard on the Sunset Strip when she pulled into valet parking at the Mocambo. She tossed her keys to the attendant and headed inside the nightclub. CV and Harley were close behind.

The club's Latin American theme featured walls lined with glass cages holding cockatoos, macaws, seagulls, and parrots. A big band was playing a sensual mambo and the dance floor was packed.

CV badged the maître d and told him they wanted a table as close as possible to the blonde who just came in.

"You mean Miss Loden?" asked the man in black tie.

"We do mean her. Who's she meeting?"

"She comes here two or three times a week and listens to the music. Sometimes she'll leave with an actor or musician, usually, though, she comes alone and leaves alone."

Just then, the band stopped playing, the dance floor cleared, and Ella Fitzgerald stepped out from a flat and took the microphone. She opened with an original song, "A-Tisket, A-Tasket," and the crowd immediately began clapping. Then everyone remained rapt and silent while she performed. During this time, the maître d had managed to seat the detectives two tables north of Dinah Loden. She was sitting alone, smoking a cigarette with red lipstick on the business end. She nervously turned the pack over and over in her left hand while sipping her drink with her right. Then she studied her watch. Harley checked hers. It was 8:55 p.m.

THE NEXT HOUR passed in this fashion. The detectives were ordering straight Cokes. Dinah Loden ordered another drink with an umbrella, pulled the cherry out and nibbled it, then checked her teeth in her compact. She reapplied her lipstick. At one point, she left her things on the table and worked her way around to the powder room. Harley followed, always keeping two people between. She waited outside the powder room, pretending to be waiting for one of the wall phones.

She returned to her table before Dinah, knowing that her drink and cigarettes and lighter were still waiting. Sure enough, five minutes later, here she came, beaming and smiling at the crowd, her newly-applied fire engine red lipstick lighting up her part of the club.

Just after ten, a new party arrived. The men, three of them, were wearing capes and black tie, the women were in gold lame and diamonds and all were happy, trilling, pushing and shoving amongst themselves and insisting they had a table at the front for "Ella's" eleven o'clock show. Harley recognized two of the men, crooners known to be living the party life every night when they weren't holding forth in Las Vegas and New York. She thought one of the women was Marilyn Monroe but the hair wasn't platinum blonde so she couldn't confirm.

Two tables were pushed together, one of the men spun around and whispered something to Dinah, she turned her chair around and joined their party. Harley's heart fell: they evidently wouldn't be leaving the Mocambo any time soon.

By midnight, the party was destined to move on. Dinah and her friends stepped out to the valets, had their cars rounded up, and set off for the Beverly Hills Hotel with Harley and CV several cars behind Dinah's yellow 'Vette. Harley followed Dinah and the others to the rear entrance of the hotel. They parked and headed for Bungalow 4, widely known by the cops to be the bungalow favored by Howard Hughes, a man of distinct habits. As Harley parked at the far end of the lot, CV said, "Private party. We might be in for a very long night. Why don't you head into the Polo Lounge, see who turns up there, and I'll stay here and watch the back."

"Good enough," Harley said. "I need to use the powder room again anyway."

She headed inside, pulling her jacket down as she tried to guarantee there would be no print-through by her holstered gun. The maître d offered to seat her, but Harley opted for the bar instead. He gave her a funny look—a woman alone arriving after midnight would usually mean a hooker looking for a late-night roll. But Harley didn't fit the profile and the bartenders were quick to serve her a Coke with a stirrer.

Harley watched the door that connected the Lounge to the hotel proper. So far, none of Dinah's party had appeared, but she was willing to wait on the off-chance Dinah herself breezed in.

By one o'clock in the morning, Harley was satisfied Dinah was ensconced in Bungalow 4, probably suitably sauced and well on her way to bed with one of the gentlemen. Harley paid her tab and left the same way she had arrived.

Outside again, in the rear lot, a security officer gave her the side eye when she strolled by, mistaking her yet again for an off-the-meter prostitute. She tossed her head and made her way to the end of the hotel until she was sure she wasn't being watched, then hurried back around the far corner, entering her vehicle with the dome light turned off.

CV was wide awake and drumming his fingers on the arm rest.

"Anything?"

"Nothing. You?"

"Somebody left in the Lincoln. But her 'Vette is still parked, and she hasn't left in another car."

"Good, then. What do you say we go busting in and arrest everyone for deviant sexual behavior?" Harley joked.

"I'd say you and I are guilty of the same thing. Then we'd be hypocrites and I hate hypocrites."

"I know. So do I."

"Any more thoughts about Wendy?"

Harley lit a Camel and cracked her window. She exhaled through the opening and lay her head back against the seat. "Not really. I'm ninety-nine percent sure she's here somewhere. Let's take that up next when we finish off the Lodens."

"Assuming the Lodens don't crack the case for us."

"I know. Assuming."

Then it was quiet for ten minutes.

Harley finally spoke again. "Poor Marcia."

"I know. Wonder where they got her stashed?"

"I'm guessing the ocean. I'm sure her car's been mashed by now."

"Sure that."

"You know what I'd like to do?"

"What's that?"

"I'd like to go inside Bungalow 4, stick my Smith down her throat, and solve Marcia's case just like that. Whatta you think?"

"I think we do that. Except we grab her on the way home, not in front of Hollywood's Rat Pack."

"Agreed. I'm seriously expecting useful info from this chick. I'll be damned if she's going to talk her way out of this one."

"Seriously agree. LT said to do whatever it takes to find Marcia."

Just then, the door to Bungalow 4 opened, and Dinah Loden stepped out.

She braced her hand on the fender of her Corvette and half-supported herself along the side of the car as she made her way to the driver's door. Sticking the key into the lock proved problematic, Harley witnessed through her binoculars, but eventually she found the hole. She half-fell into the driver's seat and soon the lights came on.

"I hear that Chevy engine from way down here," CV said matter-of-factly. "This chick is lit up like a Christmas tree. We're gonna bust her ass before she gets out on Sunset and kills someone."

Harley kicked the Ford into gear and roared up behind the Corvette. She hit her red lights and sounded the siren once. Up ahead, the Corvette's taillights flared and remained lighted. The driver rolled down the window and motioned the police car to pull on past.

"Great," said Harley. "Why don't you have a talk?"

CV jumped from the passenger's seat and approached the Corvette. He immediately leaned inside, turned the keys and killed the engine. "Ma'am, please exit your vehicle."

Her eyes wide, she struggled to climb out of the car. She wobbled to her feet and then wobbled in place.

She made guns of her fingers and did a quick draw on CV: "Got me!" she cried. "Stick 'em up!"

CV asked her to turn around, which she did. He asked her to put her hands behind her back, which she struggled with. Finally, he reached around, grasped both of her hands, and pulled them behind, where he met them with his cuffs. Handcuffed and wobbling, CV held her arm and walked her to the police vehicle.

He opened the passenger-side rear door and placed her inside. The doors would remain locked as they were inoperable from the inside.

Harley turned off her red lights and pulled around the Corvette. It was parked in such a way that it was almost completely off to the side of the connecting lane. Her driving had definitely had her off-course. It would be left there until a black and white unit could come and take photographs.

Harley called for that unit, gave her instructions, and turned right on Hollywood Boulevard to head up to Wilcox. Ten minutes later, they were turning left and heading up to Hollywood Station. It was the detectives' intent to treat her arrest as a common DWI traffic stop. What the unsuspecting arrestee didn't know, however, was that she was about to be subjected to the third degree.

THIRTY MINUTES LATER, she was slouched on a chair in the inter-view room, a cup of steaming black coffee before her, and a bucket to her side. She had vomited twice but was willing to talk about anything. She had given the detectives the names of Damien Pultec and Albert Barkley, "Da'mun and Al."

"What happened when you got to Damien's worksite?"

"Mar-sha followed me. She was looking for something."

"What was she looking for?"

"I dunno."

"What happened at the worksite?"

"Don' know. I just left her there. Da'mun an' Al took her away, I guess. But she was with Da'mun."

"That's the last you saw of her."

"Yep."

"And when was this?"

"I dunno."

"Why did you take her to Damien?"

"Becosh he knew what to do with her. Mickey hates cops. I don't much like 'em either. 'Cept you're good-looking. Are you married?"

"Why does Mickey hate cops?"

"I got kidnapped and he had to pay lots of money. It made him mad."

"Why mad?"

"Becosh you—" jabbing her finger at CV— "you couldn't find me, and daddy paid lots of money to get me back. Now he hates cops. Me, I don't care one way or another."

"Well, isn't that tender," said CV.

"It's all on the machine," Harley said, referring to the tape recorder and the table-top microphone.

Harley leaned across the linoleum-topped table and seized Dinah's lower jaw in her hand. "Listen to me, Miss Stupid. Where the fuck is Marcia? I've asked you a hundred times and you keep giving me that dumb blonde look. That isn't cutting it. I want to know what those fucks did with her."

"Probably sent her home. I dunno. Nobody tells me anything."

"Oh, fuck," Harley groaned. "Dinah, where does Damien live?"

"In a trailer at the Merryland Subdivision. He takes care of daddy's equipment. He's got a gun for robbers."

"How do you know he's got a gun?"

"He showed me. Itsh a rifle."

"You mean a shotgun?"

"I dunno."

"Who lives with him in the trailer?"

"Mr. Barkley lives there. I think they're engaged." This, with appropriate giggles and unintelligible additional comments that only a drunk would appreciate.

"All right, CV. Let's get a jailer in here and deposit her ass in the drunk tank. Unfortunately, we won't be around when she sleeps it off and comes to."

"We're going to the job site."

"Yes, we are. We hit the trailer in the dark before those two know we're coming. Little Miss Priss here is going to warn them as soon as they cut her loose tomorrow at court."

44

At four a.m., the trailer was completely dark. It was a moonless night in the country with a low cloud cover, so ambient light and starlight were non-existent. "Perfect night for a raid," Harley whispered to CV when they parked and exited their car 300 yards away.

He didn't respond. Before leaving Hollywood Station, CV had checked out a Remington shotgun and a pocket full of shells. If there were any gun battle, it would be brief and the need for additional ammunition would be unlikely, given the nature of the surprise they would bring.

"Anything that jingles in your pockets, leave in the car seat. Leave it unlocked. We might return in a great hurry. Or with prisoners. Either way, we don't want to deal with locks."

They whispered back and forth as they proceeded back along the road to the trailer. As they neared, the place loomed larger and larger in the dark until it appeared to have the same shape and size as a railroad boxcar.

"Pray there are no dogs," he whispered.

"That prayer went out five minutes ago," she whispered back. "Hold on. What's our plan?"

"Our plan is to wait until they shit, shower, and shave and come outside. Then we take them into custody."

"I know that, but what if they run? Usual procedures by the book? Or are we going off-book?"

"Meaning?"

"Look, these are the guys who very likely murdered my partner and buried her body where she'll never be found. I want to shoot them as they come out and be done with it. But I think Chall expects a little more discretion than that."

"Although he was encouraging results more than justice."

"Exactly, didn't he mention something about having the mayor up his ass?"

"Harley, I like your idea. We plug them when they step outside, scalp them, and burn the bodies."

"Well," she whispered, "that's one end of the spectrum. No, seriously, if they make a break for it?"

"I say this," he whispered back. "We've been told they have a gun, so the chances are they're armed. They are suspects in a first-degree murder case. If they break for it, we shoot them."

"That's what I plan to do," she said. "Thanks for the talk."

They were within 100 yards when she said this. It was time to go silent.

She led the way. It was to be her kill.

Then they were 100 feet away. They stopped and listened. They sniffed the air for the smell of coffee brewing or cigarette smoke—anything that might indicate someone was up and around. Hearing and smelling nothing, they closed on their target.

At fifty feet they stopped again, engaging all their senses to detect if someone was awake. Then they left the asphalt for the dirt alongside the gravel path leading up to the trailer. She was able to discern the outline of trees along the backside of the unit. Maybe oak, maybe cottonwood, she couldn't tell.

Now they walked abreast in case they needed to shoot.

At twenty feet, CV's hand suddenly shot up. He'd seen or heard something. He motioned Harley to get down. Her knees cracked as she squatted on the dirt. Her eyes strained across the space separating them from the trailer. She listened for any sound. She heard it, then. A night bird. In the trees. CV patted her shoulder and indicated he was clear with what he'd heard, and it had been the bird and they could now move.

Just ahead was a small set of steps leading up to the door. A white handrail bordered the left side.

The detectives split apart at the steps, one going to one side, one to the other. They placed their backs against the trailer and stood there, waiting. CV's shotgun had a round in the chamber. Harley's pistol was fully loaded, checked and rechecked. She held it muzzle-down, the frame against her right thigh as she shot right-handed. She had the right side, CV the left. If the perps failed to obey her order to freeze, or if they made any move to evade or attack, CV would level them from behind with his semiautomatic shotgun.

She looked back east. She could've sworn she saw the first hint of light on the eastern horizon. She blinked once, twice: maybe her eyes were playing tricks. Maybe there was no light. She occupied her thoughts with these observations. It was the only way to stay in the moment.

The time was 4:32.

FIFTY-EIGHT MINUTES LATER—AT 5:30—the sound of a clock radio buzzing then playing music—split the air. The detectives heard a voice inside the trailer call out, "Rise and shine, asshole! Time to build a house!"

The detectives used the sounds inside the trailer to mask the shuffling of their own feet as they fought against the numbness from standing immobile for an hour.

Twenty minutes later, the door opened. Pultec came out first, followed by Barkley.

"Freeze!" cried CV and Harley simultaneously. Harley continued, "LAPD."

The men turned, saw the guns on both sides, and stopped moving.

"Raise your hands!" Harley commanded. By now, CV was behind the men, his shotgun muzzle moving from one back to the other. Evidently the men understood, because neither moved an inch.

Harley came around behind and handcuffed the larger man. She then took CV's cuffs and handcuffed the other.

"Names!"

"Damien Pultec."

"Al Barkley."

"I'm going to ask this one time. If you give me the truth, we won't hurt you. But if you withhold, we will hurt you. Tell us what you did with the woman detective. Now!"

"Fuck off," said Pultec. "You can't prove anything."

"That's your final answer?"

"Fuck you."

"Where are the keys to that backhoe?" She was indicating the Wain-Roy backhoe parked beside the far end of the trailer.

"Fuck you."

She inserted the muzzle of her gun into Barkley's ear.

"Our lieutenant doesn't care if you're alive or dead when we bring you in. I'm going to ask you, Al Barkley, one time and then I'm going to shoot you in the knee. Where are the keys?"

"Fuck you."

Harley placed the muzzle of her gun against Barkley's kneecap and pulled the trigger.

The roar of her gun split the morning and echoed across the surrounding hills. Barkley collapsed to the ground, on his side, crying out.

"That's one stiff leg. Or maybe you'll just bleed to death if we're delayed. Where are the keys?

"On top of the air filter," Barkley moaned. He was rocking back and forth on his side, his hands cuffed behind, his kneecap shattered and bleeding through his khaki trousers.

Harley approached the machine. She had operated the same model for her father at his construction site. She swept her hand across the air filter. She immediately located the keys and climbed up into the seat. The engine turned over, caught, and she used the levers to lift the bucket up from the ground. After several attempts, she managed to turn the machine and drive it back to the suspects.

She partially lowered the bucket and hopped down, leaving it running. Then she went behind Pultec and removed his cuffs. She put her gun against the back of his head and marched him up to the machine's long arm.

"Stand here and don't fucking move," she ordered. Then she raised his hands to either side of the overhead arm and cuffed him so that his hands and arms were cuffed on either side. She then climbed back aboard and moved the levers. The arm started to lower, which would've crushed the man, but she managed to stop it and go the other way. The lifting arm raised Pultec off his feet so that he was dangling beneath the arm of the unit as his cuffs slid at first then gripped the arm where a ring stopped his slide. He cried out in sharp pain, hanging by his wrists and the longer he was there he cried even harder.

She went back around, facing him.

"Now, tell me where you put the woman or so help me God, I'll shoot you in both knees and leave you here until you die."

His wrists had to be on fire with the cuffs digging in. He struggled to keep from kicking out, which was making his pain worse every time he scissored his legs in agony.

His head slumped to his chest. He had passed out from the pain.

Harley climbed aboard once again and lowered the boom until the man's feet touched the ground. She grabbed a hose, spun the spigot, and blasted the man's face. He sharply came around, sputtering and gasping for air as he stared glassy-eyed at his captor.

"Tell me where she is," Harley said through clenched teeth.

The man surrendered to the agony.

"In the cornfield at the end of the road."

"Pultec, shut your fuckin mouth!" cried Barkley.

"All right, you're going to take us there. CV, let's put Mr. Hurt Knee in the truck. You follow us."

CV prodded Barkley up on his good leg and dug his shotgun in the man's back. He hopped up to the Dodge.

"The keys are in it," Barkley panted in pain.

CV shoved him into the cab on the passenger's side. Then he lay his shotgun in the bed of the pickup and climbed into the cab. He removed his .357 magnum and jammed the muzzle against Barkley's side.

"Don't fucking move."

"I won't, I won't move."

"Too fucking bad."

Harley mounted the backhoe and again raised the boom. Pultec's feet left the ground and he shrieked in pain. Then she found her way through the gears and the machine began moving forward.

Out to the lane they went, turning right without stopping and proceeding in the direction of the cornfield.

"Tell me where!" she ordered Pultec.

"At the—at the next turn-in!"

She wheeled the vehicle up to the cornfield at the end of the lane and stopped.

"Now where?"

"In the center. But please take me down first. The cornstalks will kill me."

"All right, but first tell me this. Did you give the detective a chance like that? Or did you just dig a hole and push her in?"

"We let—we let her...run."

"Not good enough. Hang on, Mr. Pultec! Oh, that's right, you are hanging on already. Here we go!"

The machine lurched ahead, crashing through the corn, stalks flying by after they poked and stabbed at Pultec dangling from the long arm, the bucket fully raised. This went on for a good thirty seconds until they came to the spot Harley instantly recognized. She saw Marcia's grave and understood. She saw Marcia's terror and felt her pain—what she could of it. She pulled to a stop, leaving the man dangling from the arm. She jumped down with the engine yet running.

"That's her."

It wasn't a question, but Pultec answered. "Yes."

"Who dug the hole?"

"I don't remember."

"Who dug the hole!"

"I did."

"Who pushed her in?"

"Barkley did. She never saw it coming."

"What about the two male detectives? Where are they?"

"At...the other...side of the field."

Pultec passed out from the pain. Harley had the information she had come for, found the grave she had hoped not to find, and had the man's confession. She'd also found Sullivan and Black. That would develop as well.

CV had followed them into the cornfield and was waiting inside the truck at the edge of the small clearing.

She approached the driver's side.

She shouted over the engine, "I'll put him in the bed and climb in with him. Let's head for our Ford."

"Gotcha," shouted CV. "Shout if you need help."

She stopped as she was turning away. She turned back around. "Do I look like I need help?"

"Harley, you know what I meant."

"I do. Forgive me, CV. This is more than—"

Her words broke off as she returned to the backhoe. She climbed up into the operator's seat and lowered the bucket. Her first impulse was to crush Pultec under the arm, but she resisted. But she promised herself she would be there when he ate the gas in the green room at San Quentin.

She'd be in the front row, watching and smiling.

45

Both wrists were broken, and his arms dislocated at the elbows and shoulders. Three ribs were displaced. The pain was unbearable, so the ER doctors loaded him up with heavy injections of painkillers. Which rendered him unconscious. Pultec was then taken to a separate ward in the hospital and cuffed to the bed by his ankles. He wasn't going anywhere as he would be groggy with morphine for several days.

Albert Barkley was a different story. He was taken to the OR, his knee repaired, and returned to a private room to recover. He also was cuffed to his bed rails. Again, morphine took away the pain and left him just conscious enough to answer her questions.

"Who killed Ira J. Spielman?"

"No—no—we didn't kill him."

He denied the murder for an hour, even when Harley twisted his injured knee.

She finally turned to CV. "I don't think these bums did Spielman."

CV shook his head. "I don't either."

Lieutenant Chall, looking grim, entered the room.

He sat down in the visitors' chair and folded his hands.

"It's her. The stupid bastards took her hands and her teeth but left her shield in her jacket. She was buried with her shield."

CV shook his head. "Figures."

Harley's eyes welled with tears.

CV embraced her. "I know," he whispered. "Let it out."

Harley averted her face as she left the room, depriving Barkley of the satisfaction of seeing her tears. She made her way up the hall to the visitors' waiting area and sat down hard on the two-cushion gray couch. Then she broke down. She cried and cried with Chall and CV on either side of her.

"CV," Chall finally said, "take her home and take care of her. I'll see you both next Monday at first-watch roll call. You both need some time. By the way, Dinah Loden admitted complicity in taking Marcia to her killers. She's being charged with conspiracy to commit murder. The judge refused to set bail."

"All right. I'll take her now."

"The family will call me about the funeral. I'll call you with the plans as soon as I know."

As they left, tape recorders were being set up and confessions were being recorded from Pultec and Barkley.

There were no games this time around.

Pultec, confessing, kept watching the door to his room.

Asked the detective, "What are you looking for, chum?"

"The crazy woman. Is she coming?"

"It depends on how honest you are. Tell me again about digging the grave."

BY THE THIRD day after the arrests, Harley's abject grief started to lift. A ray of sunshine got through.

CV had been feeding her chicken noodle soup and grilled cheese sandwiches—the extent of his culinary talents.

But it turned dark again, for it was Saturday and time for Marcia's funeral. The day dawned rainy and cold, the gloom thick enough to require lights and wipers. CV and Harley were picked up by Chall and driven to the church.

Marcia's family and co-workers crowded the church as all available officers and detectives from LAPD filed into St. Andrew's Holy Redeemer. Mass was said and the rest of the memorial followed.

Services at the graveside were attended by an honor guard with bagpipes and ribbon badges on chests clad in LAPD blues.

Harley fought back her tears in the cemetery, trying to be strong for Marcia's family. But she tossed the first pinch of dirt onto her partner's casket, lying below in the newly-dug hole, and then the dam burst. She wept openly and without shame until CV and Chall walked her back to the long line of waiting police vehicles. No other officers had left the cemetery and wouldn't until after she left.

They returned to her home in Lieutenant Chall's police cruiser, where Chall bade her goodbye.

"You did well," Chall told her, leaned and gave her a hug, and walked away. "I've never hugged another police officer during my entire watch, some eighteen years," he told them. "Extraordinary times call for extraordinary measures."

"Thank you, Lieutenant," Harley said. "For everything."

The lieutenant turned to leave, but then turned back around. "Hey, you've still got four days to find that daughter. What do you say?"

Harley straightened fully upright. He was obviously ignoring the original thirty-day rule as it had already been much longer. "Copy that, sir."

"Good. Get it done. Let me know if you need an extra day or two."

"Copy that, sir."

HARLEY CRIED ALL the rest of that day of the funeral. CV held her, on the couch, and in the kitchen while waiting for coffee to percolate, in the bedroom where she tried to nap and couldn't, then in bed where she shivered and cried out, waking up in violent, cold sweats three different times.

After a fitful night's sleep, she awoke the next morning and announced she was finished. She would cry again for Marcia, but not until later, because now only three days remained for her to find Wendy and bring her home.

46

Harley paid for 100 prints of Wendy's most recent picture. She planned on leaving it at every hospital in LA. as well as other obvious places where needy persons met providers. She had no reason to think Wendy would be anything other than needy because of her age, lack of education, youth and inability to get an adult job, and the other strikes against someone like her.

Harley and CV split up the rest of Monday afternoon and took the pictures to Traffic Divisions all across the county. They asked each —and each eagerly agreed—to leave pictures at train depots, Salvation Army homes, rehab centers, and food-stamp offices in LA. The accompanying cards asked anyone who thought they had spotted Wendy to call Harley at the LAPD office. All shift commanders gave the case a priority that first day: Harley was one of them and she was counting on their help.

Harley stayed late after work, manning the phone line. Then it happened: a call came in at 9:25. The caller was a traffic cop in Malibu who swore he followed a young girl into a house along the beach. It had been thirty minutes ago, and she still hadn't come back out. He had gotten a good look at her face after writing her a ticket for speeding. He was ready to swear the girl was the one in the photograph. Harley demanded the address and tore downstairs with CV in the lead, ready to drive.

They headed toward Malibu then west. An hour later, they arrived at the address, drove slowly beyond, and parked four doors down. The dome light in their Ford was switched off when they opened their doors and began creeping along to the address on El Camino Way.

Harley rang the doorbell. The detectives heard it chime just inside the closed door. No answer. After a thirty-second wait, she rang it again. Still no answer. So, Harley rapped her knuckles hard on the screen door, making it rattle against the frame for extra oomph. But there still was no answer. So, they crept around back. Japanese lights were strung across the yard and a record player, somewhere near the French doors, was playing the Four Preps' "Dreamy Eyes." Cigarette embers glowed around the dark edges of the yard. Fifty yards west, the Pacific Ocean pounded the sand. Harley wasted no time boldly walking across the yard and up to the wet bar where couples were gathered, talking and laughing. She pulled out her badge and ID and coolly laid them on the bar. Then she produced one of the Wendy pictures.

"Anyone seen this girl?"

Heads shook *no* and voices grew quiet.

"Well, I was told by another police officer that she entered this house not forty-five minutes ago. He's been watching down at the corner and hasn't seen her leave. Anyone seen her now?"

Again, no one claimed to have knowledge. Then, just as Harley was about to turn on all outside lights and begin taking statements, a small voice from just inside the French doors spoke up. "It's me you're looking for."

Harley jerked around and swept into the house though the open French door. She switched on a light. If it wasn't her double, it was a damn good copy, Harley would tell the cop who called her. Because the young girl had Wendy's dark hair, cut short like Wendy liked to wear her hair, a sweet movie star nose and bright white teeth, and she even—as Harley checked her out—returned Harley's attention with a look of disdain. She didn't get it: this one didn't even know her and already looked like she loathed her.

Harley sighed and backed away. "We've made a mistake, miss. Sorry to bother you."

Then the girl smiled, and Harley almost broke down, she so resembled Wendy. "I'm sorry but I got a ticket tonight for speeding. My dad's gonna kill me and I'm afraid to go home."

"Really? Do you need me to call him for you?"

"You'd do that?"

"Sure, I would, if you think it might help. Does he know you're attending this party?"

"Yes, it's his partner's son's birthday. My dad is a surgeon and Dr. Ischner lives here. They open people's heads up for a living." She giggled at that notion.

"Let's find a phone and let's call your dad."

FIFTEEN MINUTES LATER, Harley and CV were headed back downtown. They split up at Hollywood Station and took their separate vehicles home. The next morning, Harley was back to manning the phones at five o'clock. No calls had come in overnight; the log was clear.

Then, at 6:16 a.m., the phone rang abruptly, bringing Harley almost to her feet as she had been dozing.

"Detective Ellis? This is Delano Matrice. I run a mom and pop grocery here in City of Industry. I just saw your girl named Wendy. And I think I know where she stays."

"Give me an address, please. I'm on my way."

"My address is 1344 N. Wiley Street in City of Industry. She's in an apartment upstairs just across the street. I can see her right now in the window. Hurry, there's several people moving around in there. They might be leaving."

Harley went out and jumped in her unmarked Ford and headed east on US 101 toward City of Industry. She thought better of running Code 3 with lights flashing because it wasn't an emergency by law. Still, she drove aggressively at a high rate of speed in the inside lane.

But traffic was heavy on this weekday morning as rush hour was underway. She found herself stuck behind a pickup truck brimming with cantaloupes, some of which would tumble into the roadway, causing Harley to swerve and brake to avoid colliding.

Harley finally made a left onto Hacienda Boulevard and headed north four blocks. Then a right and another left. She found Daniel's market on the corner, a small mom-and-pop with the customary Coke and Sunshine Bread signage. Pulling up in front, she sat for several minutes in her vehicle, observing the building directly across the street. Downstairs was a laundromat and upstairs there appeared two side-by-side apartments. The windows were open on both and the light morning breeze was toying with the curtains, moving them outside then in and outside and in. She finally decided she had no option but to have a look.

She climbed out of her vehicle, pocketed her keys and waited for a break in traffic so she could jog across. The downstairs door was open and led immediately to a stairway with a landing a dozen steps up. She double-timed the steps, turned at the landing, and kept going another four steps. At the top were two doorways, one left and one right. She knocked on the one on her right and it swung open. She stuck her head in and called, "Wendy?" Then again, louder this time. No answer. She stepped inside.

A quick survey of the interior confirmed her first suspicion: someone had cleared out of the place in a great hurry. She went to the stove and held her hand over the burners. One of them was still warm. Then she snooped. It was a single bedroom on the street side with living room, kitchen and bathroom in the rear. Held to the refrigerator door by a magnet was a hookup appointment from Southern California Edison. Sure enough, it was addressed to Wendy S. Miller. Harley wondered how many Wendy S. Miller's there would be in all of Los Angeles. Especially ones who'd abandoned a playpen and rickety baby bed. Somehow the occupants had been tipped off and fled.

Gone again.

So, there was nothing else to do but keep looking, keep hoping for a call.

47

"All right," said Devonna Stacey, MD. "According to my chart, you've been to see me twice already and I thought we might need three sessions. This would be visit number three. How have you been?"

Harley looked around the doctor's office, trying to decide where to begin. "I lost my partner. Murdered. How do you think it's been?"

"I'm sorry. I heard that. It was a bad question. Forgive me."

Harley took her head in her hands and leaned her elbows onto her knees. She rocked there for several seconds, fighting down her rage and pain. Then she pulled herself together and spoke as calmly as she could muster.

"I've been okay. I'm working a homicide case that might involve my daughter. That's bad."

"How involved?"

"Didn't I tell you last time? The Spielman case?"

"The movie producer? Your daughter might be involved? How's that possible?"

"She screen-tested there. It turns out, he assaulted her. Now we've found evidence she might've been involved. It was her letter opener."

"This is the man who was stabbed in the ear with the letter opener?"

"That's right. The letter opener came from my Wendy."

"How's that working for you, investigating someone you love?"

"Lieutenant Chall is going to take me off the case. Unless I can clear my daughter."

"Have you had any luck finding her?"

"Not much. I've come close a couple times. Well, once, I actually spoke to her. But she disappeared again. We're still looking."

"Harley, the first time we spoke, you'd had a moment when you imagined seeing your daughter."

"I remember. Hasn't happened again."

"Any hallucinations or visions at all? I need to be clear about that."

"Nope, nothing."

"I'd really need to know if that happened again."

"What would you do?"

"Hard to say. It would depend on the situation, what happened, exactly. And it would depend on you. We'd definitely need to take steps to reduce stress. That would be one aspect of any treatment."

"Nothing like that happening. I do have a male friend now."

"A boyfriend?"

"Not a boy. He used to be my partner. We rode around in the same unmarked vehicle for two years. We went out together as friends maybe twice a week. But then he called me up and asked me to dinner. It was sweet."

"Did it go any further than dinner?"

"Who wants to know?"

"This is confidential. LAPD knows nothing we talk about."

"We spent the night together."

"How did that make you feel?"

"You know what? It felt really goddamn good. I hope my Lieutenant doesn't fuck it up but it's probably inevitable."

"Would it present any problems at work?"

"Probably not. Lots of kidding and teasing, I'm sure. Romance travels like ink in water at a police station."

"What about Angelina? How does it affect your living situation?"

"She's so busy with work and shopping second-hand for maternity things we hardly see each other. Whatever it means for any of us, it's good for her, too."

"Okay, let's talk about your stressors again. We know about Marcia and that's enough of a loss for an entire lifetime. But you have even more. First, your daughter is missing."

"Check."

"Second, you're working with a new partner?"

"Check."

"Third, your partner is now your new romantic partner?"

"Check."

"Fourth, you have a house guest. A young, pregnant woman."

"Check."

"Anything else?"

"I went to Mexico and met with a very bad man. He's threatened me and my family. Then Marcia went to San Quentin and saw this man's brother. The Juarez man is going to kill me if I don't get his brother out of San Quentin. I can't do it—it's not possible."

"So that's another stressor, that's five. Harley, any of one of these is enough to be disruptive to someone's life. And you've got five all at once. What do you do to help with the pressure? Has your drinking picked up?"

"No."

"I think you told me that on paydays you have two drinks or three?"

"Two. That hasn't increased. I just do what's on my desk every day. What else is someone gonna do?"

"Taking responsibility is huge. That's doing the right thing. Do you feel like an anxiety medication might help?"

"And make me into a robot? No, thanks, Doc. I respect you and all, but the meds are a no-no for me. I need to be on every day."

"I understand. I appreciate your need to be sharp every day. Do you have any vacation time coming up?"

"Not really. Can't really afford to go anyplace anyway."

"Well, what would you like to have me do for you?"

"Just not make me come back. I don't need it."

"Tell you what, Harley. You come back if you want to. No more pressure, not from me. You decide."

"I won't be back unless they make me."

"They won't. I'm going to tell them you're finished here."

"God, thank you."

"All right, Harley, Goodbye, now."

"Goodbye."

48

Wednesday and Thursday passed with three false leads, one on a new registrant at an apartment complex and one during a traffic stop. The third came from a social worker who had noticed Wendy's name on the book at Smart Step Daycare in Van Nuys. Harley and CV headed for the address.

In the side yard were jungle gyms, a merry-go-round, and several swing sets. Children were squealing and giggling at play, romping all around under the watchful eye of three workers stationed strategically around the fenced area. The face of the building was done in river stone and a ten-foot tall cartoon bear was attached to the roofline. The detectives went inside and badged the woman behind the desk.

"Detective Ellis looking for any child last name of Miller. Do you have one here?"

"Oh, yes, a new child. Let me get his name. Yes, he's Bobby Wendell Miller. Mother is Wendy Miller. Is that the one?"

Harley's heart raced. "Yes," she said weakly. "That's the one."

CV stepped forward. "Can you tell us what time the mother is returning?"

"Let's see. He's registered today for seven a.m. to four p.m. The mother works—do you want her work number?"

CV wrote down Wendy's work number.

"What does the mother do?"

"She's working as a waitress at the End Run. It's a family-owned cafe about two miles from here. Shall I call them for you?"

CV shook his head. "No, that isn't necessary. I'm going to wait here with Bobby while my partner goes down and speaks to the mother. Please write down the address of the End Run."

The woman looked it up in the *Yellow Pages*.

Harley grabbed up the address and exited the daycare. The End Run was very close. She told herself what she was going to do, reminded herself that this was official police business and that her options were limited to one.

She parked at the space nearest to the Roman columns making up the facade of the End Run, then hurried inside.

She knew Wendy the instant she saw her, even though she was looking at her from the rear. The size, the hair color, the posture, the tilt of the head while she was taking an order. There was no doubt. Mothers know their daughters even in silhouette.

Harley crept up behind, removed her handcuffs from the back of her belt, and clapped the cuffs on first one wrist then the other.

The girl turned, terrified, her hands cuffed behind her.

"What!"

Harley shook her head once. "I'm placing you under arrest for the murder of Ira J. Spielman. Please come with me. You'd be smart not to resist."

WENDY WAS silent the entire ride back to Hollywood Station. CV drove; Harley rode shotgun, holding the one-year-plus grandson on her lap. The prisoner, Wendy Miller, sat forward in the rear seat, handcuffed behind her back, quietly crying. Finally, she said, "His daddy took off. Please don't put him in foster care. I'm begging you."

"He won't be going into foster care," Harley snapped.

They pulled into the LA County Jail and introduced their prisoner into the system. Harley was surprised at her own reaction to the entire process: she really didn't have anything to say to her daughter. She was emotionally wrecked, physically exhausted, and now had a new grandson whose needs had her mind a million miles away as she planned for him. There would be a bed, a playpen, a diaper pail, bottles and warmer, food, diapers, diaper pins—the list in her mind was endless and relentlessly cycled through her thoughts.

But there was, ever present in the swirling storm in her head, also the Wendy problem.

CV DROVE her home with the baby and took off for FedMart with a long shopping list. Grandmother and grandson were left to fend for themselves for the first couple of hours, alone. The daycare had returned the dozen diapers the mother had provided as required, along with several bottles, and jars of baby food. It wasn't much, true, but it was enough to get by until CV returned with supplies.

She then called Lieutenant Chall.

"LT, Harley here. I took my daughter into custody and picked up my grandson from daycare. He's here at my home."

"CV called. Social Services is making an emergency placement of the baby with you, Harley. I see no reason why that won't become permanent once the court is finished. Regarding your daughter, I've turned the case over to Tommy Jones. You are relieved of it."

"Will there be bail?" she asked, even knowing there was no money for bail and even knowing Wendy, the runner, didn't belong out on bail anyway.

"The District Attorney won't agree to bail, you know that already. The grand jury will vote a true bill first thing in the morning."

"My Lord. I do know that."

"One more bothersome note, Harley. I'm concerned about your safety. We both know what Reuben Ordañez said would happen to Wendy if you failed to get his brother, Matin, out of Q. Now that Ordañez can find her, he can reach her."

"Sure. He can reach her even easier in jail."

"I'm afraid so. I'm going to call and request she be single-celled for the time being. But that won't last. She's not special in the eyes of the LA County Sheriff. Just another prisoner to them. But I'll do what I can for as long as I can."

"Thank you, LT. Let me talk to CV about Ordañez. I know we'll take some precautions going in. Let me see what we come up with."

"I don't think you're personally at risk, but watch your back, Harley. You and CV both need to watch your backs."

"So. You know about me and CV?"

Long pause, then, "Please. I'm a detective."

She shook her head, said goodbye, and hung up.

Yes, he—they—were the police. And it was Chief Parker's town, Los Angeles.

Not the kind of town where a thug like Ordañez was going to be able to make waves.

He was already way out of his league.

49

Harley took two days and rode the train up to San Quentin. She left Bobby with CV at her place. Plus, she had Angelina, who loved helping with the baby. CV had older kids of his own and was well-versed in all the routines.

This time she wasn't going to see Matin Ordañez. This time her visit was with Bubba Lee Necco of South Los Angeles. She had busted Bubba for armed robbery while working Vice, interestingly enough, when he beat a john half to death who refused to pay one of his girls. Bubba, who was as big as an NFL fullback, was mean, brawny, and dangerous. Out in the real world he was always strapped both with a .44 magnum gun and a barber's straight-edge razor. He didn't mind killing and, it was said at his sentencing, he got a thrill out of maiming for life. Now he was doing a twenty-year stretch on a second conviction and his young wife of 22 was already moving on. She had two of Bubba's kids, and Bubba, who was only 24, was dying every day over his loss. He would have done anything to get out of San Quentin and back to his family and the streets.

Which is where Harley came in, as the cop who took him down.

She passed quickly through Q's security points and, once inside, told the guards she was there to see Leon "Bubba" Maxwell. Ten minutes later he was led into the room, wrist-chained, waist-chained, and leg-ironed. He was locked to the floor loops and left to talk to Harley.

"Hey, remember me?"

"Only every night when I'm thinking of someone to murder."

"Well, that's good to know I'm in your thoughts."

"Lady, I don't know what the fuck you want, but I ain't dropping a dime on anyone. If you need a snitch, you got the wrong guy."

"I don't need a snitch. I need a big strong sociopath. Like you."

"Yeah, well, fuck you, too."

"Hear me out, Leon. I have something good for you."

"Go on."

"The warden tells me you don't come up for a probation hearing for another seven years. He also tells me you've got a wife and two little kids. One of those kids is named Leon, like his daddy. I'll bet you miss those guys."

"Well, fuck the warden and fuck you. Guard!"

"Hold on, hold on. Let me finish. Seven years. I can make it happen next month."

"Do what?"

"I can get your parole hearing set up one month from now."

"I been a model citizen."

"That's the problem. I don't want to see a model citizen. I want to see you be an animal."

"Why would I be your animal?"

"Because there's a man in here who's threatening to kill my family."

"Fuck him, too."

"That's right, fuck him, too. But I need more than words. I need you to put the hurt on this man."

"Like how bad?"

"I need broken bones and a stab wound. Just don't kill him or we're both in serious trouble."

"Let me see I got this. Hurt this guy, break something, slice him open, don't kill him, and I'm up for parole in one month?"

"That's it. Bingo, you're about to get out. You're my collar so I get to call that shot. Is Bubba in or is Bubba out?"

"Lady, I don't owe you shit. But I owe my family. Give me this busted-up mother's name."

"Matin Ordañez."

"Who is he?"

"The brother of some very bad people in Mexico."

"Those assholes? I put the hurt on those assholes, too."

"I like you, Bubba. We make a deal and you even offer to throw in some freebies. That's solid."

"When do you want this mofo half-dead?"

"By tomorrow night."

"What cell block is he?"

"He's being moved into west, just like you."

"How I know him?"

"He's going to be sitting across from you at supper tonight. He's Mexican, he has a teardrop tattoo under his left eye, and his front tooth is gold. He's very large."

"Shit. I can make this chump my bitch 'fore I'm through."

"No need for that. Just hurt him when no one's looking. You know how to do that?"

"You foolin' with me now?"

"How about this. Stab him in the upper arm. Break an arm or a leg. Bust his nose. But don't kill him. Deal?"

"Deal."

"Good, then we're done here."

"Hey, what about they catch me?"

She smiled. "Nobody's going to be looking. The guards are all going to be on the other side of the cafeteria. Just be sure you take your regular seat. The new guy across from you, that's Matin Ordañez. Now say his name."

"Mr. Fucked-up."

"Perfect, you've got it. I'll be back next month for your parole hearing. I'll recommend. And when you get out, don't you fuck up again. If you do, ain't nobody coming for a third-strike loser. Got me?"

"Go on, lady. Before I lose my cool."

"See you, Bubba. Have fun."

"I always havin' fun."

She then took the bus into the city and enjoyed a quiet night in a marked-down hotel. Room service, some TV, and at midnight she called the San Quentin infirmary.

"This is LAPD Detective Harley Ellis. Do you have a new patient there by the name of Matin Ordañez?"

"We do. Busted up pretty bad, Detective."

"Tell me."

"Both arms broken, a stab wound in his upper left shoulder, one eye badly bruised and an ear half-bitten off. They're wiring his jaw together. A disaster."

"Who got fingered for it."

"You know how it is here, Detective. Nobody saw anything."

"All right, good night."

She hung up.

An hour later, she finally reached Reuben Ordañez in Juarez.

"Listen, tough guy. You remember you threatened my daughter?"

"You didn't forget!"

"Check up on Matin. He's in the hospital with broken bones, a stab wound, and an ear torn off. I put him there and I'll do it again if anything ever happens to my daughter. If my daughter is in an automobile accident, your brother dies. If she falls down ice skating, your brother dies. If she cuts her foot at the beach, I'm coming for your brother. Are you reading me so far, asshole?"

"What the fuck?"

"You've got it. Now you get down on your knees and start praying my daughter didn't burn herself cooking today. And you call your brother and tell that stupid asshole he's never getting out of prison."

"Lady—"

"Hey. I told you to lock the doors, that I'd be back. Remember?"

"You said that, but—"

"No buts. Start praying for my daughter after you call your brother or I'll have my people go in tomorrow and break his legs, too. Now pray!"

"You think that stop me?" it came out of Ordañez like a low, animal growl. He was backed into a corner and ready to flail his way out.

"Maybe. But let me add what will. I talked to Matin. He told me everything I wanted to know about you. I learned your kids' names, where they live, mothers' names, where the mothers live, schools, everything Matin knows I now know. You hurt my kid, I hurt three of yours. You threaten my kid, I threaten yours. I know about Esmeralda in Cabo. I know about Jimi in Mexico City. I know about Denisse and Genni and Michaela in Juarez. I even know about your twins in San Diego. And I know about your brothers' kids. And your sister's kids. I know it all. Now you call that brother of yours and ask him whether I'll come after someone named Ordañez. If they don't have his jaw wired together yet I'm sure he'll tell you about me. What's our rule, Reuben?"

"This is business. No kids."

"There you go. No kids, no way, or I'm coming to Mexico."

She hung up, smoked a Camel out on her small deck, and went to bed.

50

When she went to visit Wendy, she didn't go there on an official call. She went just like every other civilian. No special interview room, no special favors. They spoke through Plexiglas in the visiting room, black phone on either side.

Wendy was brought into the visitors' room wearing an orange jumpsuit that had stenciled across the back *LA County Jail*. She was neither timid nor bold, just together.

She picked up the phone and looked her mother in the eye.

"How's Bobby?"

"Bobby is with me and he's just fine."

"I didn't do it."

"The evidence says you did."

"What evidence is that?"

"They found your letter opener buried in his ear. They found your monogrammed scarf on his couch. They found your pregnancy letter. It all adds up to you being there."

"I didn't do it."

Harley sighed. "You're going to have to do better than 'I didn't do it.'"

Wendy's face clouded up. "Why don't you ever believe me? You never did!"

"Wendy, it doesn't matter what I believe. What matters is the evidence in the case. The police who investigated the crime scene found a letter opener that said 'Wang's Hardware' along the blade. That's where you were living, in Las Vegas."

"Bobby gave me that letter opener. I wasn't living there yet."

"It doesn't matter if it was before or after. Mr. Wang says you were in his store trying to get some way to seal your toilet. He gave you a letter opener."

"He did not! Yes, I was in his store but that was because Robert Ray gave me the letter opener with the name of the store. Advertising works. I went in there because of it."

"Your monogrammed scarf was there, too. The one I gave you."

"Someone took it out of my purse. Or I lost it. I don't know. But I know I didn't leave it there. Mr. Spielman raped me there and my purse was never opened. And I sure as hell didn't take it out and leave it before I ran off that day."

"Why did I pick you up at the Morning Glory cafe that day? Why weren't you out in front of Capitol Films?"

"Because Annalee said we should ride the bus down and get some coffee. Spielman had done the same thing to her before."

"Tell me what else she said."

"She said she had to get the part. The state took away her baby for non-support and she needed the Gayle Howard part to get the money to get her baby back. Or her little boy, I forget. We talked and I had coffee and went to the bathroom and cleaned myself up in there. He slimed my genitals, the fucking bastard. Then I cried and cried in there."

"When you went to the bathroom, did you take your purse?"

"I don't remember."

"Think hard. This might be important, Wendy."

"No, I didn't take it. I felt him leaking out of me and I knew I'd be in the stall, wiping. I didn't want my purse in the stall on the floor and I didn't want to leave it on the bathroom counter with the stall closed. So, I left it on the table because Annalee said she'd watch it."

"Did Annalee know you wanted the Gayle Howard part?"

"She heard me say it. Yes, I wanted it."

"Was she the kind of girl who might rob your purse while you were gone?"

"What? What are you saying? She was very nice."

"Unless she took your letter opener out of your purse and took your scarf out of your purse and killed Spielman. If she did all that, she's not so nice. Why would you even say that?"

"Because—I—I—"

"You're what?"

"I'm living with her. Or was. She took me in."

"What?" said Harley, incredulous. "You just might be living with the girl who killed Ira J. Spielman!"

"Not now, I'm not. Now I'm living in the LA County Jail."

"How did you ever find Annalee?"

"We traded numbers at the cafe. She said to call her sometime. When I got back from Vegas, I called. Then Robert Ray ran off with Annalee's sister. He went to Phoenix to serve coffee at the Baboquivari with his new girlfriend. It's very complicated."

"Look me in the eye, Wendy."

Wendy looked her mother in the eye as only a daughter can.

"Tell me you didn't do it."

"I didn't kill Mr. Spielman."

"All right, I believe you."

"Are you going to help me?"

"I'm going to go talk to Annalee. What address do you have?"

Wendy gave directions as she didn't know the street address. It was only a quarter-mile from Smart Step Daycare.

"Tell me what Bobby likes to eat."

"He loves apricots. He hates peas. He's good with a warm bottle anytime. He has to have one at bedtime or he' up in the middle of the night and wakes you. He has a favorite stuffed animal at Annalee's, a Goofy doll I got him at Disneyland. If you have a pool, he loves to wade and splash. Before bedtime he wants to be held. He loves to play patty-cake. I have a version I call South Chicago Patty-cake where it's very speeded up, which he loves. That's about it. He's a good little boy and I miss him terribly! What will they do with me in here? Will I go to prison?"

"You'll go to juvie. You might be kept in juvie until you're twenty-one."

"That's five years! Bobby will be six years old then! He won't even know me!"

"Yes, he will. I'll bring him for visits. You'll be able to work up to overnight visits with him. I'll make damn good and sure he knows his own mother."

"Thank you, thank you."

"Of course, I'll do that for you. You're still my daughter and I love you more than anything, Wendy. You're my baby."

"Mama, I'm sorry how I acted. I've been so mean to you."

"Well, we'll move on from that. We have lots of years yet to make up for lost time. But first, I'm going to go have a moment with Annalee. I've got some things to ask her."

"Goodbye, Mama."

"I'll be back every day you're here. Keep your chin up."

"All right."

51

Harley headed to Annalee's after she left the jail. The drive up into the hills took forty-five minutes, given the traffic. Then, when she was sure she'd found the right place, a young woman told her no, Annalee wasn't home. She said she worked the swing shift at Universal Dynamics. Harley drove back down out of the hills and took Sunset Boulevard to Echo Park. The company was huge, with several warehouses and a dozen eighteen-wheelers backed up to loading ramps, loading boxes the size of refrigerators.

Harley found the front door and went inside. Two women were banging typewriters. Harley walked up and badged the one with the green mascara and flecked lipstick. She looked up glumly when she saw the badge. "Who?" was all she said.

"Annalee Johnson," said Harley, "she works swing."

"Lemme look her up on my Rollie." She spun the dial on her Rolodex. "Yes, all right. She's in building two, lathe operator. I'll call for someone to walk you over, officer."

Harley had a chair and waited. Ten minutes later, a white-haired gentleman wearing brown coveralls over a white T-shirt entered through the back. "You're the police officer looking for Johnson?"

"I am."

"I pulled her off the floor. She's out back, waiting to talk. We can put you in one of our empty offices. Follow me."

Harley followed him down a long hallway and then, just as they were about to exit the building, he stopped and popped open a door. "In here, Ma'am."

Harley went into the small, empty office, and switched on a light. There was a steel desk and four chairs. She took the one facing the door and sat forward with her notepad at the ready.

Minutes later, Annalee Johnson sauntered in. She was sweaty, wearing a kerchief on her head, and her hands were quite dirty. Harley shook her hand and Annalee removed the kerchief from her head. She finger-combed her hair and blew out a burst of air up at her bangs. "Hi, Mrs. Ellis. I hear you arrested Wendy. That's too bad."

"It is too bad, Annalee. You want to know why?"

"Why?"

"Because the crime lab says your fingerprints are on the letter opener that killed Mr. Spielman." Harley was bluffing but came across genuine.

"My prints? *My* prints?"

"That's right. And your prints are on Wendy's monogrammed scarf, too. So why don't you tell me what really happened with Mr. Spielman."

Annalee's face fell. Her eyes were downcast and her forehead crinkled.

"I didn't get the part he promised. I was supposed to get Gayle Howard."

"So, what happened?"

"I don't know. They just never called. Now I'm working to get my son back from the state."

"How old are you, Annalee?"

"Almost twenty."

"You were how old when you had your son?"

"Just fifteen. My uncle got me pregnant."

"Did you kill Mr. Spielman because he didn't give you Gayle Howard?"

"I went to talk to him a second time. I met Wendy again and this time I took a letter opener out of her purse when she wasn't looking. And I took a scarf I knew she had. Then we went to the studio. She went in first and came out crying. She told me she didn't get the part and he'd told her to stay the hell away from Capitol Films. Then it was my turn to go in and talk to him. This time, I let him have sex with me. Then I asked about Gayle Howard. He said no. I still had the letter opener in my purse, and I whipped it out and swung it at him. I'm very strong in my hands, I'm a metal lathe operator. He ducked but it caught him in the ear, and he stood straight up and keeled over on the couch. I pulled open my purse to grab my bus transfer and run. But then I saw Wendy's scarf. I only stole it because I wanted it. I didn't do it to hurt Wendy. But then I thought, Oh, what the hell, and I tossed it on the couch. By then he was dead."

"Go on."

"The secretaries weren't around. So, it was easy to just leave. I ran down to the gate, my bus came, and I was gone in a flash."

"Would you write out what you just told me."

"I guess. It isn't fair for Wendy to be in jail. And she's got her son and I don't have mine. She should be with Bobby. Give me your paper."

Harley slid her notepad over with ink pen. Annalee began writing. Every so often she'd stop and examine a fingernail and then continue. Twice she dug an index finger deep into her ear. "Filings," she said. "Very fine bits of metal. They get in my ears, up my nose. I have to shower as soon as I get off."

"Sure."

Five minutes passed and finally Annalee laid aside the pen. Harley read the confession. Just as she'd said, she admitted murdering Ira J. Spielman.

Harley tucked the notepad back inside her jacket pocket. "I guess you know what this means?"

"Yes, you've gotta take me to jail?"

"Yes."

"How long will I be there?"

"Depends if they process you as a juvie or as an adult."

"If I'm a juvie, can I work during that time?"

"They have jobs, yes."

"And I can save up enough to get my son?"

"I'm sure there's always a chance of that."

"If I don't have to pay for a place to live and pay for food, maybe I can save even more. Do they need lathe operators?"

"Annalee, I'm going to put these handcuffs on you. I'll put them in front. It's department policy, otherwise I wouldn't use them at all. And I'll have to make you ride in the backseat of my car."

"Department policy again."

"Exactly."

"Should I clean out my locker?"

"What's there?"

"A book I'm reading and my lunch pail. We already had lunch so it's empty."

"All right, then, let's go."

"Don't let that woman out front with the green eyes ask me anything. She already hates me."

"I won't. We'll just walk on past and be gone."

"Thank you, Detective.

52

CV questioned Harley about Annalee's confession. He reminded her there weren't any fingerprints on the letter opener or the scarf. She smiled at him and brought him another cup of coffee. Then she took Bobby from Wendy. The missing daughter was now found, released from jail, and sweetly reasonable about things with Harley. Harley went to her rocking chair. It was a bentwood, purchased from Yellow Front for the exact purpose of rocking her grandson.

A second rocker exactly the same was occupied by Angelina, who was breastfeeding her little girl. The baby kept falling asleep and Angelina kept jiggling her awake to finish her feeding.

Harley rocked her grandson and watched his mother sitting across from her working the *Times* crossword puzzle in the Sunday morning edition. Wendy had been out of jail for six months and was looking for a new job in the Help Wanted section. She was tired of waitressing and wanted something more. Her mother wanted her to finish school, but Wendy first wanted to pay some bills she had left here and there during her travels. She had already filed for annulment of her marriage from Robert Ray, as well.

"What's a seven-letter word for slight or trifling?"

"Minuscule," said CV.

"That's nine. Anyone else?"

"Small, tiny, trite? But seven letters? I'm sure I need time for this one," Harley said.

Two small suitcases waited by the front door. Another cup of coffee and they'd be on their way to Las Vegas.

A wedding was just hours away.

HARLEY GOT her transfer to Robbery Homicide Division. Lieutenant Chall told her he owed her that. Even more, he said she'd earned it. But she'd no longer be partnered with CV—thanks to the departmental policy against spouses serving together. The rule was meant to leave one parent alive if tragedy struck partners on duty. Her new partner was a woman named Janice Reiman. She was coming over from Vice and joining Harley out of Hollywood Station.

CV was promoted to office duty. He had passed the lieutenants' test and was just waiting to see if a promotion came through. He hated the desk already. The promotion would change all that.

Damien Pultec and Albert Barkley were in east wing—death row —at San Quentin. Their time would come.

Tommy Jones and Ivan Sharp worked up the case against Annalee Johnson. Her lawyer claimed the killing was in self-defense, that the so-called victim was in the process of raping her when she lashed out with the letter opener. A sympathetic Juvenile Court judge agreed, and she was committed to incarceration for a period of six months while her family situation was reviewed and revised. In the end, her son was returned to her on the condition that she not violate the law and support her child. There would be weekly reviews of her living situation, as well. Universal Dynamics hired her back but this time on the day shift, so the little boy was in daycare while mother worked at her metal lathe.

Capitol Films was sued by eleven young women who all came forward and made claims against the company for failing to properly supervise Ira J. Spielman. The story made national headlines. The country was shocked at their courage and enraged at Spielman and Capitol Films. The "LA Eleven" alleged they had been assaulted and abused by Capitol's employee. The grand sum of eleven million dollars was sought. Two of those claimants were Wendy Ellis and Annalee Johnson. Neither girl ever screen tested in Hollywood or anywhere else again.

Mickey Loden was indicted on charges of mail fraud and insider trading after the stock of his publicly traded company tanked and he sold short two days before. He went to trial in federal court, was convicted, and eventually served forty-nine months in Leavenworth. He was then charged with conspiracy to murder in the case of Marcia Meriwether; this was after the feds were finished with him. He pled guilty and was sentenced to twenty-one years at San Quentin, but he avoided the death penalty. His lawyer claimed he wasn't aware Pultec and Barkley intended to murder Marcia Meriwether, he had only instructed them to "Get rid of her," meaning, he cried in court, "to send her on her way."

Wendy's million dollars—minus the lawyer's one-third—was in the bank, earning interest. She planned to leave it untouched until

Bobby started college. Until then, mother needed a career. She was looking at serving in the U.S. Navy. A career in Shore Patrol was calling.

THEY ARRIVED at Somewhere In Time Wedding Chapel just off the strip in Vegas at noon that day. Thirty minutes later, Harley and CV were married. She wore a white summer dress with blue daisies, he wore a white shirt with bolo tie featuring a scorpion embedded in plastic, courtesy of the chapel's gift store. Neckties were mandatory and CV had left his in Los Angeles, so the scorpion served. Pictures were taken; the bride wore a corsage on her dress, also purchased from the chapel's gift shop. The two witnesses were Ralph and Charmaine Ellis, her in-laws, who had flown in to give Harley their blessing and be there for her when she rejoined the world. They cried at the end, then everyone laughed and went to lunch. Ralph and Charmaine left to catch their return flight to LA.

Harley and CV then went to their hotel, checked in, made love on the heart-shaped bed of the honeymoon suite, then retreated downstairs to the pool.

Drinks were ordered and suntan oil was spread.

Harley was lounging in her hat and sunglasses when she suddenly sat up and touched CV, on the next lounger over, on the arm.

"Trivial," she announced. "Seven letters meaning trifling or slight. Trivial."

"Try to get some rest," he yawned. "I plan on keeping you up dancing until sunrise."

"There was no such thing as trivial in our pursuit."

"You did everything you could to save three. We only got two. What a great loss, our Marcia."

Harley stood and jumped into the pool at the deep end. She then swam the crawl end to end before climbing out and lying back on her lounger again.

She crossed her arm over her eyes and soon drifted off. She remembered thinking, later, how ready she'd been right then to stay up with her lover all night.

Just after midnight, she called the warden at San Quentin. It was done. Damien Pultec and Albert Barkley were no more. Harley's eyes filled with tears. "Marcia," was all she could say to CV.

"I know," he said gently. He bent and kissed the top of her head.

They danced until two and then went to bed.

They slept like best friends sleep, curled around each other, drifting in each other's dreams, touching yet apart.

THE END

FREE BOOK FOR EMAIL SIGNUP

Signup for my email list and receive a free Thaddeus Murfee book today! Your email will not be spammed and will only be used to notify you of new book releases, book sales, and free drawings, so please signup now.

—John Ellsworth

ABOUT THE AUTHOR

I'm an independent author. I'm independent because I enjoy marketing, selecting covers, reader communications, and all the rest. But I do need you to tell others about my books if you like them. Also, if you liked *No Trivial Pursuit*, would you please leave an Amazon or Goodreads review? It would mean a lot to me.

Presently, I'm working on my 31st novel. I published my first book, *The Defendants*, in January 2014. It's been a wild ride and I was self-supporting four months after my first book came out.

Reception to my books has been phenomenal; more than 2,000,000 have been downloaded in 60 months. All are Amazon best-sellers. I am an Amazon All-Star every month and a *USA Today* bestseller.

I live in San Diego, California, where I can be found near the beaches on my yellow Vespa scooter.

Thank you for reading my books. Thank you for any review you're able to leave on Amazon.

Website and email:

ellsworthbooks.com
johnellsworthbooks@gmail.com

Made in the USA
Middletown, DE
02 July 2020

11881007R00199